CARDS OF DEATH BOOK 5

THE FIFTH PORTAL

TAMARA GERAEDS

ISBN-13: 9798651410057
Cover design by Deranged Doctor Design
Editing by Ambition Editing LLC

PREVIOUSLY, IN CARDS OF DEATH

So much has happened, I sometimes think a year has passed instead of a couple of weeks.

Here's a quick recap of the most important stuff in case you feel as lost as I do.

Me and my friends have been doing everything we can to prevent the Devil from escaping from Hell to rule over Earth, using the Cards of Death and our powers to save souls. Bad luck, fake friends and several curses have caused us some trouble along the way, but we're not doing bad. We've only lost one soul so far.

We also had to kill our 'friend' Simon, but the other traitor, Paul, is still alive and probably planning something awful.

Vicky has two curses to deal with, and we found out one of them was put on her by Gisella's aunt, who wants the Book of a Thousand Deaths to bring her daughter back from the dead. So we're hoping to at least lift one curse soon. The second curse on her has something to do with someone touching her grave. Every time that happens, she is pulled into a memory but also closer to the Shadow World. I'm afraid I'll lose her if she gets pulled much further.

Taylar's unfinished business is something we'll

have to deal with soon, because it's slowly killing him. For real this time.

Meanwhile, I've been watching Maël and wondering why she hates to eat. Although none of the ghosts need to eat or drink anymore, food gives them comfort. But not Maël. I've been meaning to ask her about it, but there's never a good time when you're busy fighting Lucifer.

Good things have happened too. D'Maeo got the parts of his soul back that were stolen by the black void that killed him. We found a secret room in the mansion, and in the room, we found the Bell of Izme, made by the iele, a fairy folk. There's also a porthole in the secret room, leading to the hidden tunnel in the silver mine, where I found Dad's notebook and a strange dark portal. With the bell, we can close the portal that the demons are trying to open. Where it leads to, we don't know, but it can't be any place good.

The iele came to get the bell back from us. They weren't very friendly, but in the end, I managed to convince them to let me keep it for a while. They will be back to collect something in return though.

Mom is fine again, thankfully, but Trevor won't rest until she's by his side. I'm sure of it. Mona will have to keep a close watch on her. I'm glad we were able to reverse Trevor's spell to spy on us, but I'm not so sure it actually worked. I guess we'll find out soon enough.

CHAPTER 1

Ever since my battle against the Devil started, my luck seems to be running out slowly. So when Quinn shows up telling me he has come to deliver bad news, I expect the worst.

All faces turn to him as he appears, tall and dark in his human form, and looking more worried than I've ever seen him.

"Quinn has some bad news," I say before anyone has the chance to greet him. I want to know what he's come to tell us as soon as possible.

The smiles forming on the others' faces falter.

The angel lets out a heavy sigh and rakes a hand through his short curls. "I'm sorry, guys. I've been sent to tell you your actions have disturbed the balance between good and evil. Fix it or the world is doomed. Everything will shatter. All life will be lost."

Jeep takes off his hat and wipes it several times,

even though there's no dirt on it.

"Bad news, huh? That was an understatement," he mumbles.

We stand there frozen between the protective circle and the back door of Darkwood Manor, and it's as if my brain has completely shut down. And it's not just me. There are blank looks all around me.

After a long and awkward silence, I finally manage to push some words out of my throat. "I don't get it. We saved the fourth soul. How can that disturb the balance? We're supposed to save those souls, right?"

Quinn nods solemnly. "Yes, you did well. But you also did something else."

When he doesn't continue straight away, Gisella steps closer and places her hands on her hips. "Spit it out already. What was it then? What did we do wrong?"

His mouth twitches up a little as he looks at her, and I think back to a few minutes ago, when everything was still great, when Charlie and I were feeling happy because of the awesome girls we're dating. Judging by the start of the grin on his lips, Quinn must be thinking the same, but his gaze is overshadowed by sadness.

A cold wind pulls at my clothes, and dark clouds roll in, as if the weather already knows what Quinn is about to say. Or is it just me, unconsciously changing it to fit my mood?

Either way, I'm growing impatient. "Just tell us, Quinn." After all, I've still got some luck left.

Whatever this is, we'll fight it, like we always do. I have to believe we can.

Quinn presses the bridge of his nose. "Apparently you sent some people and a small army of demons to another place?"

Coldness grabs my chest, but it's not the wind this time. "Yes, we did. We cast a spell to make anyone who attacked us disappear. Why?"

"They ended up somewhere they shouldn't have. You'll have to get them back, or kill them if you must, before it's too late to restore the balance."

Warmth floods back into my body. *There's still hope.* "Sure, we can do that. Where are they?"

His shoulders move up, causing my newfound hope to shatter. "I don't know. This is all I was told. We're not supposed to interfere." He gives me a small smile. "Bringing you this message was the best I could do."

I shake my head. *No more negativity. No more doubts.* "It's fine. It's enough. We'll figure it out. We always do."

His smile widens. "That's the spirit!"

And, without warning, he vanishes.

"Isn't he a perfect ray of sunshine?" Gisella remarks, finally lowering her arms.

Feeling the need to defend my friend, I say, "I think he's as frustrated as we are at not being allowed to help much."

I look around for support, and thankfully, most of the others nod in agreement.

But my breath catches in my throat when my gaze falls upon D'Maeo. Something dark moves in his eyes. I squint against the sunlight as the clouds above us part. D'Maeo swats at something in front of his face, and a fly buzzes off. I let out a silent sigh and turn. "Come on, guys. Let's sit down and eat something first. Some of us need the energy."

Vicky pushes me aside in a mock race to the kitchen.

"And some of us need the happiness," she calls over her shoulder.

Mona follows, smiling again now that she's able to return to what she's best at: spoiling us rotten.

"How about some waffles?" she suggests while her sparkles already pull the ingredients out of the cupboards in the kitchen.

Taylar hurries past me. "I love waffles."

"Who doesn't," I answer just as Maël gestures for me to go inside.

"Right," I say, "you don't."

Her look of composure is immediately replaced by one of hurt. She goes a shade more transparent, and her golden headpiece seems to lose its shine.

I stay where I am while the others file into the kitchen and keep my eyes on Maël, who doesn't move either.

When we're finally alone outside, I try to conjure a reassuring smile. "I'd like to talk to you, Maël. I think it's time you told me why you've got such an aversion to food."

Her jaw is set tight, making her look more like a stubborn princess than a queen.

"Is that an order, master?" she asks rather coldly.

"I don't want it to be. I'd rather you tell me because you want to, because you trust me."

She looks away, studies the rays of sunlight dividing the lawn into dark and light patches.

"Please, Maël," I beg. "You saw what happened to Taylar because of his unfinished business. I just want to do what I can to keep everyone safe." Gently, I place a hand on her shoulder. "Including you."

"I know." She walks over to a tree stump and sits down. Her shoulders are no longer pulled back proudly, her head not held up high in confidence. When I see the change in her, I know I've made the right decision. There's a heavy weight on Maël's shoulders, and we need to lift it.

I kneel down next to her. "Please tell me everything."

CHAPTER 2

"I had been a queen for years when I made my first big mistake," Maël begins. "We had been moving our camp every month to avoid the Spaniards."

I frown. "Spaniards? I thought you used to live in Africa."

She gives me a knowing smile that makes me feel young and ignorant. "I did. It was the year 1501, I believe, when the Spaniards started shipping African people to their country to work as slaves. They were especially fond of the free tribes, since there were no masters to deal with, no one to pay or to fight to get what they wanted." She pats my hand. "Did you not learn this at school?"

"I'm not sure," I answer truthfully. "I wasn't into history that much."

Another sad smile. "But you are now?"

"Well, it's a different story if you know someone

who used to live in the past."

Finally, her eyes sparkle a little. "You make a good point there. And anyway, history books are not always correct. I think a lot has been forgotten, changed as it was passed on or simply misunderstood."

I sit down on the grass and fold my legs in front of me. "Tell me more, please."

Her gaze grows distant, and I wonder if in her head she's stepping back in time.

"We were able to stay out of the Spaniards' way by moving around and sending scouts out every day. This meant, however, that there were not enough men left to go hunting. I appointed two of the men to teach some of our women how to hunt. They were against it, but I was their queen, so they did as they were told. It turned out the women were good at it, and soon, everyone forgot how unusual it was for them to hunt."

While she speaks, I try to form pictures in my head of how it must have been. Groups of scarcely dressed people huddled around fires where animals were roasted or cooked. Children on the laps of their mothers, spears resting against a nearby tree, songs rising into the sky. I've seen it in movies countless times, but I have no idea if it was really like that so long ago. Maël's dress certainly doesn't look like it was made in the sixteenth century. It's quite fashionable now. And her golden headpiece would look great on the head of a famous singer.

Maël smiles down on me. "You look like you have

wondered off. Am I boring you? Do you want me to get to the point?"

I shake my head feverishly. "Not at all! I was just trying to imagine what your life was like and wondering whether all those movies I've seen got it right."

She holds out her hand. "I can show you, if you like?"

In a second, I'm on my feet. "Definitely!"

She touches my arm when I sit down next to her. Just before the bright flash pulls me into the memory, I squeeze my eyes shut.

I'm glad I haven't eaten yet, because the food would've been pushed out for sure. The feeling of my stomach rising to my throat is much stronger than the previous times I was sucked into a memory. Now it feels like my insides are on a rollercoaster with a blender at the end of it.

I bend over when I stop moving and retch. Inside me, everything is on fire while at the same time a knife is thrown around.

Shivering like crazy, I try to straighten up. Maël jumps to my rescue and pushes me onto a rock.

"I apologize, I should have warned you. Travelling to a memory of so long ago can be uncomfortable."

"Uncomfortable?" I pant. "That's… what you… call this?" I swallow hard and wrap my arms around my stomach. "Horrible is a better description."

Maël taps her staff against my foot. "Look over there. That might make you forget your discomfort."

Groaning softly, I look up. Several feet away from us, there's a camp. Low, wide tents made of something black are set up in a neat line, partly hidden from sight by several trees. The sun is setting. It paints the sky with orange. In the distance, I can hear children laughing, and there's a faint smell of fire.

"When your insides have settled, I can show you around," Maël says.

I look up at her, and I notice her back is straighter than usual. Her skin glows in the fading light, and there's longing in her eyes.

"Are you happy to be back?" I ask her, pushing myself up without trouble.

She inhales the humid air and closes her eyes. "Yes and no." She starts walking with confident, royal strides. "Come on," she calls over her shoulder. "It is almost time."

Time for what, I wonder, but I don't ask, because from all corners of the camp, people are emerging, all going in the same direction.

Maël takes her time following them, but she makes her way around obstacles so easily that I struggle to keep up. Tent lines, food bowls, weapons, toys, everything has been dropped, and I almost trip several times before finally arriving in the middle of the camp, where a fire is crackling and about sixty or seventy people are gathered, all facing the same way.

"They all look so beautiful," I whisper when I come to a halt next to Maël.

She smiles without turning her head. "Yes, especially today. You see, we have a wedding."

"Can we go closer?"

"Of course. We cannot be seen anyway. But we are not here to watch the wedding, Dante."

My shoulders sag. "That's a shame. I would've liked to see it."

She looks down at me with fondness in her eyes. "Maybe some other time. Now watch."

The women and children around the fire start cheering as several men approach, with fully painted bodies in red and gold. One of them is covered in white flowers. His face is a work of art, decorated in white paint that forms intricate patterns.

"Did people marry out of love here?" I ask Maël.

She shakes her head. "No, usually a suitable husband was found through what you could call wedding trials. The boys had to compete with each other to get the girl. Unless, of course, it was someone of a high rank. Then my father, the king, would match two people."

Another question rolls out of my mouth before I can stop myself. The more she tells me, the more I want to know. And now, I finally have the opportunity. "But that was before you became queen, right? Was it common for women to become leaders of the tribe?"

She sighs without a sound. "Not at all. And we were not exactly called kings and queens, but since I did not know the translation of the African word for our rulers, when your grandfather asked me who I was, I settled for queen, which is pretty close to the truth. Now, I am used to the title." She turns away from her tribe to face me. "But to answer your question, I became the leader because I had to. We used to dig gold for Mansa Kambi, the ruler of Mali, but one day, we were ambushed by another tribe. There was a great demand for gold, and too many people digging for it. We lost more than half of our tribe that day, including my father and many other strong men."

The tears in my eyes reflect hers as I imagine the hurt she must have felt. The hurt she still feels now because of it. "That's horrible. I'm so sorry, Maël."

She swallows and continues her story. "Since there were no men strong enough to compete for leadership of the tribe, and there was little time to decide, I was elected unanimously by the elders to become the leader."

"Why wasn't there much time?" I ask.

"Because we had to find another way to survive quickly. Digging for gold was not an option anymore, unless we wanted to travel for miles. Our village had been raided, and we barely escaped death. The men began to argue amongst themselves over leadership, since none of them was really fit enough to challenge another. Being the king's daughter, I had been taught to hunt, and my father still trained me several times a week in battle before he died. So I could take on any of the men left."

"And you had your power, right?" As far as I know, all of the ghosts had their powers when they were alive, but you never know. Magic varies from person to person.

She gives me a small nod. "That too. If someone was too fast for me, I could slow down time to defeat them. But my father taught me to use my magic only when I had no other choice. True strength lies in knowing when to use which power."

"Did you ever use it against someone in your tribe?"

"A couple of times, at the start of my rule. Some men wanted to test me or prove they were stronger than me."

I grin. "And you showed them they were wrong."

"I did." There's no joy in her words. It's just something she had to do, nothing she is proud of. It must have felt a little like cheating to her.

My eyes flick back to the approaching men. They don't look happy, like they should. I'm about to find out what Maël wants to show me here, but I want to know what led to this moment first.

"So, what happened then?" I urge her.

"We built tents and started moving." She gestures at the homes around us. "It took some getting used to, but we did okay. The men hunted. The women took care of the children and the camp and gathered fruit. But Mansa Kambi was not happy. He knew some of us had survived and wanted us to work for him again. He sent over some of his soldiers to collect us." Her gaze drops to the ground. She grabs her staff with so much force that the skin around her knuckles tightens. Her jaw is clenched.

I'm afraid to ask what happened next, but after a short, pained silence, she continues.

"They used so much force. They hurt my people for not moving fast enough. They bound everyone, even the children. At night, we had to take care of the torn skin on their feet. We were not allowed to hunt or even search for food. When two of the children died, I could not bear it any longer. They had not bound me. I was the only one they respected, although mildly." She blinks several times. A single tear rolls down her cheek, glistening in the light of the fire. "I tried to talk to the soldiers. I told them we would cooperate if they treated us well. They refused, said we were traitors and would be slaves for the rest of our lives." She purses her lips. "I could not let that happen. I could not lead what remained of my tribe to a life like that. They did not deserve that."

I want to ask her what she did, but my voice has left me. My throat is dry, because for the last couple of minutes, I've forgotten to swallow.

To prevent tears from escaping, I avert my eyes. Silence has fallen upon the camp, as two of the men lead a skinny teen boy to the fire. He's limping, and his face is covered in dirt.

Maël is watching him too. She lets out a heavy sigh and finishes her story quickly. Whether it's because of the approaching boy or the hurt inside her, I can't tell.

"I used my power to free everyone and kill the soldiers. The men wanted to help me, but if we were ever caught, I did not want them to be punished for it. So I took care of them, hid the bodies and we left without a trace. From that moment on, my tribe followed me without question. We moved around constantly, and half of the men acted as scouts while half of the women joined the hunt. We managed to evade Mansa Kambi's soldiers and followers, and we were quite happy. Until my first mistake."

When she doesn't continue, I turn my head. Regret is painted in streaks across her face as she watches her men lead the scrawny boy to the fire. "Watch," she whispers.

Together, we step closer. The boy has sunk to the ground, too weak to stand without the support of the men that led him here. More than a hundred eyes fall upon him as he looks around in fear. The silence is almost palpable, and because of it, my heart shoots up to my throat when a loud drum is heard.

The crowd parts immediately and bows as a commanding presence steps out into the open.

She looks more beautiful than I've ever seen her. Her hair is long here, golden ribbons braided through her dark locks, her face decorated with elegant gold and red patterns. She's wearing a long, red dress with beads necklaces draped sideways over her chest.

"Wow, you look so beautiful," I gasp. "And so… different than anything I've seen in my history books."

The Maël I know chuckles softly. "Like I said, history records are not all complete or correct. Sure, some tribes wore simple clothes, but we were quite fashionable."

I shake my head incredulously. "Very fashionable! I never would've guessed you lived so long ago. That dress you're wearing now will make lots of present day women jealous."

She laughs out loud when I gesture at her black dress with the golden flowers and add, "That is, if you lose the cape."

She takes a small bow. "Thank you for the compliment, Dante. Now, pay attention. You wanted to see, so watch."

With slow but determined steps, sixteenth century Maël makes her way to the boy on the ground. He watches her with wide eyes full of fear and admiration before bowing. The rest of the tribe stands up and forms a circle around the both of them.

The queen addresses the two men that brought the boy here. She asks them something, but I don't understand the words.

"What did you say?" I enquire, without taking my eyes off the scene.

"Who is this, and why did you bring him here," Maël translates.

The two men bow to her again. When they answer, they don't just look humble, but apologetic.

"They say they found him, weak and almost starved to death," Maël explains. "He claims to have

19

escaped an army from another country that took most of his tribesmen on a boat to Spain."

I rub my arms to drown out the cold suddenly spreading through me. "That poor boy."

"Yes, poor boy." Maël's voice trails off, and it takes a while for her to continue.

We watch as her former self orders some food. She gives it to the boy and gestures for him to leave. An old man joins her. He looks worried and seems to plead for her not to send the boy away. I wait for Maël to translate, but she remains silent. Her mouth is a thin line, and her eyes, sad again, don't leave the boy for a second. Eventually, the same men that brought him in help the boy to the edge of the camp. There, they watch him until he slowly vanishes in the dark.

"This was the first we heard of slaves being transported to another country," Maël finally says. "We had heard of Mansa Kambi's soldiers tricking traitors like this. That is why I sent him away. The next day, the scouts found him, only about a mile from the camp. His throat was slit, and the mark of a traitor was carved into his forehead."

CHAPTER 3

Her voice is hoarse by the time she reaches the end of the last sentence. I get an overwhelming feeling to comfort her, but when I put my hand on her arm, she strides off. She goes straight for the crowd, that has burst into song at a simple hand gesture from the old Maël. The children form a line from the bride to the groom and throw petals. The wedding is about to begin.

Expecting Maël to watch the ceremony up close, I follow her, but she suddenly turns left, passing tent after tent.

"Where are you going?" I call after her.

She stops when she reaches the border of the camp, and I hurry to catch up.

There's nothing but sand in front of us and mountains in the distance. The acacia trees, that give the tents some cover and shadow, provide the only green for miles.

For a moment, we just stand there, staring at the wind that picks up grains of sand and moves them around aimlessly. Other than that, everything seems quiet.

I can almost feel Maël's pain. "You know it wasn't your fault, right? Kings and queens have to make tough decisions. They make mistakes, just like everybody else." I place my hand on her arm again, and this time, she doesn't move. "You couldn't have known. Your people knew that, didn't they?"

Her nod is barely visible. "Maybe."

I stare into the distance and wait for her to continue her story. But she doesn't speak, and when I follow her gaze, I understand why.

"Is that normal?" I ask, even though I know the answer.

Without responding, Maël raises her staff. Her right foot moves a bit back, creating a better balance for her.

She's ready to fight, and that confirms my fears. "We're under attack."

I imitate her fighting stance and conjure a ball of lightning. "Will our powers even work here? Aren't we supposed to be immune to anything from this memory?"

Just like mine, her eyes follow the sand that falls from the sky in waves, quickly forming the shape of a giant snake. "I do not think this is part of the memory. I have not seen this before."

I throw the lightning into my left hand and fumble for my Morningstar behind my waistband with my right. "You mean, something followed us in here? It must be really strong then, right?"

Maël tilts her head. "No... I do not think it followed us."

She raises her staff a little higher as the sand snake dives down.

In a reflex, I throw my ball of lightning and my Morningstar at the same time. They both soar straight for the snake's head. It seems oblivious to the danger approaching and keeps coming. The Morningstar hits it first, making the head explode into tiny grains that tumble down. A millisecond later, the lightning hits it. The sparks that fly everywhere blind me.

It takes a couple of blinks before I can see again, and my stomach turns upside down with a jolt.

The sand snake is still coming. The bits of it that have fallen down are sucked back up and disappear into the tail.

I reel in my Morningstar and throw it again, but this time, the sand snake avoids it easily, moving its body up.

"What do we do?" I ask over the noise of the moving sand.

Maël doesn't answer, and when I turn my head, I see her lips moving. The tip of her wand is glowing.

She's trying to slow down time.

"It's not working! Nothing is!" I yell at her. The urge to step back pulls at me, but I can't leave Maël here on her own. Who knows what this sand creature will do to her.

Maël suddenly drops her arm. "Maybe we are not supposed to fight it."

I feel my forehead wrinkling as I raise my eyebrow at her. "What? Of course we are. It's attacking us."

"Maybe not. I sense something... hesitant about it."

The mouth of the snake opens and comes at me full force.

I duck just before the sandy jaws snap shut.

"Oh yes," I mock, "very hesitant."

The snake is moving around us lazily now, leaving enough room for us to move a little, but not enough to escape.

I keep my eyes on the grainy body, making sure it doesn't touch me.

Maël uses a different approach. She is standing absolutely still, letting the sand inspect her from head to toe. She shivers. "I know where this came from."

"What? How?"

"It showed me."

The sand snake backs up a little, tilts its head and moves back to me.

I put away my Morningstar and take out my athame instead, waving it in front of me to ward off the sand. "Is it dangerous?"

It snaps at my weapon and nearly rips it out of my hand. Grains of sand jump onto my arm and crawl to my neck. It itches like crazy, and every grain seems to hiss at me. I whirl round and round in an attempt to get rid of the sand, waving my arms in the process.

Maël stops me mid-turn.

"I am not sure," she says, calmly wiping the sand off my arm.

"Well, this should give you a pretty good idea," I respond, holding up my arm, which is covered in a bright red rash.

She shoots me a small smile. "I have a feeling it does not attack unless provoked. Try putting away your weapon."

The snake's head hovers in front of my face, and my hand tightens around my athame.

"Put it away, Dante. Trust me," Maël says.

The snake slithers closer through the air with a deafening roar, making it almost impossible to hear what Maël is saying.

"Put it away," she repeats, and I lower my weapon.

The snake tilts its head and… starts to vibrate.

"What's it doing?" I whisper, not daring to move.

Maël puts her wand back into her cape and smiles when the snake vibrates harder. The roaring of the moving sand is replaced by a growing rumble.

My breathing goes faster. "Is it going to explode?"

"No." Maël chuckles. "No, Dante, it is purring."

My jaw goes slack. "It's what?"

"Putting away your athame will make it even happier. Try it."

"Are you sure? It's probably just getting ready to eat us."

She chuckles again. I have to admit, I love the sound. "Yes, I am sure."

The muscles in my arm protest when I lift my shirt and put my weapon back behind my waistband, where it lies coldly against my skin.

The rumbling gets louder, and the sand snake seems to smile at me. Then it nods, as if to express its approval, and takes off in a whirl of dust and heat.

With one hand pressed against my chest to slow down my heartbeat, I turn to Maël. "What on earth was that?"

"That was the beach from the lost continent of Mu."

"Come again?"

Surprise flares up in her eyes. "You have never heard of Mu?"

"Not of Moo and not of any beach that can do that." I stretch my arm and point at the swirling sand that's now barely visible in the distance. "What is Moo, the land of cows?"

She shakes her head at me. "Very funny, Dante. No, it is Mu, written with a 'u', and it is a continent that popped up between Asia and America in the early nineteenth century."

With the sand snake far away, but still in sight, I relax a little. I lick my lips. "How can a whole continent just pop up somewhere?"

"Well, Mu is actually a part of Purgatory. But it has a will of its own, as you can see, and one day in 1822, it managed to escape and settle in the Pacific Ocean as a new continent. Everyone could see it, even non-magicals. If you look it up in the history of the non-magical world, you will find that the whole thing sank about a month after it appeared. Ruins were found at the bottom of the ocean. But the magical community knows that Mu got taken back to the Underworld by Charon, the ferryman. Several people saw it happen. Nobody knows for sure, since Charon has never been very conversational, but the story goes that Mu wanted more power and, therefore, moved to Earth to rule over people. However, the Beach of Mu is strong, and it warned Charon, who came to get the continent and place it back where it belongs."

My head is spinning, or maybe that's just a remnant of the sand whirling around me. "You're saying this Mu can move on its own? So, it's alive?"

She takes out her wand again and peers at the sand moving along the edge of the camp on the other side. "Yes, you could say that. And as you can see, the Beach of Mu can move on its own too."

"What about Purgatory? I thought that didn't exist. We have Heaven, the nine circles of Hell, the Underworld and the Shadow World, which is the world between life and death, basically. So, what is Purgatory then?"

The purring gets louder again as the sand comes circling back to us. It dives at us, and we duck to avoid it. My hands sting as it touches the snake, but one look at my arm tells me the rash is already gone.

"Purgatory is the place where impure souls go,"

Maël continues as we watch the sand soar through the sky above us. "Those who are not bad enough for Hell and not good enough for Heaven end up there, and they can be purified. Purgatory is part of Tartarus and Mu is part of Purgatory. It is the place where the souls wash ashore."

The tail of the snake hits me in the neck, and I double over. I land on my knees hard and grit my teeth. "Okay, that's it. I've had it with this thing. You say it's harmless, I say it's about to swallow us whole." I focus on cold and imagine the grains of sand freezing one by one.

The snake hisses as frost wraps around its tail.

Maël aims her staff at me. "Do not anger it!"

I try to answer, but my words come out slurred, stretched. "Wwwwhyyyyy noooooot?"

"Because it is wired to punish those who keep using violence."

The snake's head appears in front of me out of nowhere. It isn't smiling anymore, and the purring has changed back to an angry roar. I can't move anymore. The grains of sand crawl around faster than before, changing the shape of the creature from long and slender to short and bulky. Arms pop out of its new torso as it looms over me.

I want to scream to Maël to release me from her time lock, but I can no longer produce any sound.

All I can do is watch in horror as the African queen lays her staff on the ground and gets down on one knee. *Has she been taken over by an evil entity? Why is she letting this happen?*

The sandy head, which now resembles a lion's, is inches from my face. Its hot breath makes my head burn. I pull away, inch by inch and way too slow to save myself. Tears form in my eyes, not just from the physical pain, but also from the thought that one of the ghosts in my Shield is leaving me to die.

"Mighty Beach of Mu," Maël says, her nose touching the ground, her empty hands stretched out in front of her. "Please give this boy another chance. Sorrow and a heavy burden have tainted his mind and faith, but in his heart, he is good."

Well, that sounds a lot better. Maybe she's still herself after all.

The lion closes its mouth and whirls around to face her. It roars at her, and she flinches a little.

Softly, she continues. "I know you have the ability to look into his heart, probably better than anything else in the universe. Please judge him yourself and kill him if I am wrong."

What? I gasp, but the sound is only in my head. Tears now crawl in pairs down my cheeks. *She is lost. Why else would she suggest killing me?*

I force myself to keep my eyes open when the sand lion turns its attention back to me. I will face my fear and my death if I have to. And I will fight, even if it is in slow motion.

Of course, that's all just wishful thinking, because as soon as the lion moves in, I close my eyes in a reflex. My chest contracts heavily as the sand penetrates my flesh and moves around inside me. My eyes bulge, and my heart stops beating. I feel weightless as I fall sideways and hit the ground. Inside I'm screaming and fighting, but not one muscle moves on the outside, except for my eyes, that slowly blink open. I breathe out and lie there, staring straight ahead, not able to suck in new air.

Maël! I scream without sound. *Fight the evil that makes you do this. Stand up and help me!*

She doesn't. She just sits there, her head touching the ground, her eyes closed.

My insides itch like crazy, and my mind gets fuzzier with every second that ticks away.

I'm dying. Cold spreads through me as the realization hits me. *I'm actually dying.*

CHAPTER 4

The dark has taken over most of my vision when the wriggling inside me changes. I can feel the grains of sand moving faster.

This is it. It's sucking the last bit of life out of me.

My fight is over. There's nothing left in me to fight with. No breath, no energy, no strength.

All I have left are blurry thoughts. *No pain... universe... gone... wrong...*

I can no longer feel my body, and my sight is completely gone. With everything around me black as night, I can't tell whether I'm asleep or awake. Dead or alive.

Suddenly, I wonder what will come next. *Will I go to Heaven? Or to Hell, because I failed to save the world? Or, much more likely, will I get caught somewhere in between, in the Shadow World, or left on Earth to take care of my unfinished business?*

Maybe I can finish my battle against the Devil as a ghost?

I smile, even though I can't feel my lips. I'm not sure I even have a mouth anymore.

Hey, my thoughts are coherent again! That must mean I'm dead. Floating around in space until someone decides what to do with me. No tunnel of light yet.

I try to turn my head, and a heavy feeling washes over me. The darkness around me spins, or maybe I do. I'm not sure. Something pats me on the cheek and words tumble out of my mouth. "Please don't take me to Hell. Let me go back to Earth. I have to stop Lucifer."

"You *are* on Earth, silly boy. Or your body is at least." There's another pat on my cheek. "Come on, Dante, open your eyes. The Beach of Mu has left."

"I'm not dead?"

"For a moment, I was afraid you had left me," Maël's voice answers. "But no, you are not dead."

Carefully, I open my eyes. The bright light reminds me of the tunnel I was looking for only a minute ago. But we're still in Africa, sitting at the edge of Maël's camp, in her memory.

She holds out her hand to me. "Come on, get up. You are fine now." With ease, she pulls me to my feet. "The sand is gone."

Rage courses through me as I remember her words to the sand lion. I pull myself from her grip and fall right back down, my legs too wobbly to hold me, but I don't care. I stab my finger at her. "You betrayed me! How could you do that?"

32

Her eyes grow wide. "Excuse me?"

"You told that sand to kill me."

She folds her arms over her chest. "Really, Dante? Of all the things I said, *that* is what you focus on?" She shakes her head, the look on her face resembling that of a disappointed mother scanning a bad school report. "It was ready to write you off. It thought your violent behavior could not be unlearned. I acted before it could take you out. And I had to make it convincing."

The rage churns inside me, and I ball my fists.

"Listen, Dante," Maël continues. "I understand where your suspicions are coming from. You knew your friends Paul and Simon for years and never suspected them to be evil. You have known me and the others in your Shield for a very short time, and we are asking you to trust us unconditionally. But we are really fighting for you. For you and the world. You must trust us, Dante."

"I do trust you!" The words come out strangled, forced, but I know they're true. *I trust Maël, I trust my whole Shield, so why did I say those things to her?*

She smiles at me, oblivious to the confusion rolling around in my head. "Do you really? You lost faith in me rather quickly back there. The first thing you thought was that I had handed you over to some evil entity."

"But I didn't." The fear I felt just minutes ago washes over me, and tears spill from my eyes, this time at normal speed. "I didn't lose faith."

She drops down beside me and takes my hand. "What is going on with you, Dante? Tell me."

Bile rises to my throat, and I swallow. "I'm not sure. But I'm telling you, I never lost faith in you, not deep inside. There's just something…" While Maël squeezes my left hand reassuringly, I lift the other and study it. I tell my fingers to move, and they do. "There's something inside me."

Suddenly, I'm sure of it. "Something was controlling my thoughts. Trying to screw with my mind? To drive me crazy?" More tears fall down as my whole body starts to itch. I grab Maël's shoulders with both hands. "There's something inside me!"

The usual calmness that radiates from her doesn't help me now. I'm almost hyperventilating from panic.

She looks me in the eye. "Take a deep breath. Nothing is inside you, Dante. It is just the feeling of that crawling sand coming back. But it is gone. It searched your heart and saw nothing but good there. You are safe."

"No…" I shake my head so hard everything spins. "No, Maël, it's something else. Something made me doubt you, and when I woke up, something made me angry. Angrier than I've ever been. It was… It felt like…" I search for the right words to describe it. "It wasn't me."

Her eyes bore into mine, searching. The confidence I usually see in them is wavering.

Finally, she nods. "You are right. Something is wrong."

A chill creeps up my spine. "I was kind of hoping you'd say I was hallucinating."

"I think I know what is going on, Dante."

"Okay." I take a deep breath. "Tell me."

"You remember what Quinn told us? That the balance between good and evil has been disturbed?"

"Of course."

"I suspect that the consequences of that are graver than we thought. That Beach of Mu escaping from Purgatory again is just a small part of it. You see, every molecule in existence can be pushed to either good or evil." She waves vaguely at the sky. "Every particle in the universe, whether floating around or part of a living being, can be manipulated. Pulled to one side or the other."

I shiver. "You mean, even inside us?"

"Exactly. Normally your heart and mind control those molecules, but when the balance is tipped off, particles from outside your body might be able to pull you in another direction on their own."

She pushes herself up, wipes the sand from her dress and holds out her hand. "Come, we have to go home and discuss this with the others."

I take her hand and let her pull me up. It's a relief to find my legs steady again, even though my heart is pounding like crazy.

I close my eyes and prepare for the jolt of traveling back to Darkwood Manor.

When nothing happens, I peer through my lashes. "We're still in your memory."

"Shh," Maël hisses.

With my lips pressed firmly together and my heartbeat deafening in my ears, I wait.

Still nothing happens.

Eventually, Maël lets go of my hand. Her next words hit me like a bulldozer. "We cannot leave."

My heart almost stops. "We're trapped here?"

Maël keeps patting her dress with her hands. "For now."

I stretch out my hand to her. "Try again."

"I don't think—"

"Just try again, Maël. Please?"

She must be able to see the fear in my eyes, because she gives in without another word. With my hand held firmly in hers, she closes her eyes.

I follow her example and try to send good vibes through my arm. *This will work, this will work.*

Then I hear a familiar voice. "Dante, can you hear me? Maël? Answer me, please!"

A worm of worry wriggles through my stomach. It's not just the panic in Vicky's voice that triggers it, I can also feel her dismay. It hangs over us like a heavy shroud.

When I open my eyes, it's not just Vicky's face that greets me. The others are gathered around us too, and they all look equally distressed. Even D'Maeo and Mona, who are not easily shaken.

"Maybe we should just leave them for a while," Gisella suggests. "They'll come back eventually. Maybe it's a long memory."

Vicky straightens up with balled fists. "They've been sitting here like statues for an hour already! That can't be normal!"

Gisella looks away. "No, it can't be," she mumbles.

With a smile, I reach out to Vicky. "Hey, it's okay. We're back. Sorry we took so long."

Vicky stares back at me with tears in her eyes.

"What if they never come back?" she whispers.

"Babe! What are you talking about?" I stand up and wrap my arms around her. "I'm right here."

My heart stops beating when I don't feel anything. I pull back and reach for her hand, but my fingers go straight through hers. My eyes search for a reaction from Vicky, but she's staring at something behind me.

When I turn to see what it is, a soft moan escapes my lips. "No!"

I lean over my own body, sitting eerily still on the tree stump, with closed eyes.

"Am I dead? Am I a ghost?" I ask Maël while the others continue their conversation, oblivious to our presence.

The African queen studies our friends and our still bodies and shakes her head. "No, you are breathing. It is like I said: we are stuck."

"Okay, okay, so we need a way to fix that." *Stay calm, stay positive. We'll find a way back.*

My breathing slowly steadies, and I step away from our panicked friends.

Maël follows. "Do you have any ideas?"

It's more wishful thinking than an actual idea, but I can't let pessimism pull me down again.

"Yes," I say as confidently as I can manage. "Can you take us back into your memory and show me everything you intended to show me? I think that's the key to getting back."

She frowns but doesn't protest. She takes my hand, and with a modest flash, we're transported back to Maël's home country.

We exchange a relieved look, and I squeeze her hand. "Step one complete. Are you ready to show me the rest of your story? I still don't know what any of it has to do with you hating food."

Her mouth twitches. "You will see soon enough. Hold on."

CHAPTER 5

Maël raises her staff high and mumbles incoherent words. Everything around us spins. The sky above us turns from dark to light and back in seconds, and the desert before us moves up and down in waves. As dizziness hits me full force, I close my eyes and grab Maël's hand tighter.

After only a couple more seconds, her mumbling stops, and she lets go of me. "You can open your eyes now."

I stumble back when I find her whole tribe in front of me, rows of bare backs inches from my face. The old Maël's voice rings out loud and clear, but I can't see her.

"Come on," the ghost queen says. "Let us take a closer look."

We move around the circle until Maël comes into view. Two tribesmen are standing next to her with a young man between them who looks as if he's about to collapse. Maël nods at a woman, who hurries over and hands the man a bowl of water. He gulps it down with a grateful look on his face, and when he's done, the queen says something.

"I am asking what he is doing here," Maël explains.

The man looks up at her with frightened eyes.

"He is giving me almost the exact story the boy did. He escaped an army that took most of his tribe to work as slaves overseas. Another man was with him, but he died from dehydration a couple of days ago. He is asking for shelter until he is ready to move on."

When he finishes his plea, Maël stays silent. The whole tribe seems to be holding their breath. The old man I saw before steps to her side and whispers something in her ear. *He must be one of the elders.* The queen nods and opens her mouth to deliver her verdict, but one of the scouts guarding the man objects before she can utter one word. He speaks urgently, supporting every word with frantic gesticulations.

Maël listens patiently and consults the elder again briefly.

While they talk, present day Maël turns to me. "The day we found the boy with the traitor's mark, I vowed never to make the same mistake again. I am repeating my words now, to my people." She listens as intently as her subjects do when the queen finally speaks, and translates. "We will not let malicious people change us. We will not be made into a suspicious, vengeful people. Instead, we will show love to friends and enemies alike."

Cheers rise up from the crowd, and they bow to her over and over.

"Feed this man and give him clothes. We will speak with him when he is rested."

With a resigned look on her face, Maël beckons me. "Come on, let us follow them."

We watch as the man is lead to a small tent. They leave him alone to wash up and give him clean clothes, food and water. Two tribesmen stay outside to guard the tent.

"Do you want to go inside?" I ask Maël.

She twirls her staff around in her hand, her eyes glued to the tent.

"Maël? Are you okay? If this is too hard for you—"

She blinks several times before shaking her head. "No, I have to show you. Even if we were not stuck here, I should show you. You have a right to know, and maybe…" She leans on her wand so heavily that it sinks into the sand. "Maybe I need to see it too. Maybe it is time to put these demons behind me."

And with that, she strolls past the guards and into the tent.

I'm glad to find the man dressed. He's stuffing pieces of meat into his mouth at an incredible speed.

"Wow, he must be really hungry," I comment, not knowing what else to say.

Maël walks in circles around him, studying him

from all sides. "Yes, he really got into his role."

"What do you mean? What role?"

"I let this man into our camp because of the mistake I made with that boy. I did not want another innocent person to die because of my misguided distrust." She moves closer to the man, her staff held in front of her, as if she's afraid of an attack. "One mistake, and it led me to take in someone we should have killed without mercy." With her jaw clenched tightly, she tries to poke him with her wand, but it goes through him. He doesn't pause his munching for even a second.

With a sudden but graceful turn and a swoosh of her cape, Maël heads back out of the tent. "Come, I will show you what happened when we trusted him."

Once again, we move forward through her memories.

When we come to a halt, everything around us still looks the same.

"How far did we go?" I ask.

"Three weeks and four days. That is how long it took for him to gain our full trust and prepare his evil plan."

A rock lands in my stomach at the sound of her bitter words.

When she turns, I grab her arm. "I'm not sure I want to see this."

"Me neither," she says, and she strides to the center of the camp, where her double is sitting by the fire, dressed exactly like the Maël I know so well. Her

42

hair is also shorter now, like it is today.

I swallow several times, but my throat is still dry. *Am I about to witness her death? Oh crap, I hope not.*

"That is him," Maël says, pointing at the man sitting next to her copy on the ground.

We watch as the two of them exchange stories and carve spears.

"I am so glad you saved me and took me in," Maël translates, when the man speaks. "If you had not, I would not have been able to do this."

Former Maël smiles at him. "Do what?"

He smiles back, but in a creepy, knowing way that gives me the chills.

Maël must see it too and sense the hate suddenly emanating from him, because she jumps to her feet, pulls out her wand and aims it at him.

"What did you do?" Maël's translation comes out choked, and I brace myself for what's coming.

"Nothing you can fix," the man answers, his grin growing wider.

Then the screaming start. Cries of alarm and pain ring out through the camp.

Old Maël turns and runs, but we are glued to the spot, watching the satisfied glint in the traitor's eyes.

More screams erupt from the tents all around me, and when I turn to find Maël, I see her crouched down beside a young woman, who is clutching her stomach and wailing like a tortured bear. Blood drips from the corner of her mouth, and she grabs Maël's dress, gurgling something I don't understand.

The queen jumps to her feet, takes a look at all the moaning and screaming people around her, crawling from their tents or collapsing mid-run, and picks up the wand she dropped.

She mumbles the incomprehensive words I've heard several times now, and I pray with all my heart that she will be able to turn back time and save all these people. But the glowing of the tip of her wand we're both waiting for doesn't come.

A roaring laugh close to me makes me jump.

The traitor approaches, his face a mask of satisfaction and hate. He lifts his hand and shows Maël a small shiny stone.

"Looking for this?" Maël translates his words. "Your staff will not help you any longer… queen."

At the last word, his mouth twitches, as if it leaves a nasty taste on his tongue.

Maël is on her feet in a split second when she sees the tiny stone between his fingers. "You treacherous—"

He smiles gleefully as she flings herself at him. Without much trouble, he holds her back using his free hand while the other is above his head. The stone catches the sun, and although it is only the size of a pea, it manages to blind me for a second. In that second, the screams around us turn into moans of agony.

I blink to clear my vision, just in time to see Maël hit the traitor on the head with her staff. The stone—some stowed away knowledge in the back of my mind tells me it's a plume agate—bounces from his hand when he falls, and Maël dives forward to grab it.

But instead of picking it up and putting it back between the entwined twigs where it probably belongs, she drops down on her knees.

First, I think the traitor has tripped her, but then she doubles over. Her wand slips from her hand, and she lands on her side, breathing heavily. Drops of sweat pop up on her forehead, and she coughs violently.

Laughing loudly, the traitor gets to his feet and takes his time to pick up the agate stone.

"I am so glad you liked my soup," he grins, looming over Maël. "Of course, you did not ingest as much poison as your loyal subjects." He tosses the stone in the air. "That would have interfered with my plans for you."

"What a horrible man," I say to the Maël standing next to me. "He poisoned your whole tribe? Why?"

There's no answer, and when I turn my head, the ghost queen quickly wipes away a tear.

I bite my lip. "I'm so sorry, Maël. If it's too much for you to watch, we can leave. I understand why you hate food now."

"No." Although her voice is hoarse, the word comes out briskly. "I can do it."

I nod, although I'd rather not see more of this myself. But I'm sure it will be over soon. Maël is in no position to fight this man off. It will only be a couple more minutes before she dies along with everyone she's ever cared about.

I blink away the tears forming in my eyes. If only I could help her. But her fate has already been determined.

CHAPTER 6

"I will fast forward a bit," Maël says to my surprise. "And while we watch the last days of my life, I can tell you the rest of the story."

"Days?" I rub my ear to make sure I heard her right. "He kept you alive for days?"

She raises her staff, and now that I know what to look for, I see the agate hidden between the twigs at the top. That is where the sparkle comes from when Maël uses her magic. I'm glad it's intact again.

I put my hand on her arm and everything starts to move again, but slowly now, so I can keep watching.

"He made me watch them die, all of them," Maël whispers. She gestures at the space around us, and I watch the traitor flit in and out of view, throwing one person after another onto the ground around the campfire. Maël slows down time a bit, so we can see him roll in a cart filled with bodies. Most are like

47

dolls, motionless and limp, but some are still moving as he throws them down.

The old Maël tries to crawl to them, to help them, but she can barely move herself. Pain distorts her face no matter how hard she tries to hide it from the few people who are strong enough to open their eyes. I see her lips moving when the traitor returns with another load of bodies. He puts them all in a circle, leaning against each other to keep them upright, as if they're just enjoying a night around the fire together.

"What did you say to him?" I ask.

She shakes her head sadly. "I begged him to have mercy on my people. I told him that whatever we did to hurt him, it was my fault."

I swallow to keep my tears back. "What did he answer?"

"He said: 'Oh, I know it is all your fault. Their punishment will end soon, do not worry. You, on the other hand, have a long way to go before your suffering stops.' And then he just sat down next to me until they all died, and their bodies started to rot." She raises her staff higher. "It might be better to look away now."

I obey immediately, the sight of the dead around us already making me nauseous. Not just because of the way they look, but mostly because of the cruelty of it.

"Why?" The question slips from my lips before I can stop it.

"He told me it was because we abandoned our

work for the king. We lived off his land, killed his animals and drank his water, and we did not give anything back. He thought about selling us all to the Spanish, but he figured we would be too stubborn to do as we were told. He was told to punish us, so he did."

"Told by the king? By Mansa Kambi?"

"That is what I thought at first, but during our travels, we had heard about neighboring countries trying to take over our land. The king needed all of his subjects to fight for him, and we had slipped through the net several times. We wanted to remain an independent tribe, which is why we were moving closer and closer to the border of Mali, hoping to find a better home somewhere else. We could have made it, if I had not trusted this man."

"What was his name?" I'm not sure why I'm asking her this, but I suddenly want to know.

Maël shakes her head sternly. "I cannot give you his name. He is not worthy of a name anymore."

I nod, although I'm not sure I understand.

"Having a name gives you power, just as using someone else's name can sometimes give you power over them. You knew that, did you not?"

"I've heard of something like that, I think."

"This man is not worthy of going by any other name than traitor." She lowers her wand and sighs. "The end is near now."

Her wand trembles slightly, and without thinking, I grab her free hand. She tenses, and I expect her to pull free, but she doesn't. It feels a bit weird, as if our roles have been reversed, but at the same time, it feels good to know she needs me as much as I need her to survive, even if it's only for a few minutes.

Maël sucks in her breath, and I focus on her old self, lying very still by the fire. I'm glad we can't smell the decay around us. A pack of hyenas is munching on a couple of bodies. The tracks in the sand tell me they've taken a few with them already.

I try focusing on something else, but it's the only movement I can see. The traitor must be out hunting, or maybe he's sleeping in a tent nearby. It's almost nightfall, and the first shadows are creeping into the camp.

When Maël from the past moans softly and lifts her head a little, the hyenas look up from their meal. One of them moves closer and sniffs Maël's head. She tries to shoo it away, but she is barely able to move her arm or make a sound.

Two other hyenas join the first one. Maël gathers up all the strength she has left and rolls over, closer to the fire. The predators growl in frustration, and two of them return to easier prey. But the remaining animal is persistent. It has set its mind to this fresh snack, and it won't give up until it can sink its teeth into it.

"Oh no," I mumble, covering my mouth with my free hand.

The old Maël stretches her arm to the staff leaning against a tent. When I narrow my eyes, I can see the stone has been put back. If she can reach it, she might be able to freeze time and escape.

But who am I kidding? I already know she's going to die here. Even if her outfit didn't match the one her ghost copy is wearing and her hair wasn't exactly the same, I can feel it in Maël's energy. Her sorrow and rage seep into my body like lava flowing from a volcano. Maybe it's because she's squeezing my hand. Maybe it's because we're in her memory. Either way, it's as if my emotions have tuned into hers. It makes me want to turn around and run. Too bad I'm the one who asked to see this. And we can't go home, so I'll have to keep my feet firmly on the ground and see this through.

Just when I'm convinced the hyena will sink its teeth into Maël's shoulder and drag her away from the fire, a loud metallic banging echoes through the camp.

In the blink of an eye, the pack of hyenas is gone. Except for the one looming over Maël.

I have to give it points for determination, but when the traitor comes into view, slamming a wooden spoon against a bowl, it gives up and takes off. The traitor keeps making noise while he shouts something at the fleeing animal. I imagine it meaning something like 'get out of here, I'm not done with her yet!'.

When he finally stops his drum solo, I can hear the hyenas howling in the distance.

I can't help but let out a sigh of relief. At least it looks like Maël won't get ripped apart by wild animals.

Unfortunately, whatever the traitor has in mind can't be much better, judging by the sly grin on his face as he kneels down next to her.

He laughs shrilly when he sees the staff, that has fallen over and is now lying inches from Maël's hand. He picks it up and places it out of her reach, against the side of the tent. Then he vanishes inside and comes back with a bowl of water.

I expect him to give it to her, but instead, he dumps it over her head.

She splutters and tries to turn away from him, but he grabs her shoulder and pushes her on her back.

"What is he saying?" I ask Maël.

"Wake up, fallen queen, it is time to die."

The woman on the ground splutters some more, but keeps her eyes closed.

The traitor laughs and draws a spearhead from his belt. He grabs Maël by the hair and pulls her into a sitting position.

She opens her mouth, but her scream is cut off when the man drives the spear into the back of her neck.

I avert my eyes, bile rising to my throat. "No…" My head moves from left to right, as if denying what I saw makes it less true.

"Look." The queen ghost next to me lets go of my hand and tears her gaze from the scene before us.

Her hand moves to the curls that reach the spot where her cape is attached to her dress. She pulls them up to reveal a red scar.

I knew there was something in her neck, but I was always afraid to ask. Not just because of Maël's feelings, to be honest, but also because I was afraid it would be something like Vicky's scar, something attached to some kind of curse.

"How is this possible?" I ask her, studying it before she lets the curls fall over it again. "I thought with a ghost everything looks the way it did when you died. But the wound has healed. There's only that scar."

The muscles in her jaw move, and I'm afraid I've asked too much now.

"I'm sorry," I start to say. "You don't have to—"

She shakes her head. "It is okay. You have a right to ask." She points at the two people in front of us. "Watch."

I'm afraid to turn my head back, but I just want this to be over, for both of us.

Maël is slumped in the man's arms, blood trickling from the wound in her neck.

"Do not die yet," ghostly Maël translates the traitor's words with a cold voice I barely recognize. "You need to suffer some more."

The man pulls the spearhead out and places his free hand inches from the wound. A blue glow floats from his palm into Maël's neck, closing the wound.

I almost lose my balance and grab Maël's arm for support.

"He's… he's healing you?" I stutter.

A shiver runs through her. Tears free themselves

from the corners of her eyes. "He kept me alive for days with some kind of magic. Made me watch them all rot and get eaten by the hyenas."

It feels like someone is squeezing my throat shut.

"I'm… I'm so sorry… so sorry, Maël," I stammer, swallowing over and over to prevent myself from throwing up.

"It is not your fault," she says dryly.

"I shouldn't have made you tell me. This must be… horrifying for you to relive."

She whirls around so suddenly that I almost fall over again. But she grabs my shoulders with both hands, her staff falling in the sand, and brings her face close to mine. "No, you were right to ask me. Because I see it now."

"See what?" I ask, my mouth going dry again.

"Everything happens for a reason, Dante. My father dying, me becoming queen, the mistakes I made, you making me come back here, us not being able to leave this memory sooner. It is all part of the plan."

My mind is blank. "What plan?"

"Everything happens for a reason, Dante. Everything," she repeats.

Then she lets go of me and smiles. "Come on, it is time to try to get back again. We have work to do."

CHAPTER 7

We prepare to leave, or at least try to. Me with a mind that almost boils over, Maël with a surprisingly determined look on her face.

The tip of her wand, or what I now know to be the plume agate stone, starts to glow, and I glance around one more time. I take in Maël's home and vow never to forget what was done to her. Not that I ever could. The image of the spearhead piercing her skin is etched into my brain.

But now I see something else.

"Wait!" I call out.

The staff stops glowing when Maël's eyes follow my pointing finger.

"It's the sand again, the sand from the Beach of Mu."

"Another reason to leave this place," the ghost queen answers solemnly. "We cannot restore the balance from here."

"But look! It's beckoning us. Or at least, I think so." Doubt flares up, but I squash it. "What if it wants to lead us to a place that needs our help?"

"Earth needs our help, Dante. We should get back to it."

The sand snake curves and winds through the sky impatiently. When we don't move, it quickly draws closer. Its head stops inches from my face, but this time, I don't flinch. I'm not afraid of it anymore.

It jerks its head as if to say, 'Follow me'.

"See?" I say to Maël. "It wants to show us something. We should follow it."

"I am not sure—" Maël starts, but I interrupt her.

"What if it leads us to a way to defeat Satan once and for all? Or to a place where our friends are trapped?"

She starts to protest again, but I raise my hand. "I'm sorry, Maël, but I have a very strong feeling about this. My gut tells me to follow this sand, so that is what we're going to do."

She gives me an inquisitive look before nodding. "You are right. It is wise to listen to your inner voice."

The wave of sand shoots up to the clouds, twirls and dives back down.

I chuckle, all my fear for it gone now. "Looks like we made it happy."

Watching the sand dance ahead of us awakens the hope that has been pushed from sight. Yes, we're stuck here, but we won't be forever. And Maël is right, things do happen for a reason. We were meant to be in this memory when the Beach of Mu escaped Purgatory, because it is supposed to lead us somewhere. And for the first time since this whole crazy, magical ride started, I look forward to finding out where fate will take us. I've seen so many extraordinary, weird places that I can't help but wonder what else is out there. Of course, it could be as terrifying as the Shadow World, but I have to believe we can defeat whatever comes our way. I *do* believe we can. After all, we were chosen to keep the Devil in Hell and there's a prophecy that says we will win.

Without warning, another part of that prophecy nags at my thoughts. The sacrifice that's needed…

I shake my head and focus on the sand again. *We will find a way to win without sacrificing anyone.*

"What are you smiling so brightly about?" Maël asks with a frown.

"Just thinking about all the amazing things I've seen so far. Some beautiful, some ugly and frightening, but all of them mind-blowing."

She tilts her head. "That is one way to look at it."

I press my lips together and munch over an answer. "You know…" My mind wanders back to the life I led before I inherited Darkwood Manor. Before Dad died and Mom was suddenly cured of her fits. "Before I met you guys, I wasn't happy. Sure, compared to how it is now, life was pretty easy. All I had to worry about was Mom and school. But everything just seemed so…" I kick at a stone, and it flies straight up. I catch it with my foot and drop it back into the sand.

"It all seemed so pointless," I finally confess. "I didn't contribute anything to the world, and the days just dragged on, one after the other. Every day more of the same meaningless shit."

"And now you are the only one who can save the world," Maël adds.

"Right." I grin. "It went from one extreme to the other. To be honest, this is a bit too much. I really don't want the fate of the whole world resting on my shoulders, but at least I mean something now." I wait for a response, but it doesn't come.

I give Maël a sideways look. "You know what I mean?"

When she turns her head to me, there are tears in her eyes. "Yes, Dante, I know what you mean."

"Oh… I… I'm sorry," I stutter. "That was… thoughtless of me. You know what it's like to be responsible for a lot of people." *And also what it's like to lose them all.*

Her curls jump from left to right as she shakes her head. "It is fine, Dante. I understand what you are saying. And you are right. There is so much more in this world than we know, and even the evil side of it is beautiful, in its own way. Every battle we win makes us stronger and takes us one step closer to our goal."

I know that her goal is not only to save everyone

on Earth, but also to make up for what happened to her tribe. To cleanse her soul, or whatever you want to call it.

"You are one of the bravest people I know, Maël. I'm proud to call you a friend and a part of my Shield, and I know you will succeed." There's more I want to say, but the words get stuck in my throat.

"Do not lose that wonderful smile now, Dante," she says, touching my cheek briefly. "You are right to be optimistic."

Her words bring my smile back, until I search the sky for the Beach of Mu.

My mouth falls open, and my feet refuse to take me any further. "Wow."

The sand is floating near a dark hole in the sky, surrounded by a circle of light.

"It is a portal," Maël says. She sounds a bit surprised.

"Of course." I chuckle. "How did you think the beach got into your memory?"

She starts walking again, and I follow so hastily I almost trip.

"It could have teleported."

I nod, my eyes glued to the light in the sky. "Yes, I hadn't thought of that. But it didn't."

My heart goes in overdrive as we approach the portal. Inside, something is moving. Trying to escape maybe? Craving a bite of human flesh?

I suppress a shiver and come to a halt next to Maël under the gateway to who-knows-where.

"Now what?" I ask, my voice hoarse with unease. *Maybe this wasn't such a good idea after all.*

But it's too late to change my mind, because the sand comes soaring down. The snake head smiles at me as if to say, 'Don't worry, I've got you'. The next moment, I'm floating. Further and further up I go, lifted by the grains of sand. Soon, Maël is hoisted up beside me. Inch by inch, we get closer to the dark portal.

"What are those things?" I ask, my voice trembling.

I can make out scaled animals the size of rats dashing along the edge of the blackness, dots of light escaping from their pointed snouts. Their short legs move so quickly you can barely see them. I'm glad they don't seem to notice us, but getting closer to them makes me nervous.

"I think they are keeping the portal open," Maël muses. "Look at the specks of light they spit out. They are all absorbed by the circle of light."

So, they're not going to eat us alive. That's good to know.

Maël seems to read my mind. "Not every ugly thing is evil, Dante."

I don't respond, because suddenly we're moving faster. It's as if the portal is sucking us in. I can feel it pulling at my legs.

The blackness is now only inches from my nose. I squint in an attempt to make out anything other than the strange creatures and the sand swirling around me. But there's only darkness. As soon as we're pulled into it, coldness prickles my skin. Everything gets hazy for a minute, and all sounds are muffled, as if we pass through a large bubble.

Suddenly, I'm looking at myself. I try to stop moving, but I'm pushed closer and closer to my reflection.

"What's happening?" I ask Maël hoarsely. "What is that? Some kind of shapeshifter?"

A tiny light flickers above us, and I can see Maël's arm reaching out to a copy of hers. Her reflection does the same.

"No, don't!" I call out, struggling to stay still myself.

Too late.

The ghost queen is yanked forward. Within seconds, she has merged with her copy. She blinks, shakes her head and flexes her fingers. Then she smiles at me. "There is nothing to worry about. These are our bodies. We are leaving my memory, which means we need our bodies back. Just step into yours."

"Are you sure?" My voice trembles as I take in the Dante in front of me. *There's something strange about him. He's me, only… empty. Does that mean Maël is right? Is it really my body? Or is it something dark getting ready to swallow me?*

There's no more time to think about it. I slide forward until our noses almost touch. No matter how much I want to close my eyes, I don't. If this is an evil entity, I want it to know I'll fight for my life until there's no strength left in me.

I'm pulled off my feet. My breath is cut off, and for a moment, I hear two heartbeats instead of one. I struggle to free myself, but the pull is too strong. Shivers run through me like electricity. I clench my fists. Everything gets dark. *Is it over? Did it kill me?*

"Open your eyes," Maël's voice says.

I do and look down. Everything looks normal. I'm just me. Carefully, I run my fingers over my face. Nothing weird there.

Maël places a hand on my arm. "You are fine."

I stay still and try to feel around inside myself, searching for something that doesn't belong. Nothing moves. There's only one heartbeat.

Slowly, I breathe out and nod.

The ghost queen smiles again. "Are you ready to continue?"

"Yes."

She steps forward, and I follow.

A dull world awaits us on the other side of the portal. We step out onto a path of black grit.

"Any idea where we are?" I ask Maël.

She shakes her head.

The sand leaves us no time to find out what kind of world this is or to adjust to the cold climate and scarce light, taking off so fast it's out of sight in a second.

"Wait!" I call out. "We can't move that fast!"

My words echo in the emptiness, and I bite my lip. Maybe shouting wasn't a very wise thing to do here.

A soft clicking awakens in the distance, followed

by a high-pitched wail.

I rub my arms and blink until I can make out the outline of the path.

"Okay, let's go," I say quietly.

We walk along the winding path, the clicking behind us driving up our speed.

I can see a bit more now, but that doesn't make me feel any better. On both sides of the dark path, there's nothing. No buildings, streets or plants. Nothing moves, except for something that looks like thick, grayish snowflakes falling from the sky. They never touch the ground though, just hover in the air as if they're waiting for something.

I drive up the pace some more.

"Do you see the Beach of Mu anywhere?" I whisper to Maël.

With her staff still pointed at the strange snowflakes, she turns her head to me. "No, I cannot see much here at all."

My eyes search for the end of the path, but it seems to go on forever. "I feel like Dorothy entering Oz."

"Who?" she whispers back.

"The girl from…" Behind us, the clicking gets louder. "Never mind."

We urge our feet to go faster, almost running now. The grit snaps and crackles under our feet. The pieces seem to get larger the further we go. They shatter when we step on them, slowing us down more and more.

I slide down one particularly large piece that doesn't break under my weight. Maël catches me just in time. The clicking is deafening now, and I risk a glance behind me.

A horde of beelike creatures is gaining on us fast. Their bellies give off a soft red glow, which illuminates the source of the noise: razor sharp fangs, like those of a stag beetle, slam together as they open and close their mouths hungrily. Transparent wings as large as a crow's, with pulsing red veins, carry the guinea pig-sized bodies forward.

We'll never make it in time to wherever the Beach of Mu has gone.

I conjure a lightning bolt in each hand. "Can you slow them down?"

Maël has already lifted her wand. The tip starts glowing as she mumbles the words of her spell.

The clicking grows more furious, as if the monsters know what we're trying to do. Their wings beat twice as fast, propelling them closer to us at double the speed.

I lift my hands to release the bolts. Just before I can, a heavy weight lands on me, knocking me over.

The bolts splutter and die, and I scrape my hands on the grit when I try to break my fall.

I roll over to get rid of the clicking monster on top of me while I fumble for my athame.

A second body slams into me, making me drop my weapon. Not knowing what else to do, I cover my head with my arms and roll myself into a ball.

"Freeze them!" I yell, although I'm sure Maël won't be able to hear me above the racket the creatures are making.

Something lifts my shirt and tickles my back while something else ruffles my hair. I nudge my power core again for more lightning when I hear another sound. It's that high-pitched wail again, but it doesn't sound so fierce now. It's more like a hesitant question.

Carefully, I lower my hands. Something slides along my leg, but it's not a violent touch. It's soft. As if it's examining me. Red light shines above me, and I slowly look up.

One of the bee-monsters hovers just above my head. Its beetle-like head is tilted.

"Hello there," I say softly.

Its belly shines brighter, and it lets out another inquisitive wail.

I try a small smile. "I'm not sure what you're asking, but you don't have to worry about us. We're not here to hurt you. We're just passing through." *I hope.*

With a sudden jolt, it comes down and touches my face with its fangs.

It's only now that I notice the clicking above me has stopped. All except this little fellow is silent.

"Maël?" I ask carefully. "Are you okay?"

"Yes," she whispers back. "They are performing some kind of scan."

"Could they be friendly?"

The beetle-bee in front of me grabs my shirt with its legs and pulls.

"Do you want me to get up?" I ask it.

It lets out another wail, and the light in its belly flickers.

When I push myself up, it lets out an excited shriek.

Slowly, I lift my hand. "You scared me, but you're not so bad, are you?"

It nudges my hand, and I stroke its side. It feels cold and solid, like steel.

The rest of the horde circles above us, taking us in with interest. Some of them hover down for a closer look, and I pet a couple more.

"Did you see what the path is made of?" Maël asks. "It is not grit, like I thought it was."

"It's not?" I look down and swallow when I see it.

The red light from the beetle-bees shines down on the path. I shiver when I remember landing in that. Maël is right, it's not grit at all. It's a collection of shattered skulls. They're too dark to be human, so I assume they're from some kind of monstrous species. The skulls come in every size, from tiny as a mouse's to bear-big. The ones we're standing between aren't all trampled yet. Most are still intact or just missing chunks.

I throw a ball of lightning in the direction we came from and see that the further away it goes, the smaller the pieces become. Before I can think about why that is, the beetle-bee pushes its fangs against my cheek again, asking for attention.

I stroke its belly and it clicks happily.

"They look ferocious, but I think they don't see us as prey. They were probably hoping to find more creatures like the ones covering this path."

I smile when I turn my head and see Maël petting two bees at once. "Those monsters they hunt must be even scarier than these guys. I wonder what they look like."

Maël turns around and freezes. "I have a pretty good idea."

CHAPTER 8

The beetle-bees start clicking like maniacs. The racket hurts my head, but I forget about it the instant my eyes fall on the monsters in front of us.

There are at least two dozen of them, only one leap away from us. I didn't think it was possible, but they are uglier than anything I've seen so far. They look like black retrievers gone wrong. Really wrong. Their heads are covered in dented black metal. Shiny double spikes stick out horizontally where their ears should be, and the gray saliva dripping from their toothless mouths form soggy beards. Every drop that falls on the path burns away a piece of the skulls lying there. Thick, spiked legs support the bodies covered in half ripped-off flesh and black metal plates. They have something resembling boils on their backs that look like they will burst any second. Their eyes move around constantly in the sockets with a creepy grinding noise. That is the only sound they make, and it barely rises above the increasing racket the beetle-bees are producing.

They are waiting for something.

"Can you freeze them?" I whisper to Maël.

"No," she answers, almost inaudibly. "My power does not work. I think my memories sucked too much energy out of me."

With my hands behind my back, I conjure two balls of lightning. "Then I guess we're fighting."

The moment I throw the balls, the beetle-bees dive forward, crashing into the metal dogs like battering rams. The ground vibrates from the force of the collision. The clicking decreases, but the high tones coming from the dogs' open mouths almost rip my eardrums.

My teeth crunch as I grind them together in agony.

More lightning flies from my hands, and the noise drops a couple of tones, making it more bearable. My aim is a bit off, because of the beetle-bees floating between us and the monsters, but I manage to hit a few more of them. They go down whining like broken robots.

I take out my Morningstar and swat halfheartedly at the bees blocking our path. "Move out of the way!"

They look back but stay where they are, clicking furiously at the monsters, as if to intimidate them.

"Why aren't they fighting with their mates?" I wonder out loud.

One of the bees blocks the path of a dog monster

that hauls itself at it, grabs the edge of the metal on its head and rips it off.

I turn away as half of the dog's head comes off, and the body drops onto the path.

The bee soars back to its place between us and the fight, and suddenly it hits me. "Are they protecting us?" My voice sounds just as incredulous as I feel.

"I believe they are." Maël sounds as unaffected as always. "We can turn back to the portal if you like?"

My mouth drops open. "What? No! The Beach of Mu was leading us somewhere."

"It was leading us into the arms of a monster army," she states coldly.

I rub the spot between my eyes. "I can't believe that."

"Then why did it leave us, Dante?"

Searching for an answer that makes sense, I stare in the distance behind the raging monsters. That's when I see it.

I recognize the figure dressed in black immediately, even though she's moving really fast.

My mouth curls up in a wide and relieved smile, and I whip out my athame and grab my Morningstar firmer to join the fight.

"I know why it left us," I say to Maël, and I nod in the direction of the incoming whirlwind that contains my girlfriend. "It went to get help."

I gently tap the beetle-bee in front of me on the side. "We want to fight."

Both of them move out of the way, and as I dive

70

into the battle, I hear Maël calling out behind me. It sounds like 'this is not our battle to fight', but I ignore her. I'm looking forward to bashing in some of these ugly skulls and adding the pieces to the path.

Vicky dashes in from the other side, with an equally murderous look on her beautiful face.

I keep my Morningstar from unraveling, so I can hit the metallic snouts from up close, while swinging my athame around. Flesh rips, and blood sprays all over me, but I don't care. With every monster I slay, I get a step closer to Vicky.

There are only three more black dogs between us. I prepare to drive my Morningstar into the chin of the one looming over me, but two bees grab it and sink their fangs into its eyes. Since all the other dogs are kept occupied by the swarm of beetle-bees, I now have a moment to watch Vicky fight.

And that's when I see something isn't right. There's a hungry glint in her eyes that doesn't suit her, and she lashes out like a wild animal. When she bites a chunk out of her opponent's throat, I try to back up. But I'm pressed in between the struggling bodies. Fangs scrape my arm, and I duck just in time to prevent a ripped-off bee's head from hitting me in the face.

When I look up, Vicky is staring at me with bared, bloody teeth.

She's having another fit.

"Listen to me, Vicky," I plead. "I am not the enemy." I try to sound soothing, but since I have to yell to be heard over the noise of the raging battle, my words come out angry.

She licks her lips slowly, and for the first time, the gesture provokes tingles of fear instead of desire.

Her head jerks from left to right with sickening cracks as she scrutinizes me. It looks like she has a hard time deciding whether she should attack me or not.

"Remember who you are, Vicky," I yell. "We're on the same side. I love you!"

She opens her mouth, as if to say something, but all that comes out is a low gurgle. Blood trickles from her lips and down her chin.

Something hot breathes in my neck, and I duck, my Morningstar moving up to smash the monster behind me.

It anticipates my move and jumps back, only to leap at me the moment my Morningstar misses its head. From the corner of my eye, I see another black dog advancing from my left. I fold my fingers tighter around the hilt of my athame and use the momentum of the Morningstar to turn and hit my attackers at the same time. I'm halfway when I see Vicky launching herself at me with outstretched fingers. Her blue eyes have turned a shade of red. Hunger and murder shine through them.

Everything seems to slow down when I adjust the trajectory of my weapons to prevent hitting Vicky while I try to step sideways in time to avoid her as well as the two dogs.

I'm too slow, or maybe my enemies are just too fast for me. The spikes of my Morningstar scrape one of the dogs' shoulders, and my athame misses the second dog by inches. They both keep coming, even more eager to rip me to pieces now. Meanwhile, Vicky opens her mouth, ready to sink her teeth into my neck. Unable to change my course again, I keep turning. As a last resort, I drop my weapons and conjure two lightning bolts. I don't want to hurt Vicky, but I have to take out these two monsters before they get a chance to grab an arm or leg.

Suddenly, several things happen at the same time. One of the dogs lunges for my arm. Before I can hit it with my lightning, a beetle-bee flings itself at it and knocks it out of the way. Two people scream at me to duck. The first is Maël, who stabs the second dog in the side. It keels over, and its jaws snap shut next to my foot. When I turn my head, I see a ball of grease soaring through the air, undeniably from Charlie. It hits Vicky on the back of the head, and she turns with a beastly growl. Gisella somersaults toward her, slashing a couple of throats with her blades on the way. She lands perfectly on her feet, like the werecat that she is, and raises her blades, ready to fight Vicky.

I forget everything around me. If a plated dog attacks me from behind now, I will be dead in seconds, but I can't get myself to care. For a split second, I think Gisella is here to save me, but with her blades ready to slice up my girlfriend, I know I am wrong. All I can think is that I shouldn't have trusted her. She's not here to stop Vicky, she's here to kill her. She is, after all, half evil witch, half werecat, a deadly combination. The red light from a passing beetle-bee is reflected in the metal of her weapons. With Vicky in almost solid battle mode, she will not survive a knife through the gut.

I leap forward, the remaining bolt in my hand fizzling out like faulty fireworks. "No!"

My mind freezes. Everything around me gets hazy, except for the spot where Vicky is standing. A sharp pain shoots through my ankle, but I ignore it. I don't care about dying anymore. After all, what would life be worth without Vicky?

Seconds before I reach her, another grease ball hits the side of her head. She stumbles sideways, making me miss her and knock straight into Gisella.

As fighting dogs and bees jump out of our way, we land on the skull covered path. Gisella's blades have turned back into hands during our fall, but as soon as we hit the ground, her weapons glint again. I try to catch my breath and wrap my head around what just happened. Gisella has already recovered. Her arms move up. If I don't defend myself, she'll cut off my head.

Somewhere close, Charlie's voice rings out. "No!" He finally understands, like I do now, that his girlfriend is a traitor. She used him to get close to me and my Shield, waited for the perfect opportunity, and now she's ready to end us. I know this, yet I find myself unable to move. My body feels light, empty.

My brain doesn't obey anymore, no matter how hard I yell at it to do something. Fire a lightning bolt at her, hit her with hail, flood the whole path with a tsunami. Anything is better than waiting for my final seconds to pass. But I can't even bring myself to close my eyes.

My heartbeat stutters as Gisella stabs with all her force. There's a loud yelp, and a heavy weight falls on us. Our heads bump painfully, and I breathe in sharply.

"Dante?" Gisella sounds panicked. "Dante! Are you okay?"

Another voice joins hers. I know it's Charlie, but my head is spinning so fast, and my heartbeat is so loud that I can't do anything except keep still.

The weight is lifted off me, but I don't feel any better.

"Dante! Answer me!" Charlie's voice changes volume with every word he says. Loud, soft, loud, soft. "Take care of Vicky," he says, and wilt a jolt, I sit upright.

This can't be happening. Charlie is trying to kill Vicky too?

"Wow, easy." Two hands support my wobbling body. "We've got this, don't worry."

"No!" I shout, but it comes out hushed.

"Relax, the dogs are defeated. The few that are left are running away with their metallic tails between their legs."

"Don't kill her!" I moan, bile rising in my throat. I

try to find Vicky and Gisella, but the world keeps tilting.

Charlie strokes my back. Maël walks up to us with a concerned look on her face.

"Why would we kill her?" Charlie asks. "Vicky is fine, Dante. Come on, take a deep breath. I think you hit your head pretty hard there. And you're losing blood."

"Gi-Gisella. She cut me."

He lets out a sigh. "She did no such thing, Dante. She risked her life to save you and Vicky. That's what she did."

"But… but…"

"Now shut up and sit still so I can bandage your ankle."

My eyes flick to my feet. There's a large gash in my ankle. Blood oozes out of it.

"Lie down," Vicky's voice says next to me.

I turn my head and keel over. Everything spins, and fog rises before my eyes.

"Easy, babe." Her voice sounds sweeter than ever. Her face appears above my head, and I squint to make it out. The smile on her lips is a concerned one, but the traces of blood on her face turn it into something creepy.

I blink until she gets clearer. "Are you okay?"

She snorts. "I almost killed you, and you're asking if *I'm* okay? You must have bumped your head harder than I thought."

Gisella kneels down next to Charlie, who is

struggling to tie a piece of cloth around my ankle. "I've never been any good at this," he huffs.

I try to make out Gisella's face, but my vision is still blurred. Although the panic inside me has died, I'm not entirely sure I can trust her.

She pushes Charlie gently aside. "That'll do. Let me take care of the rest."

The rest?

Fear flutters in my chest. Vicky must sense it, because she takes my hand and squeezes it.

"Stop worrying. Gisella and Charlie just saved us both," she whispers in my ear.

"It is the imbalance of the universe," Maël says. "It has affected Dante too. His molecules are fighting inside him, sending him the wrong signals and magnifying his doubts."

The werecat slash black witch places her hands on my ankle. "Let's see if I can stop the bleeding through the bandage."

A sharp sting shoots through my leg, and I yell. Three beetle-bees appear above my head, clicking hesitantly.

I try to raise a hand, but I need it to keep myself steady.

"It's fine," I pant, and I briefly close my eyes when the pain soars up to my neck. "It's fine. She's healing me." *I hope.*

Gisella takes off the bandage again and admires her work. "Okay, the bleeding has stopped. You'd better lay down again. The wound is deep, so this is not going to be pleasant."

As I put my head on Vicky's lap, I meet her eyes. *Please read my fear. Please make sure she doesn't kill me.*

She bends over me and kisses my forehead. "Don't worry, I'm here."

I give in to Gisella's touch while thoughts of friends and enemies whirl through my head. This girl wouldn't be the first to betray my trust. Paul and Simon did, after years of friendship. They were just waiting for the right time to get me out of the way. Waiting for instructions to kill me. How lucky that the Devil underestimated my powers. If he hadn't, I would've been dead long before my powers even awoke.

An itchy feeling in my leg brings my thoughts to a sudden halt. Gisella has healed me once before, and I remember what it felt like, so I grit my teeth in preparation. The itch is accompanied by the sense of a hundred ants sinking their little teeth into my flesh. Soon, their number is multiplied by two, and it feels as if they're marching right into my leg. The skin pulses while they feed on my flesh.

"Almost done," Gisella says from somewhere far away.

Finally, the feeling of the little legs and teeth subsides. Since I hate to find my leg gone, I avoid looking at it. Instead, I look up at Vicky, who becomes clearer with every second that passes. She's frowning at my leg, and I can't help but smile. I know she's watching it become visible again bit by bit.

"That's an amazing gift you've got there, Gis," she finally says, letting out her breath.

The werecat smiles, but her face is pale. "Thank you."

Charlie rubs her back. "Are you alright?"

"Fine." She swallows. "Like I said, it was a deep wound. It took a lot of energy to heal it."

She swats Charlie's hands away when he tries to help her up. "I'm fine."

But she isn't. She sways on her feet as much as I did a couple of minutes ago.

I look at my leg, which bears no scar or other sign of damage. Even the blood is gone.

The world is clear again, and the mist pulls up from my brain. Above us, the bees click happily. Several feet away, Maël is standing guard.

Guilt washes over me.

I get to my feet and pick up my weapons. "Thank you, Gisella. I'm sorry I doubted you."

She shakes her head, leaning on Charlie to stay upright. "It's fine, I understand. My genes might suck, but I guess I'm stronger than them."

I raise my hand for a high five. "You rock."

She grins and hits my hand. "Thank you. How does your leg feel?"

I jump up and down and twist it in all directions. "As new."

"So we're ready to go home?" Vicky asks, handing a pack of cookies to Charlie, which he rips open immediately.

"Not quite." I stare in the distance. "Maël and I were following a wave of sand."

"The Beach of Mu," the ghost queen adds, as if that explains everything.

"It was leading us somewhere when we bumped into these horrible dogs." I gesture at the skulls under our feet.

Vicky taps her lips with her finger. "I don't know what a Beach of Mu is, but a giant sand hand appeared through a portal. We followed it and it led us to you."

"That must have been it." I give my friends a grateful smile. "I'm so glad you guys are here. We were worried, and we couldn't get back." I wipe some dust off my pants and sleeves. "How did you find us anyway?"

Vicky shakes her body like a limbo dancer, and all the stains disappear. Her hair is no longer a mess, and her teeth are an innocent white again. I blink at the sudden change, but she acts as if nothing happened.

"Of course we couldn't leave Darkwood Manor without you, so we tried the spell to call you to us, but it didn't work," she explains. "Thankfully, when we used the reversed spell, it did take us through the portal. It wasn't hard to take Charlie and Gisella with us. Holding their hands was enough. The spell was somehow disturbed while we travelled through the portal though, but the sand was still with us to lead us to you."

"Did you leave the others at home?" Maël asks,

picking up her wand. "Or did something go wrong?"

"We all came," Charlie answers with his mouth full of cookie. "But we were attacked when we arrived. We decided half of us should follow the sand, since it seemed in a hurry to lead us somewhere. That's why D'Maeo, Jeep and Taylar stayed behind."

My mouth falls open. "You left them in the middle of a fight?" I start walking. "We have to go help them!"

The three beetle-bees follow me immediately, clicking and buzzing. They seem eager to throw themselves into another battle, and when they call to the rest of the swarm, the others join us.

Vicky catches up with me. "I'm sure they're fine, babe. And the sand is probably fighting with them. It turned back as soon as we reached you."

"Then why haven't they joined us already?" I ask tensely.

She picks up her pace, worry falling over her face. "That's a good question."

CHAPTER 9

Even though we go as fast as we can, the walk is long. Even the beetle-bees have ceased their clicking as the fog moves in on us. Every few seconds, I look back to check for more monster armies. Charlie, Gisella and Maël do the same.

Eventually, I break the uncomfortable silence. "How's Mom doing?"

Vicky entwines her fingers with mine. "I think she's okay, considering all the scary stuff she's been told lately. You know how crazy the magical world is, and she found it all out in one day. That you and your Dad have powers, that magic and monsters exist and that Satan is trying to take over the world. She's shocked but dealing with it."

"Good."

She raises her voice to get the attention of the others. "The fog is getting thicker. Something is moving inside it."

We slow down, and I conjure two balls of lightning for more light.

"How much further is it?" I ask, without taking my eyes off the slivers of dust drifting closer.

"We should be there by now, right?" Vicky looks back at Gisella and Charlie, who have come to a halt.

Suddenly, Charlie's eyes grow wide. I follow his gaze and grab Vicky's arm when I see two eyes loom up in the fog.

In a reflex, I pull Vicky toward me and shoot a ball of lightning at the eyes. It hits an invisible wall and bounces back. Several skulls on the path explode, and we throw up our hands to shield our faces. Pieces of black dog rain down on us, but all my attention goes to the dark figure emerging from the mist.

It looks like a man, but there's so much dust covering him and fog swirling around him that it's hard to tell for sure. It could also be some kind of elemental or monster.

"What is that?" I whisper to Vicky, who is squinting into the mist as well.

She shakes her head.

The beetle-bees start clicking louder as more eyes blink into view. I reach for my weapons and try to find a better foothold on the path. My heartbeat goes up at the thought of having to fight more creatures like the black dogs.

The figure steps onto the path and shakes some of the dust off.

"Now!" I yell, and although none of this was planned, we all charge at the same time. Gisella with her blades held out in front of her, Charlie throwing his balls of gel, Maël swinging her staff like a kung fu master. Vicky and I are less elegant. We just charge in, yelling at the top of our lungs and lashing out with our weapons. The clicking of the beetle-bees above us is so deafening that at first I don't recognize the voice shouting at us to stop. Then an arm covered in tattoos emerges from the fog and grabs my wrist. My Morningstar, already thrown, keeps going, and the momentum pulls us into the mist.

It takes a couple of seconds for my brain to put image and memory together. Meanwhile, I fight like a rabid dog to pull myself free.

"Ouch!" Finally, the hand around my wrist lets go. Then everything in my brain clicks together, and I freeze.

"Wait."

No one responds. Of course they don't. They're all completely caught up in this fight, and every sound is lost in the racket the flying creatures are making.

I stand up straight and look around. I can't see the path anymore. There's nothing but mist around me, with the occasional red glow of a passing beetle-bee.

Something grabs my ankle, and I scream.

"It's me! It's me!" Jeep's face appears inches from my nose, and I let out a sigh of relief.

"I'm so glad to see you." I suppress the urge to hug him. Instead, I try to shake of the fog that's clinging to my clothes. "I'm sorry I tried to kill you. The only thing we saw were eyes, and they just looked… scary."

Jeep smirks at me. "I know, we can be pretty intimidating. Anyway," he gestures at the impenetrable air, "we have to stop the others from trying to kill each other."

"Hang on." An idea sparks in my mind, and before I can think it through properly, I find myself reaching up. Something bumps into my hand and clicks angrily.

"It's me!" I call out to it as I pull my arm back in.

The bee zooms down. I can't make out its face, but I see the red glow from its belly.

"Stop attacking!" I yell. "These are our friends."

It looks at me for a few seconds, then takes off.

"I'm not sure that worked," Jeep says matter-of-factly.

"Try to reach the others," I tell him, and after I pick up my Morningstar, we both go in different directions.

The clicking continues, feeding my fear that my friends are not only slaughtering each other, but are also still being chased by the beetle-bees.

"Guys!" I yell as loud as I can. "Stop fighting!"

It's as if my voice bounces back from a solid wall.

I keep walking, my weapons tucked away again, and my arms outstretched. A shiver runs through me when I think of the possibility that we're not alone here. Anything could jump us as long as this fog makes it impossible to even see our own hands.

Then my fingertips find something soft. Fabric. Hair.

"Hello?" I yell, wrapping my hand around a shoulder. "It's me, Dante."

A thunderous voice answers me. "I know who you are."

A burning sensation starts in my fingers and spreads through the rest of my body, making me yelp and drop down onto my knees.

A giant shape looms over me. Fire explodes around its head, and I gasp for breath as I try to push myself back, away from it.

I have no doubt in my mind what this is, or rather who it is. I've seen and heard him before. He tortured my mother, threatened to kill me and everyone I love. But he's supposed to be in Hell.

So how did Lucifer end up here, in front of me?

CHAPTER 10

Is this another premonition?

I'd like to convince myself of that, but when I check out my surroundings, I know it can't be. I'm still in the same gray world, with thick fog clogging up my throat. *What would be the odds of getting a premonition about the exact place I'm standing in?*

"Dante Banner," the voice thunders. "I'm glad I found you here."

I scrunch up my nose. "I wish I could say the same."

He roars with laughter. "You're funny. I almost wish I didn't have to crush your skull."

Anger flares up inside me, pushing aside my fear. I haul myself to my feet and face Satan. He's in his monstrous form, a dark, massive shape with orange eyes that bore into mine. Heat emanates from him with every breath he takes, and flames shoot out of his ears, which is why I can see him through the fog.

"You try, and I'll destroy you," I say. I concentrate on the lightning ball spinning in the palm of my hand to hide my fear.

"Oh, you cute little human." Satan shakes his head. "You think you have a chance just because you saved some souls."

I release the ball and conjure another. Lightning breaks up the fog between us, but the Devil keeps laughing. With a simple snap of his finger, he crumbles the ball to dust.

"Stop that for a minute, will you?" he says, almost friendly. "There's not much time."

"There's plenty of time," I retort with venom in my voice, "because you are never going to win this."

I concentrate on his large, black head with the protruding horns and think of ice as hard as I can.

"No seriously, stop." His voice is calm, but it reverberates through my stomach. When I blink, he's changed into his tall, dark-haired human form.

He leans over me and reaches for my head.

Ice, ice, ice. Please freeze him!

"Relax, I'm not going to kill you. Yet."

I look up. His hand hovers above my head. The scales from his monstrous form shine through the skin, but there's not even a trace of ice on it.

His index finger pokes me so hard in the forehead that I tumble back. Before I can get up, he leans over me with a stern look. "Sit still for a minute and listen." He tilts his head, waiting for me to make another move. I don't.

"Good." His grin is so big I fear it'll tear his skin. "I've got a proposition for you."

In an attempt to regain my dignity, I cross my arms. "The answer is no."

"Don't test my patience, Dante Banner." He raises his voice, and I turn my head when a foul stench escapes his lips. "I may not be able to kill you in this projected form, but I'm starting to feel the urge to try." He straightens up to his full length and looks down on me as if I'm nothing more than an ant. "Now shut up and listen. Your family has been trying to sabotage my plans for years. This has never ended well for you, and it never will. My rule over the Earth is drawing nearer. I admire your efforts to stop me, but eventually, you will go down just like your father and grandfather did before you."

I roll my eyes and sigh heavily. "Is there a point to this speech?"

He brings his handsome face close to mine. The heat rising up from it scorches my skin, but I keep still.

"My offer is to let you live. We can play this game a while longer, but to be honest, I'm fed up with it. There are more enjoyable games to play. Games we could play together."

I snort and almost believe my faked confidence myself. "Somehow I doubt we have the same taste."

"Oh, but I think we see eye to eye on some subjects. For instance, how do you feel about murderers, rapists, torturers and such?"

I press my lips together.

His throated laugh makes the ground tremble. "You try to hide it, but I can see the disgust in your eyes. What if I told you you could punish them all? All of those sinners."

He's almost got me tempted, but of course I know it's too good to be true. Still, I play along. "That would be great. And then what?"

"I will let you find and punish every sinner on Earth. I get just a couple of souls in return. Nine is all I'm asking for. All sinners too, by the way, so where's the loss in that? I get my nine, you get the rest. Do with them what you will. How does that sound?"

He gives me that creepy grin again and waits patiently for my answer, but I can tell by the way he flexes his fingers that he's nervous.

I keep him in suspense for a moment, pulling a face that hopefully says I'm mulling it over.

"Well?" he asks. "What is your answer?"

"Really?" I imitate his laughter, but it comes out weak. "You think that's a good deal?"

He scratches his chin. "Not enough, huh? What if I throw in some saved loved ones?" He places a hand on his chest. "Promise to let all the people you love live. I can even bring that feisty girl back to life for you. What do you say?"

My heartbeat goes up. My brain shows me images of Vicky without see-through skin. Vicky in a different outfit, with different hair and flushed cheeks. I would give anything to make that happen.

"See? I told you I had something good to offer." Lucifer sounds satisfied. "You don't have to answer now. I'll visit you again soon. Think about it. And decide wisely."

When I look up, he raises both hands at his sides and moves one up after the other, like an evil imitation of Lady Justice. "Save them all, kill them all. Save them all, kill them all. It's your choice, Dante."

I want to tell him to stuff it, but he vanishes into the mist.

I stay on the ground, breathing in deeply.

"Dante? Say something!"

It's Vicky. She sounds panicked.

"I'm here!" I yell back, waving my hands in front of me to part the fog.

A dark shape jumps out at me and almost crushes my lungs. "We've been looking for you for hours! Where did you go?"

I frown. My answer is muffled by her lips. She kisses me hard, and I have to push her away to catch my breath.

"I was so worried. We all were."

She finally lets go and turns around. "Guys! I've found him!"

It takes a couple of minutes and some more screaming to gather everyone. I'm glad to see Jeep, D'Maeo and Taylar with them.

Charlie flings himself at me and pats my back hard. "I thought we'd lost you, mate. What happened?"

I touch my cheeks where the sting of Lucifer's

heat still lingers. "I was here. I was just here."

Vicky weaves her fingers through mine. "We called for you. Why didn't you answer?"

"I saw Lucifer."

Every single mouth drops open.

D'Maeo is the first to recover. "Are you sure? That's not possible, is it?"

"Of course I'm sure. He isn't that hard to recognize, you know."

"But how?" Taylar asks.

"He said he projected himself here."

Vicky's hand skims my chest and face. I shake her off. "I'm fine. He couldn't really hurt me, because he wasn't really here."

She steps back abruptly.

"I'm sorry." I pull her back and kiss her. "I didn't mean to snap. It's just… let's say it was an intense meeting."

Jeep takes off his hat and dusts it off for the third time. "What did he want?"

"He offered me a deal."

Frowns all over.

"What kind of deal?" D'Maeo and Vicky ask in unison.

Quickly, I explain what Satan offered me.

Jeep bends over with laughter. "He said that?"

His laugh is contagious, and soon we're all gasping for breath.

Except for D'Maeo, who folds his arms over his chest and gives us his fatherly look of disapproval.

"Come on," I finally manage, taking in big gulps of air. "You have to admit it's kind of funny. The Devil is so scared of us that he offers me a part of his kingdom." I make quotation marks in the air at the last word.

D'Maeo nods slowly. "Yes, he's getting desperate. And you know what desperate people do, right?"

I wipe my eyes with the back of my hand and shrug. "What? Desperate things? What's he going to do, send more demons?"

The gray-haired ghost doesn't answer. He just stares at us, one by one, forcing us with his gaze to remember something important, like a teacher waiting impatiently for their students to dig into their memory of past lessons.

Maël is the first to regain her serious demeanor. Although, I have to say, she never really loosened up. She never steps out of her role as queen.

"Okay, what?" I ask them both. "What is the worst he could do after all he has already done to us? He tried to kill us and scare us. He sent armies of demons, and traitors who acted like friends. He took my mother and tortured her. What in the world could be worse than all that?"

My voice gets stronger with every word. Fear is slowly trickling back into my body, because I know D'Maeo wouldn't look at me this way if it wasn't serious.

"Beelzebub is worse," he says calmly. "And I can guarantee you, that if you say no to this offer, and we save more souls—"

"You mean 'when'," I interrupt.

He smiles. "Yes, when we do that... Lucifer will turn to his last option, his last chance to win this. He will send his right hand to deal with us. And I'm not looking forward to fighting Beezlebub."

"Right." I wipe the remains of my laughing fit out of my eyes. The fist that has been squeezing my heart a lot lately is back.

But I straighten my back and shake the tension off my shoulders before the feeling can take a hold. "You know what, let him send this Beezleguy. We're stronger than he thought, and we will get even stronger. Some of us are still learning to control our powers, and for every surprise he has, we'll have an answer. Right?"

Nobody answers, so I raise my fist to strengthen my words and try again. "Right?"

Gisella is the first to step forward and raise her fist next to mine. "Right!"

Of course Charlie follows her example, and soon the others join in. Even the beetle-bees, that have watched us silently from a couple of feet away, dash in and click their fangs furiously.

"The Devil will never win," I exclaim, and I smile as D'Maeo gives me an approving nod.

CHAPTER 11

We've walked another mile at least, the bees keeping watch in front as well as behind us, when we finally see a light in the sky and something swirling around it.

"There it is!" Vicky calls out. "That's the beach, right?"

I squint at the wriggling shape. "Yes, I think it is."

We increase our pace, but I warn the others to stay vigilant. Anything can jump us from the fog if we're not careful. Still, I feel a lot more confident now that I'm no longer alone with Maël. With all our strengths combined, we make a pretty good team. And it's nice to have the beetle-bees as back-up.

Finally, we reach the end of the path of black skulls. It takes a couple of steps to get used to even ground again. The solid sand we walk on now has red stains here and there, as if something gets killed on it regularly, then pulled down and eaten, but so far, nothing is popping out of it.

When I look up again, a snake made of sand is hovering in front of me.

"Hi there," I say cheerily. "Good to see you again! Thank you for guiding our friends to us."

It bows its head and nods at the portal in the sky, which is pulsing.

"You want us to follow you through another portal?" I scratch my head. "Are you sure it's safe?"

The snake's head nods, then moves from left to right before soaring back into the dark sky.

"Well, that's comforting," I say to the others as we start walking again.

Vicky links her arm through mine. "I think we should follow it. It seems benign."

I exchange a look with Maël. "That's what we thought too."

We walk until we're under the shiny portal and look up. There's nothing to see but the pulsing light, which seems to hold the gateway open.

Charlie sighs and conjures a large ball of grease. "Okay, let's do this. I can't wait to get out of here, you know."

Within seconds, he has built a stairway of gel. While he builds some more steps, he offers his hand to Gisella and guides her up.

I whistle softly. "I'm impressed." Then, with a grin, I add, "But there are faster ways of getting there."

Before I can finish my sentence, the Beach of Mu sweeps down and picks me, Maël and Vicky up. In one vertical movement it heads for the portal. I have to cling onto its granular body to keep myself from falling.

Once we're through the portal, it slithers across the floor to let us off. When I get to my feet, I realize we're in another unknown world, that doesn't look much better than the last. The air is humid, and the sky somehow seems to press down on me. Shivers wake up inside me at the thought of walking through more unfamiliar territory. *Who knows what else we'll run into. I don't want to find out what kind of creatures live here.*

The sand dives back down to pick up Jeep, Taylar and D'Maeo while Charlie and Gisella step from their stairway into this new world. Behind them, the swarm of bees gathers silently.

"You're not coming with us?" I ask them.

The one at the front clicks solemnly.

Maël appears next to me and places a hand on my arm. "I don't think they can. They are bound to their world."

"Then this is our goodbye," I say, and I'm surprised to feel the tug of sadness. I get down on one knee and bow my head. "It was an honor to know you all and to fight with you. Thank you for all you've done for us. Stay safe."

Next to me, Maël gets to her knees too, and soon the others follow.

The bees click softly and bow their heads. Their red bellies turn a bright yellow. Then they turn and take off.

Jeep is the first to get up. He puts his hat back on and cracks his back. "That was interesting."

When I pull Vicky back up, she places a kiss on my cheek. "I'm so proud of you," she whispers. "You're turning into a great leader."

"Thank you, babe, but I'd rather be a great fighter right now."

She tilts her head in thought. "Try to be both."

I pull her close, and she buries her face in my shoulder. "I was so worried when we couldn't wake you from Maël's memory."

"I know, I'm—"

"Guys?" Charlie nudges me, chocolate smeared all over his mouth.

Reluctantly, I let go of Vicky and follow his pointing finger with my eyes.

I swallow when I see an army of toad-like monsters the size of raccoons approaching on all fours, their spiked tails raised high. "That doesn't look good." I survey our surroundings. There's some kind of dark lake on our left and dead, white trees on our right.

I point behind me. "I say we go that way as fast as we can."

"I second that." Vicky turns and pulls me with her.

Every couple of steps I look behind me. The army of toads is following us at a lazy pace, which makes me think we're going exactly where they want us to go.

Taylar catches up. He blinks nervously as he takes

in the lake and forest on both sides and the stone path that seems to lead nowhere. "Where do you suppose we are?"

"To be honest, I have no idea. And I'm not so sure I even want to know," I respond. I point at the Beach of Mu, dancing through the air like a kite without a string. "But I guess we're going in the right direction."

We both glance over our shoulder to check on the army behind us. It's still there, but not closing in. Their fat toad legs keep a steady but slow pace, and because of that, we've slowed down a bit too.

"Where do you think it's leading us?" Taylar asks.

"To something important. Maybe to the solution to this whole 'disturbed balance of the universe' thing."

"What if it's a trick?" He rakes his fingers through his white hair and glances left and right again. "What if it's pretending to be our friend, just to lead us to our deaths?"

The thought has crossed my mind too, but my gut is telling me the sand can be trusted.

Not that my gut is so reliable. Paul and Simon managed to trick it for years. But the beach could have killed me and Maël easily, and the others too, if it wanted to.

What if it's leading us to its boss? To someone who wants to kill us himself?

"If it wants to harm us, we'll fight it," I say out loud to quiet the voice as well as Taylar.

He nods, but there's still concern on his face. I can't blame him. This world doesn't feel much better than the last. I'd be happy to get out of here soon too.

Of course, there's no such luck.

Suddenly, the sand stops swirling. It hovers high in the air for a second and then shoots back to us at lightning speed.

"What is it?" I ask, but I can already see for myself.

Straight ahead, another army approaches. It consists of fat creatures with slick and uneven skin and tails resembling spiked bludgeons sticking up into the air. A copy of the army behind us.

"I knew this was a trap!" I yell at myself.

"Stay calm," Vicky says. "Maybe they're the good guys, like those bees."

As if on cue, the toad monsters all come to a halt, rise up on their hind legs and spit out blotches of… well, probably deadly poison.

"Maël!" I point at the army behind us. "Charlie!" My hand moves to the army on our other side.

My friends waste no time. Mumbling rapidly, Maël focuses on the incoming drops on her side while Charlie throws tiny balls of gel at Spiderman speed in the other direction. He knocks the dozens of blotches out of the air like a pro, but on our other side, they're still coming closer.

D'Maeo steps up beside the ghost queen and raises his hands. His deflective power works faster than Maël's time tampering one, and after a couple of seconds, the drops fall out of the sky.

I whip out my Morningstar and conjure a bolt of lightning in my other hand. "Maël, Charlie, D'Maeo, can you get rid of any more drops coming our way?"

Charlie and D'Maeo nod. Maël is still chanting, but I'm pretty sure she's heard me. And it looks like her power is at full strength again.

"Okay…" I raise the hand with the lightning bolt above me. "Who's ready to fight?"

The rest of the group lets out a battle cry, and when I release my bolt, we all charge, half of us straight ahead, the others in the opposite direction.

The army in front of me lifts their heads again and spits out more blotches than I can count. I increase my speed and duck, but there are too many drops to evade. Moving sideways, I can avoid two more, but one is soaring directly toward me.

I hit it with lightning as a last resort. As soon as it connects with the liquid, I know this was a bad decision. The blotch blows up into hundreds of little splatters that are impossible to dodge.

I throw myself onto the ground, cover my head with my arms and prepare for the excruciating feeling of a toxic substance burning through my skin and bones.

Something hits me with force, and I almost roll over.

"Sorry!" the familiar voice of Taylar says.

I look up and find myself under his shield while poison soars straight through his transparent body.

He lifts the shield back up and examines the front. "Looks like the protection spell on it is still intact. Here, you use it." He hands it to me and storms off before I can protest.

"Be careful!" I call out after him.

"Always!" he yells back, slamming his sword into the head of the first monster he meets.

Vicky breezes past me, and I'm relieved to see the poisonous drops flying through her too. But it's too early to breathe easy, since I know it requires a lot of concentration to fight and stay transparent at the same time. One slip up, and there's a gaping hole in my girl.

One of the toad monsters crashes into my leg, pushing me over. It opens its ugly beak, ready to spit, but I bring down the shield and crush its skull. Slimy skin splatters in all directions. Thankfully it doesn't burn.

I risk a quick glance over my shoulder and see Gisella cutting off limbs and Jeep's hat soaring back to him, dripping with blood and slime. Maël still has her wand raised, aimed at the army that Vicky and Taylar are fighting. But they're not slowing down one bit. Maybe I was wrong about her strength returning.

Another weight knocks into my shield, and I shove it away while reaching for my Morningstar, which I must have dropped when I was trying to avoid the venom. Without unraveling it, I swing it down on top of the toad's head. The spikes penetrate the leathery, slime-covered skin. Its bulky legs slide sideways, and the thick head hits the ground.

It takes some strength to pull the ball out of the toad's skull, and I almost tumble backwards. I sway on my feet, and from the corner of my eye, I can see two monsters storming in from each side.

Instinctively, I conjure a lightning bolt in my left hand while aiming the Morningstar on the monsters to my right. Then I remember what happened when I blew up the venom drops and close my hand. I need a different approach. A different kind of weather condition.

"How about some nice big hail stones?" I say out loud, and I turn my eyes on the sky, imagining icy stones the size of golf balls dropping on the toads' heads. As they waddle closer, the sky gets even darker than it already was. Hail starts falling down, but it's hardly ball sized. More like Mentos.

I concentrate harder, envisioning the hail stones growing and flattening the monsters' bodies.

More hail rains down, and just like I imagined, the stones hit only the toads. Although they're not nearly large enough to do any damage, they do slow them down. Some of them squeak in pain as hail hits their bulging eyes.

I focus hard on the hail continuing to fall before I lash out with my Morningstar and whip out my athame with my other hand. I take out the two toads in front, but the others are tougher, and about a dozen others are closing in on me fast.

My heartbeat quickens as I hit and kick furiously at

anything that comes near. Pretty soon I'm out of breath. My arms are heavy, and my head hurts from trying to keep the hail pouring down.

There's too many of them. We'll never win this.

And then the thing I feared most happens.

An agonizing scream reaches my ears. This one is different from the deep ones that the toads produce. It's not a human battle cry either. It's the sound of a girl in pain. My girl.

I see her, hunched over in agony, a hole the size of a coin in her chest. Something inside of me breaks. It feels like a lid is lifted, a rope cut. All my self-control shatters in that moment. I have no more limits, nothing that holds me back. Rage boils to the surface, pushing aside any other feeling.

A loud voice I barely recognize as my own drowns out all other sounds as I raise my arms. "NOOOOOOOOOOOOO!"

It seems to go on forever, fueling the power bursting out of me.

Images of flattened toads and pieces of slimy skin scattered everywhere fill my head.

The sky above me rumbles. Solid clouds suck up almost all the light. Then the sky turns white as hail stones the size of footballs crash down. The toads jump around in panic, their screams like music to my ears. I want them all to die, die, DIE!

A deafening crash makes the ground tremble, and I sway on my feet. The haze in my head clears up as silence descends. I blink and turn my eyes back to the scene before me.

There are hail stones everywhere, slowly melting on top of bodies that are reduced to mush.

I stare at it in shock. *Did I do that?*

Then Jeep rushes past me. "Vicky?"

I inhale deeply and dive forward.

Jeep kneels beside her, afraid to touch, but I can't just leave her lying there.

She weighs less than she should, and she flickers in and out of view. Her face is contorted in pain.

When she meets my eye, her lips curl up. "I messed up, babe. I wanted to stay with you until we beat Satan, but I messed up."

"No, you didn't." My eyes burn as I pull her closer and kiss her forehead that keeps disappearing. "Just stay strong, Gisella will heal you."

I look up as rapid footsteps approach.

Sad faces look down on us. Gisella's hand flies to her mouth, and Charlie bites his lip while Taylar turns away. D'Maeo and Maël, the strongest in my Shield, just stand there with hunched shoulders.

"She's not lost yet!" I yell, all control over my voice lost.

Tears drip from my cheeks and fall through Vicky's blinking body.

I reach out to Gisella and pull at her hand. "Heal her. Please hurry."

She bows her head. "I'm sorry, I can't."

"Of course you can!" My voice is shrill.

She blinks. Her eyes are wet. "I'm sorry." She pulls

her hand from mine.

I grab her again and yank her closer. "Don't be sorry! Heal her!"

"Dante." Charlie's calm voice barely registers. "Dante, listen." He kneels down beside us and waits for me to look at him. "Are you listening?"

His shape is hazy as tear after tear wells up in my eyes. My words are no more than a whisper now. "Please help her."

"She can't, Dante. Gisella can't heal ghosts."

A soft hand touches mine. "Babe?"

I look down at my girl. Her beautiful face is a mask of pain and sorrow. The sheer thought of losing her cuts off my breath. 'Don't leave me,' I want to tell her, but all I do is cough and sob.

"It's okay, babe. I'll wait for you on the other side."

No! I can't do this without you.

Slowly she closes her eyes. My whole body goes cold as she stops moving."

CHAPTER 12

I've been sitting in the melting ice and slime in total silence for several minutes when a thought hits me. "Quinn can heal anyone, right?"

Charlie turns his head to me with a start. "What? Oh… yeah, I think so."

The clouds high above us dissolve, and I squint against the sudden bright light. "Well, go get him! Go back home and call him! Take Mona back with you too, just to be sure."

Maël clears her throat. "We still can't leave, Dante. I just tried."

"But…" Nausea rises in my throat as I wrap my arms tighter around the body in my lap. I shake my head violently. "We can't give up! Do you hear me? I'm not losing her!"

D'Maeo takes a step closer and opens his mouth, but I raise my finger to silence him. "Don't you dare tell me we all knew the risks, or that casualties are inevitable. Those are things they say in the movies. But this is real life, and this is my girl! She doesn't deserve to go like this. She's supposed to fight by my side until the end. I can't-"

My voice is cut off abruptly as Vicky's body trembles and rises an inch from my lap.

Her eyes are still closed, her arms and legs stiff, her whole body so transparent it's barely visible.

She rises a bit further, then falls back into my lap.

Before I can wrap my arms back around her, she's lifted again, pulled up by an invisible cord around her waist. The sight of her being moved like a ragdoll sends chills down my back.

Once again, the pulling stops, and I catch her.

"What's happening?" I ask, looking up at D'Maeo for an explanation.

It's the African queen that answers. She points at a bright light in the sky that's slowly getting bigger. "That is the heavenly light. It is calling her."

A sharp pain shoots through my heart. "What? No!"

Charlie rests his hand on my shoulder. "Don't panic. I think it can't get to her here."

"Why? What do you mean?" My voice is strained. Tears run freely down my cheeks, and I don't bother to wipe them away.

"Do you see the way she's pulled up and dropped down over and over?"

I slap his hand away. "Of course I see it!"

"That's the light trying to pull her in and failing."

Vicky's involuntary movements get less frantic. She's only lifted an inch by the waist now and slowly let back down. Lifted, and let down.

"I think Charlie is right," Maël says. "We are still trapped. There is only one way out of here for us, and the Beach of Mu knows where it is." She points up at the sky with her staff. "That light of Heaven does not know. It is unable to take Vicky from here."

Taylar scratches his head. "But why? Isn't Heaven like the most powerful world in the universe?"

Maël looks at him without even the slightest spark of joy in her eyes. "One of the most powerful, yes. But the balance of the universe has been disturbed." She rests her gaze on me. "We have caused a rip in all worlds, even Heaven."

Honestly, I couldn't care less about the universe getting screwed up because of us. I know it's selfish, but all I want is for Vicky to get up and give me that cheeky look I love so much. For her to tell me we'll be fine and to steal a quick kiss.

"Does this mean she's not lost yet? Can we bring her back?" I ask hopefully.

Maël gives me a silent stare before finally responding. "Perhaps."

A thought hits me. "Maybe that beach has a solution." Gently, I place Vicky on the ground and stand up. My limbs are stiff from the cold and shock, and I stretch them a little while I look around for the sand. "Where is that thing when you need it? It keeps running off."

"There." Charlie points at the sky, which has turned darker, not just because the Heavenly light has left, but because night is falling in. With every shred of light that vanishes, my body gets heavier.

"As soon as we get Vicky up again, we should find a place to rest," I tell the others.

The beach is dancing through the sky again, as if nothing is wrong at all. I wave at it with both arms. "Hey, Beach! We could use some help here!"

It responds immediately, coming down with the speed of a rocket and halting at eye level.

I come straight to the point. "Vicky is hurt. Can you help us?"

It tilts its snake head as if thinking about it. Then it slips down, wraps its body around Vicky's and hoists her up.

I exchange a look with the others, and when no one says anything, I shrug and start following the beach. "Let's go."

To my surprise, the sand snake soon turns right into the forest of dead, white trees. The moment I step from the path, cold mist clings to my hands and neck.

"Are you sure this is safe?" I call out to the beach.

It doesn't respond, leaving me no choice but to follow it.

My legs are getting heavy, and my breath creates puffs of smoke.

I come to a halt when the clouds rising from my

mouth turn into solid ice.

"What's happening?" I wave at the sand leading the way. "Wait! Beach of Mu!"

It stops and turns its snake head.

"Some of us won't be able to survive in this cold for long," I explain, rubbing my arms hard.

The snake nods before slithering onward.

I run after it. "Wait! We have to turn around."

It doesn't respond anymore, and I try to grab its tail. When my hand touches it, the grains just slip through my fingers.

With every step, the air gets colder. I can barely feel my face anymore, and no matter how hard I rub my arms or stomp my feet, no warmth reaches my limbs.

D'Maeo catches up with me. "You should turn back with Charlie and Gisella. We will follow the beach and get Vicky back."

"I… no! We…" My teeth chatter so violently that I can no longer finish a single sentence. My thoughts are getting incoherent, and from the corner of my eye, I see Charlie leaning on Gisella.

Placing one foot in front of the other slowly, I manage to turn and stumble back to them. I don't want to leave Vicky, but I'm no good to her, or to anyone, dead.

I can't believe… the beach would…

Turn… go back to warmer places…

Can't leave… have to…

"Where did it go?"

Crunching sound…. my eyes…?

Moving shadows… Figures… Voices…

"The beach, it's gone!"

Who said that? I know him.

"Take him and the others back. We'll go after the beach."

Pulling… I slide… Feel so heavy…

Bump… Head hurts…

"Dante? Can you hear me?"

Yes… am here…

Feel nothing…

"Dante? Try to stay awake, please."

Yes… Yes…

"It's getting warmer already. Can you feel it?"

Cannot feel… All dark…

"We're losing him."

Crying…?

"They will not make it, Jeep. We need to find another way."

"I can try to make a fire. The trees are getting drier here."

Crack… Howl…

Beast…?

Heat…

"Get away from them!"

Pain… Don't want…

"Maël? What are you doing? Help me!"

"No."

Crash…

"Wait, Jeep! I think they are trying to help."

"By setting them on fire?!"

Lovely warmth… want more…

"The beach is back."

Nice silence…

"Where is Vicky? What did you do to her?"

Tickling…

"No, you stay away from them. We don't trust you anymore. You almost killed them! Maël, help me!"

"Take it easy. It is helping. Let us follow it."

Wind… Tingling inside…

Peace…

CHAPTER 13

When I wake, I can't open my eyes. Or maybe I can, but everything is still dark. My thoughts are all messed up. Why, I have no idea. No matter how hard I try to remember what happened or where I am, everything inside me remains dark and fuzzy.

My throat is dry, and when I try to move my arms or fingers, nothing happens.

Maybe I'm dead.

But wouldn't I be able to see something then? Unless I ended up in the wrong place somehow.

My whole body feels sort of heavy and weightless at the same time. It feels like it's filled with cotton candy fresh from the machine. Soft and warm.

"Did he move yet?"

That voice, I know it. It awakens an urge to do the right thing, to make the person that sound belongs to proud. It's a low and serious voice, and I picture a man with gray hair in a suit. *Do I know anyone like that?* I try to summon an image in my head, but there's nothing. Not even a glimpse of a face. Just darkness.

Did someone answer this man? Maybe I briefly drifted off, because the male voice is speaking again.

"His body is warm again. He should be fine. He probably just needs some more rest. Try not to worry about it."

"How can I not worry, D'Maeo?"

Another voice. Female.

"The others are already up. Eating, training, trying to find a way back home."

Who is this? She sounds… important. Confident and in charge somehow.

"And did you see what arrived today?" she continues.

"Yes, yes." The man–D'Maeo?–sounds tired. "I saw the Cards of Death."

"If Dante does not wake up soon, we will have to save the next soul without him. And to be honest, I am not convinced that we can."

Cards of what? That sounds dangerous. And why would they need me to save a soul? What does that even mean? Save it from what?

"We have no other choice but to try if he doesn't wake soon, Maël. It will be difficult, but we are strong, and we have Charlie and Gisella at our side."

Charlie and Gisella. Charlie and Gisella. D'Maeo and Maël. I repeat the names in my head, but they don't ring a bell. The only name that means anything to me is my own. *Dante, that is my name. Right?*

A cold shiver runs through me as doubt nibbles at my brain.

My name is Dante. Dante… something.

If I could hit something now, I would.

Dante… Argh! What is my last name?

I should start easy. My Mom's name, I can remember that, right?

Susan. Yes! And my Dad is… J… Jim? No. James?

I feel like screaming.

Susan and…

Keep calm, Dante, you know this. Just take your time.

"Have you seen Taylar?" the female voice interrupts my efforts. "He is barely hanging on, and there is no one here to heal him again."

Another name I don't know. But my heart does, I feel affection for him.

But who he is doesn't matter now. I should be able to recall my own name first. The rest will follow.

I try saying it out loud. *Dante…* No sound comes out. My lips probably didn't even move.

"I know." The man, D'Maeo, sighs. "And we've had to lock up Vicky. The curse has got a strong hold on her."

"It must be this world. I know the Beach of Mu brought us here to save Vicky, and I am thankful to have her back, but this environment is not good for any of us. Maybe Dante will wake up if we take him away from here."

I block out the rest of the conversation, because

something has changed inside me. When the woman mentioned someone named Vicky, I felt something interesting. A spark, near my heart. A jolt of some kind. Energy trickles through my limbs. I try to send it all to my fingers and lift them.

"Did you see that?"

A hand on my arm. "Dante? Can you hear me?"

"He is crying."

Because I'm so happy! I can move and feel. I'm back!

"Can you open your eyes, Dante?" The serious male voice again. Encouraging and patient.

I send all of the energy from my fingers to my eyes and... nothing.

"He is still too weak. We should leave him alone to rest."

Another touch, on my cheek, I think. "Rest, Dante. You will need all of your strength again soon."

No! I don't want to rest! I want to open my eyes, to see you, remember you. And most of all, I want... Vicky. Yes, that's what I want. Another spark in my heart, and I know she is the key. The key to healing and remembering.

"Take the cards," the male voice says. "We'll have to start studying them."

I try to open my eyes, utter words and remember more for hours. The name Vicky keeps sending waves of energy through me, but still there's no image to match it. No memory.

My body and heart remember, so why can't I? What happened to me? To Dante. Dante Banner.

Dante Banner, that's it. I want to yell it. *Dante Banner*

117

is my name! Instead, I let my thoughts drift off. Remembering my full name has drained every last bit of energy out of me. All I long for now is to sleep.

CHAPTER 14

A soft hand touches my cheek. It's cold, but it still sends tingles down my neck.

The hand stops moving when I shiver. "Sorry, did I wake you?"

The voice is soft and warm. "You scared us."

Is this Mom's voice? It sounds so familiar, so like... home.

With all my strength, I pry my eyes open. A young face looks down on me, too young to be my mother. She has a sad smile, and her skin is a bit transparent. I frown when I realize this doesn't scare me. *What is she, a hologram of some kind?*

She lifts my hand and kisses it. "I'm so sorry I couldn't be here sooner, babe. I had another fit right after the trees healed me, and they had to lock me up. But don't worry, I'm here now, and I'm not leaving you until you're better." She grins. "If Heaven can't take me from you, nothing can, right?"

I try to smile back, but I can't do anything but stare. Half of what she said didn't even register. All I can think is: *this gorgeous young woman is my girlfriend? How did that happen?*

I was never the most attractive of my friends. Quinn is the one getting all the female attention, and Paul and Simon know how to behave around girls better than I do.

Silently, I study the girl. She looks a bit older than me, has a great body, slender but muscled, and blue eyes anyone would drown in. She's dressed like a kick-ass monster hunter or something, all black, half jeans, half leather, plus a bit of lace around the chest. Her black hair matches her outfit, except for the blonde tips that reach her shoulders.

She scrunches up her beautiful face. "Why are you staring at me like that? Is something wrong?"

Things click together in my head. The energy coursing through me when I heard the name Vicky and this girl calling me babe.

"Vicky?"

"Yes, babe?"

"You look so beautiful."

She frowns. "I always look like this. But thank you."

"Are you a science student?"

Now she seems simply baffled. "What?"

I lift my heavy arm to gesture at her transparent body. "If you're not, then how did you manage this hologram?"

"What are you babbling about?" Her hand flies to my forehead. "You don't have a fever. Do you know where you are?"

I shake my head, which makes me a bit dizzy, so I stop.

She squeezes my hand. "Do you know your name?"

"Yes, it's Dante Banner."

"Do you know where you live?"

I press my lips together. "In... wait, I know this." I close my eyes and try to envision my house. "Black... Blackford, Idaho, that's it. I live with my Mom on a quiet street in Blackford, Idaho."

Vicky shakes her head. "Not anymore. You moved. Don't you remember?"

"I did?"

Her eyes bore into mine. "You're not messing with me, are you? Because if you are, I can tell you it's not funny. We both nearly died just days ago."

I blink rapidly. "We did?"

Suddenly, she rises to her feet and walks away. "Guys? Come quickly, please."

A second later, my bed is surrounded by people. Vicky is no longer the only transparent one. There are four more holograms and two solid people. I smile as I recognize my best friend. His name pops into my head.

"Charlie!" *How could I forget about him when I thought about my friends earlier? And these other people, they all seem to know me.*

"Hey, mate," he says with a grin. "How are you feeling?"

"Better. So… are you all scientists or students?" I ask, really wanting to know the answer now.

Worry slides over their faces, and I swallow. "I guess neither." I rub my face and think as hard as I can. "I'm sorry, I just can't remember who you guys are."

Vicky takes her place on the edge of my bed again. "Dante, what's the last thing you remember?"

My eyes drift to the ceiling. It looks old and dirty, and it's far away. *Where are we? Is this some sort of church?* My gaze drops down, and I search for the walls, but it's so dark here that I can't make anything out.

Where are we? What happened? Who are these people?

"Dante?" Vicky's voice drags me back to my bed.

"I remember…" Images flood back into my mind. The last bell of school, stepping outside into the sun, driving home with Quinn and the others. "The last day of school."

Shocked expressions all around me. *What did I say?*

"That's not all," I hurry to say. "Quinn dropped me off at home. Mom was waiting. Susan." I smile. "And Dad…"

It hits me like a derailed train. *Dad. He is no longer with us.*

John Banner, that was his name. He died. But how?

My vision is suddenly hazy. My eyes burn. I blink, but the tears keep falling.

"My dad," I say hoarsely. "He died."

Vicky wipes the tears from my face. "We know."

"Do you know what happened to him?"

She shakes her head. "Not yet. But Dante, you have to concentrate, okay? Try to remember more. What happened after you found out your father had died?"

Hope lies in her eyes as I make the gears in my head turn. But everything is blank after that.

"You met us, remember?" she urges.

"No." It's no more than a whisper. "No, I don't remember."

A thin man in a strange old-fashioned shirt steps closer to the bed. He adjusts the black bowler hat on his head and rolls up his sleeves to reveal a set of tattoos that... move?

I push myself further up and as far back as I can manage. "What the heck are you?"

The man stops dead and gives me a hurt look. "I'm Jeep. You know me. I'm part of your Shield, here to protect you."

He takes off his hat and bows, and I let out a shrill laugh. "Okay, okay, enough of this. I want some answers."

The tattooed guy with the car name straightens up. "Well, master, I wanted to suggest trying to nudge your power core. It might spark your memory."

Master? What is he going on about? And what is that power core he's talking about?

"What am I, a machine?"

Visions of movies like Robocop and Terminator

fill my head. My throat turns dry. "Oh no, I *am* a machine, aren't I? Did you implant a chip to save me?"

Jeep shakes his head. "Oh no, it's much crazier than that. You are a—"

Charlie pushes him aside. "Stop scaring him. It's bad enough that he can't remember."

Jeep glares at him with his arms folded. "We're on a deadline, wise guy. We need his powers to save the next soul."

While I try to wrap my head around what they're saying and what could possibly be worse than finding out you're half machine, everyone starts talking at once. They're arguing about what to tell me and how, and about some kind of mission to save someone important, and to defeat... the Devil?

I close my eyes and cover my ears. A sharp pain slowly moves from the back of my head to my eyes. The voices around me seem to get louder and louder, and it hurts, it hurts.

"STOP!" I yell, throwing my hands forward.

There's a loud bang and a blinding flash, followed by the rumbling of a wall coming down.

Silence falls upon us, and I turn my hands over and over. *Did I do that?*

Someone sniggers. The girl in the red leather catsuit, standing next to Charlie.

"Well, at least he didn't lose his powers," she says cheerily.

CHAPTER 15

My head hurts even more when they finish their story.

"This must be a dream, right? Things like this don't happen in real life."

"Are you sure?" Vicky says softly, lifting my hand. "Try to imagine a bolt of lightning in your hand."

"A what?"

She smiles patiently. "You're a Meteokinetic, a Mage that can control the weather. Which means that, for instance, you can conjure a bolt or ball of lightning, ice or a tornado, a wave—"

"Or some really large hail stones to crush your enemies," Charlie interrupts. "Like you did when Vicky got injured." He chuckles. "That was great, man. You got so angry I thought the world was going to explode."

D'Maeo shakes his head solemnly. "That was pure luck. And it was a fraction too late. Vicky was already fatally injured."

I frown at him. *Is he always such a spoil sport? This just started to sound a bit better after the whole story about being destined to make sure the Devil stays in Hell.*

"He is right," the African queen says.

This woman still impresses me. Not only her royal looks and beauty, but her whole demeanor. She radiates wisdom and strength. She is a true queen, and I'm grateful to have her fighting by my side, especially now that I've lost any knowledge I had about this crazy magical world.

"Tell me what to do," I say.

The two oldest ghosts nod their approval, and D'Maeo hands me two cards. "Study these. Try to deduce as much as you can about the soul we need to save. Meanwhile, we'll keep trying to find a way home."

I take the cards from him and nod. "No problem."

When everyone turns to leave the building, Vicky doesn't move. "I'll stay with Dante to see if I can jog his memory some more."

Charlie looks over his shoulder and winks at me. "Great idea."

As soon as they close the large doors behind them, I look around. "So where are we? I mean, I know we're in some kind of unknown world, but what kind of building is this? And why is there no echo in here? It's so big, yet it sounds as if we're in a small room."

Vicky shifts on the edge of the bed to follow my gaze. "It's some kind of abandoned church. The acoustics must be different because the atmosphere differs from ours. I'm not sure whose building it is, since we haven't seen any humanlike creatures yet. Just the barren trees that healed me."

I study the side of her face, and my hand moves to touch it before I can stop myself.

When my fingers caress her cold skin, she closes her eyes. "I'm glad you're still here."

Silently, we stare at the dark sky behind the crumbled wall until my arms start to freeze.

"I wish I hadn't crushed that wall. It's getting really cold in here."

I haven't even finished my sentence when the scarce light from outside is blocked by a giant white tree. Its branches reach for a boulder, which it places back into the gap I accidentally created.

My mouth falls open. "They're fixing it."

Vicky has a pensive look on her face. "Yes, it seems important to them to help us. Maybe the Beach of Mu told them about our efforts to restore the balance in the universe."

I scratch my head. "A beach told a bunch of trees what we're trying to do, and they want to help?"

She shrugs. "Pretty much."

"And you don't find that weird?"

With a sudden move, she throws her feet onto the bed and slides closer to me. "I've seen stranger things than this."

All kinds of feelings are racing inside of me. Desire, doubt, fear, anticipation. While my fingers tingle from the cold, waves of heat rush through my chest.

I scoot over so we no longer touch and hold up the cards. "So, these tell us who is going to get killed and how?"

Vicky nods.

"And they also let us know which sin the person is going to commit if we don't stop them."

"Exactly. But we already know which sin, because we have the list from your great-grandfather's book."

"Dante Ali-something."

She grins. "Alighieri. He's famous."

"For writing a true story about the circles of Hell which is seen as fictional by people without magic," I summarize.

"Yup. And because of his story, we also know what kind of demons to expect. You see, the punishment of every circle of Hell is connected to the demons that guard that circle."

I hold up the card that's dripping. "Let me guess, in this circle the souls are punished with water?"

"Yes, so the demons will also have something to do with water. They're covered by it, they attack with it or..."

"They're made of it?"

"Possibly." She studies me for a moment, which makes heat rise to my cheeks.

"You really don't remember me?" She sounds as much fascinated as hurt.

I lift her hand, that's still holding mine, and kiss it.

"I don't, but my body does."

Her gaze drops to my pants.

"That's not what I meant," I hurry to say.

She lets out a sigh that could win an Oscar. "Shame."

She pouts, and I can't help myself. Laughter bursts out of me as if it's been cooped up for too long, in loud, choking salvos. My chest contracts as joy, relief, fear and grief try to escape at the same time. The corners of my mouth can't decide whether to go up or down.

"Oh, babe, come here." Vicky's soft voice provokes loud sobs interrupted by hiccups of laughter.

She wraps her arms around my neck and pulls me closer. "It's okay, let it all out. You've been through a lot. We both have."

I bury my head in her shoulder. Her skin is so cold, but she smells so good. I want to hide inside her and never come out.

The next thing I know, I'm kissing her neck. My lips quickly move up to her chin and find her soft mouth. All my emotions blend together into one content feeling as I softly push her back and everything around us fades away.

CHAPTER 16

I wake up in silence, tucked under the covers in the dark, and go over everything my friends have told me.

My powers. They should be my main focus now. When we find the soul to save, we'll have to fight. How can I do that if I don't know how to use my powers?

Carefully, I concentrate on the spot near my heart, the spot that is supposed to hold my magical energy.

"Nudge it softly," I mumble as I hold up my right hand.

A small flicker of a light illuminates the bed and the sleeping beauty beside me. She stirs, and I hastily move my hand away from her. With an extra nudge and a lot of concentration, I manage to make the ball of lightning drift from the palm of my hand to the ceiling. With my eyes, I steer it around the large space. The big gap in the wall is gone, and when I squint, I can make out dark marks in the stones. The ceiling is high and curved, and I think there are words carved into it. Oval shaped windows break up the walls on my left and right side. I can't see anything through them.

I pick up the Cards of Death that have slid onto the floor and study them again.

They both have moving, blue symbols, lines and skulls on the back. Plus one strange face with big eye sockets and horns on top of its head.

We haven't figured out how to remove the dripping water from one of the cards yet, so I stare at it for a while and rack my brain for a solution.

I'm surprised at how long I can keep the ball in my hand lit. I know it's only small, but the Shield told me using my powers will drain my energy, and I still feel fine. Which I'm happy about, because it's still chilly in here, and the ball gives me a bit of warmth.

A thought hits me, and I hold my hand closer to the card. Heat evaporates water, right?

Patiently, I wait for something to happen. When the dripping continues in the same rhythm, I imagine a bigger ball. It grows immediately, and I watch it intently. Of course that doesn't help one bit, and neither does the bigger ball of lightning. Tired of waiting any longer, I push the card into the light.

Nothing changes.

With a sigh, I close my hand and lean back in the pillow. Darkness envelops me, and a cold breeze brushes my face. I wonder if I'd also be able to conjure sunshine inside this building. I mean, if I can create and manipulate rain, hail and storm, why not also sunlight?

I sit up again abruptly and look at the cards in my hands. *If I can create rain out of nothing, I should also be able to* move *rain, or… water.*

I focus on the flowing water on the card until everything else around me fades into a haze. Then I nudge my power core and imagine the water rising up from the card.

I expect nothing, but I give it all I've got. In my mind, the drops flow up instead of down and take all the water with them until the symbols on the card become visible.

And then, just like that, it happens. I'm so surprised that I lose focus, and the water splashes down again.

After I've shaken the drops from my face, I try again.

The card is the only thing I see. I imagine the water rising and rising. It does, and this time, I keep my focus. Slowly, I turn my eyes to the symbols on the card. There's five of them. One in each corner and one in the middle. Every time I look at them, the small pool of water descends, and I shift my attention to keeping it in the air.

Now my energy is draining fast. Brief glances will have to do. I memorize the symbols and let go.

The water splashes back onto the card. Cold drops land on my arm and on Vicky's cheek.

She wakes with a start and glances from me to the

cards in my hand.

A smile creeps onto my lips.

Vicky pushes herself up. "Did you do it?"

"I did. Now all I need is a pencil and a piece of paper, before I forget."

With a proud but incredulous look on her face, Vicky reaches into the back pocket of her pants and pulls out what I need. "How did you do it?"

I quickly scribble down the symbols and fill Vicky in.

Her mouth falls slightly open. "That's amazing, Dante. You've just rediscovered your powers, and you can already do this? We might not be as lost as I thought we were."

"Really?"

She bends over and kisses me on the lips. "Really."

We huddle closer together and study the symbols I drew.

"So, there's wings, a tree, a thimble, a sun and a green dot," I explain.

"A fairy," Vicky says.

I shrug, not sure if those even exist.

"It could also be someone who works in a park," Vicky says. "What about the other card? Maybe we can figure it out after our little…" She throws me a mischievous look, "… nap."

The cold leaves my body in a second, and I grin. "Maybe."

I put away the water card and hold up the other one. "We've got two red scratches and a lightning bolt. One indicates anger, because that's the sin of the fifth circle. The other points to the way this soul dies, right?"

Vicky nods. "It's probably not literally lightning that—" She falls silent as the doors on the other side of the church open with a soft creak.

D'Maeo steps in. He looks at us, scratches his beard and closes the doors behind him.

"Everything okay?" I ask when he approaches with a flashlight in his hand.

"Sure." He drags an old chair to the end of the bed and sits down. "How are you doing?"

"Not bad," I say. "Although, I still don't remember anything new."

He smiles, but somehow it doesn't feel right. It's no longer affection I see in his eyes, but malice. When I focus on it, his shadow seems to grow while D'Maeo himself shrinks.

When he speaks, it's as if his voice comes from behind him. His words make no sense.

I shake my head and blink.

Everything is back to normal. Although, normal isn't what it used to be.

"Have you gotten any further with the cards?" the old ghost asks.

"We were just working on that," I say, keeping my eye on every move he makes.

He leans closer, and I watch his shadow. *Did it move a fraction later than the ghost did, or was that just my imagination?*

He holds out his hand. "Can I see them again?"

"Sure," Vicky says.

But before he can take the cards from her, the doors swing open with a squeak, and Maël appears in the doorway. "What are you still doing here? You are not even dressed yet?"

I'm so baffled that I don't know what to say.

But I don't have to, because Maël turns to the old ghost. For the first time since I woke here, she sounds angry. If looks could kill, he'd get beamed up to Heaven right now. "What happened, D'Maeo? You went in to get them, and now you are sitting here as if we have all the time in the world?"

Without wasting time, I jump out of bed and put on the clothes I find on a chair next to it. I manage to do it without falling over, glad to find my legs have their strength back.

On the chair, I also find two books, an athame and something I don't recognize. After a quick questioning look at Vicky, she nods, and I put everything in my pockets and behind my waistband. Strangely enough, it doesn't feel uncomfortable at all, but there's no time to figure out why that is. Maël is still standing in front of D'Maeo, fuming like an angry dragon.

The gray-haired ghost shakes his head as if to lose an unpleasant thought. "I'm not sure, Maël. I hurried over here, and when I stepped in, I somehow forgot why I came."

"You came here to tell them another army of

135

those foul creatures is coming. We need to leave before they reach us."

"Why?" Vicky's voice rings out from the other side of the bed. She joins the others and gestures at me. "You saw what he did last time. I think he can do it again."

"This army is a lot bigger than the two we fought before." Maël's grip on her staff tightens. "You know, the ones that killed you."

Vicky's skin gets more transparent as she swallows. "Yes, but Dante can kill them all with hail before they reach us."

The queen shakes her head. "I do not see how. He barely has any knowledge of what he can do."

"He practiced, and he just did some things I think he couldn't do before."

Maël frowns at me. "You did?"

I chuckle nervously. "Well, I don't know. I have no idea what I could do before." I turn to Vicky. "But I can't imagine being able to crush a whole army of monsters with hail. How did I manage that?"

"Well…" She fiddles with the zipper of her leather jacket. "That was because…" She looks up for help, and Jeep, walking in, finishes her sentence. "That was because your girlfriend got killed, Dante. You got really, really angry."

"Which is why I do not expect a revival of that incident," Maël continues. "And we should not risk losing anyone again. We are very fortunate to have Vicky still among us, as well as everyone else. I wish to keep it that way."

"Me too," I nod. "So let's get out of here."

I stroll out of the building and into a gray, foggy day. From every direction, I hear the creaking of branches and the moaning of something ancient. The sound gives me the chills, even more than the cold does, and I rub my arms.

"What is that?" I ask Vicky when she joins me.

"We're in some kind of ent forest. These are the creatures that healed us." She weaves her fingers through mine and leans closer. "I'm grateful they did," she whispers, "but to be honest… they freak me out a little."

I smile and kiss her. "Me too."

When the heavy doors close behind Maël, I turn around. "Does anyone know the way?"

Charlie points at the sky, where a whirl of sand drops from the heavy clouds. "That does."

My eyes follow every movement of the phenomenon while every last brain cell in my head tries to grasp what all of this means. "Is this that beach you were talking about?"

"It is. And since it got us this far and led us to these ents, we thought our best shot would be to follow it again."

My head goes up and down without my consent, and my feet move on their own. Instinct must have taken over, and it feels good. It means my brain has time to wrap itself around everything I've just learned. *Magic is real. Magic… is… real.* I say it over and over in my head, and the evidence is right in front of me, but still I don't believe it. "I'm dreaming."

Cold fingers squeeze my hand. "No, you're not."

I turn my head and take in Vicky's beautiful face. "What?"

"You're not dreaming."

Did I say that out loud? I didn't mean to.

She pulls me closer. "As strange as this is, even for me, it's all very real. So are we, so are your powers."

"And the Devil."

Her face contorts into a mixture of sadness and anger. "Yes, him too unfortunately."

"Did you… did we ever… meet him?"

"You did, just a couple of days ago. And you have premonitions about him sometimes."

"Premonitions?" If my head spins any faster, I'll tumble over. "What about?"

She wipes a dark lock of hair from her face with her free hand. "Don't worry about that now."

Don't worry about that now? It must have been really bad if she doesn't want to tell me.

A cheery voice pipes up in my other ear. "You saw our defeat. Or actually, Taylar did, when he had your powers."

I turn my head to find Jeep grinning widely at me. "We lose?"

"Not necessarily," Maël joins in. "Your premonitions give you possible outcomes in order for us to prevent them or make them happen. What Taylar saw does not have to happen at all."

"Wait." Vicky stops dead in her tracks. Her eyes scan every face in our group. "Where *is* Taylar?"

"He's right behind…" Charlie turns and falls silent. "He was behind us when we went to see what was taking D'Maeo so long."

Vicky throws her hands in the air. "And you didn't keep an eye on him?" Her voice is shrill with rising panic.

Although I don't know much about this world, or about magic, and I don't even remember who Taylar is, something dark slithers through my stomach at the thought of him getting left behind. Who knows what hides between these unmoving trees?

CHAPTER 17

When we turn back, a strange sound is added to the moaning and creaking. It resembles a heavy drumroll, interrupted by a slapping noise.

My heartbeat quickens as I take in Maël's worried face. "Is that the army you were talking about?"

"It is. We must find Taylar soon, or it will be too late to run."

"Where did you see him last?"

She walks past me and beckons us. "In the Tree Hall, this way."

On the other side of the church, there's a giant tree. The trunk is so wide you could fit a front door and two big windows in. When I look up, I can't even see the top of the tree.

Maël taps the side of the trunk three times and places her hand on the white bark. Part of it moves back, and she steps inside. I follow behind the others.

To my surprise, I find myself in a narrow hallway, with wooden doors on each side. High above us, stairs float. Where they lead, I can't tell. It's too dark in here.

My friends step into the first room to our right, where a boy of about fourteen, with white hair and see-through skin, is lying on a bed. I kneel down at his side. He's so transparent I can barely see him.

"Is this normal?" I ask Vicky, who crouches down next to me.

"No, he's fading because of his unfinished business."

I frown. "That's a real thing?"

"Unfortunately."

"Dante?" Taylar's voice is a hoarse whisper. "Dante? Is that you?"

"Yes." In a reflex, I grab his hand. "I'm here."

He lets out a heavy sigh and becomes a bit more visible. "Thank goodness. I thought we lost you."

"Never," I answer with all the confidence I can muster. "And you're going to be fine too."

"No." He curls up his lips into a vague smile. "No, I'm done. I'm joining Lleyton. You go on without me."

Lleyton? I mouth at Vicky.

"His brother," she whispers.

A pang goes through my heart. "I'm sorry, Taylar. You'll see your brother again, but not today. And not tomorrow either, if I can help it. We're getting you out of here."

He waves his hand vaguely. "It's too late. There's no energy left inside me. Let me go, Dante. Save yourself. I'm not important."

"Yes, you are!" Jeep's stern voice is loud, and the tree we're standing in stirs uneasily. I can see the walls moving.

The tattooed ghost kneels down on Taylar's other side and picks him up as if he doesn't weigh a thing. Maybe he doesn't. "Come on, we've wasted enough time arguing. We're getting out of here, all of us."

And with that, he strides out of the room, through the tree's open door and into the white woods, away from the growing noise.

"This unfinished business," I say to Vicky after a couple of minutes. "You know what it is?"

"Yes." She stares off into the woods. "His brother was killed by a pixie that was sent by a powerful man named Shelton Banks. Taylar spent the rest of his life searching for him, to get revenge, but he never did."

"And this man is still alive?"

Vicky shakes her head as if to get rid of an uneasy feeling. "Apparently. He must be really old now."

"And weak," I say eagerly. "Easier to kill."

"It doesn't always work like that with magical people, babe. Sometimes they grow stronger with age."

"But you know where to find him?"

"No, but we haven't really tried yet. There was no time."

I clench my jaw. "Well, we'll have to make time

now, or Taylar won't make it."

"None of us will make it if we don't get out of here," she says softly. "Which is what we've been struggling with from the beginning."

I wrap my arm around her and pull her close. "We'll be okay."

She barely reacts. Her eyes are locked on the unmoving figure in Jeep's arms. "I hope so."

While I search for more words of comfort, the whirl of sand comes to a halt in the sky in front of us. Next to it, I can make out a bright blue line.

"Is that a portal?" I ask with a frown. "I imagined something more like a… doorway."

Vicky stares at the line with fascination. "Portals come in all shapes and sizes, but to be honest, I've never seen one this small either."

The Beach of Mu changes into the shape of a staircase, and one by one, we climb it, D'Maeo leading the way with Jeep close behind.

At the top of the stairs, the two of them hesitate.

"What is it?" I call out.

"The portal emanates a lot of heat," the old ghost answers. "I'm not sure it's safe."

His last word is almost drowned out by the stomping of a thousand feet that suddenly grows louder and is joined by a deafening howling.

When I look over my shoulder, I forget to breathe. Gruesome monsters with fat bodies and spiked tails fill up the path behind us at an alarming speed. Their large mouths are wide open, releasing howls that make the hairs on my arms stand up.

"Time to go!" I yell, pulling Vicky along as I make my way to the stairs.

The ground trembles, and the stench of dead meat wafts our way. The sand moves under our weight as we hurry to the top of the stairs. Now I can see the portal is much more than a blue line. We were just looking at the side of it before. From up here, I can see the entrance, a circle the size of a large dining room table, lying flat in the air. Steam rises up from it, and blue flames lick the edges. It might be dangerous to touch those, so we'll have to go through the portal one by one.

"Jump!" I tell D'Maeo and Jeep, and to my surprise, they obey without objecting.

They're swallowed by the steam in an instant, and I can only hope they're okay.

Before I follow them, I wait for Charlie, Gisella and Maël to catch up.

"Go, go, go!" my best friend urges me from the bottom of the stairs, and after a deep breath and a nod from Vicky, I jump into the steaming hole.

The heat envelops me, and I'm afraid to open my eyes. The cold from the world I left behind is just a vague memory as flames wrap around me.

I clench my fists to withstand the pain surging through me. *We're all going to die in here. I made the wrong decision.*

Somewhere between the raging of the flames I hear two voices yelling. At first, I can't make out what they're saying, but as I get closer to them, the syllables start to make sense.

"Watch out!"

"Open your eyes!"

Struggling to even breathe in this scorching heat, I force my eyes open. They burn and start watering, but I focus on D'Maeo and Jeep, standing under another portal, which is drifting inches to my right in a sea of boiling lava. If I don't manage to steer a bit to the right, the lava will swallow me whole.

"Use this!" D'Maeo calls out to me, and he picks up a wooden board and places it in the waves of lava.

A second later, I land on it. My momentum carries my feet and the board forward while my upper body tumbles the other way.

"I've got you," D'Maeo's voice says close to my ear, and I feel his hands around my waist.

He pulls me through the portal safely, but there's no time to catch my breath. Vicky and the others will jump soon, and the lava carries the portal further and further away from the one we fell through.

CHAPTER 18

I step a bit further away from the edge.

D'Maeo takes in our surroundings with clenched jaws. "I don't like this one bit."

Jeep nudges me. "Turn the lava to ice."

I straighten my shoulders. "Right."

I can do this. I have to. If I fail, my friends will be swallowed by this raging heat.

With a sharp shake of my head, I get rid of the thought of warmth. It's cold I need, lots of it. Nice thick layers of ice that cover everything in sight. And a soft layer of snow on top, to break their fall.

Ice, ice, ice. I repeat it over and over in my head and imagine it popping up in blocks from the sea around us.

"That's it, keep going," D'Maeo urges me.

"A little faster would be great," Jeep mumbles, and I nudge my power core harder.

Images of large slabs of ice fill my inner vision, and I quickly cover them with loads of snow.

There's a thud, and I fight the urge to open my eyes. I have to keep my focus, wait for everyone to arrive here safely.

There's a rustling sound beside me, followed by Vicky's soft 'Thanks, babe'.

One down, three to go.

Two thuds reach us in rapid succession. Charlie's voice rings out. "Wow, great job, Dante!"

"Just a second longer," D'Maeo says. The tension in his voice is obvious, but I don't blame him. One moment of broken concentration, and Maël tumbles into the lava.

Still I can't help but look up to see what's taking her so long.

The drumroll of rapid footsteps gets louder.

"That can't be good," Charlie says, his eyes wide with fear as he looks up too.

Then the ghost queen tumbles down, and I focus on the ice and snow again.

She lands without trouble, but her staff is knocked from her hand. It slides to the edge of the slab she's standing on. When she reaches for it, a dozen shapes fall from the sky.

"Hurry!" Charlie yells at Maël as she manages to grab her wand just before it slips off the ice and into the lava.

The slab turns into a seesaw as more and more monsters fall down on it. Several of them lash out at

Maël with their tails. She knocks some into the lava with her staff, but there're too many of them, and they keep coming. Soon the ice slab won't be able to hold all this weight anymore.

"Hit them with hail, Dante!" someone yells.

"No, melt the ice under their feet!"

I grit my teeth while I try to do both at once. Cracks form in the ice under Maël's feet.

Charlie steps forward. "Let me help."

With a couple of quick wrist movements, he hits several monsters in the face with gel. They flail in an attempt to get the stuff off and knock over some of their congeners.

Maël weaves between them, swinging her staff to create a path to the floating portal.

"Hurry!" I tell her. "I can't hold the ice much longer."

More and more cracks appear under her feet while balls of gel fly everywhere, and monsters keep falling from the sky.

Suddenly, a deep, rumbling voice booms from above us. "Vic… ky…"

Without thinking I look up, my concentration broken.

Charlie lets out a panicked 'Dante!' and grabs Maël's wrist just in time.

I help him pull her through the portal as the ice breaks into a thousand pieces and goes under in the smoldering sea of lava. The piercing screams of the burning monsters hurt my ears, but they're soon drowned out by the frustrated growls of the remainder of the army that looks down on us from the world we just left.

Maël straightens up and wipes the dust and ice from her dress. "Thank you, boys."

"You're welcome," we say in unison.

I turn my head back to the portal above. "Who did that voice belong to? The one that called Vicky?"

The ghost queen steps aside to let Vicky through, who shoots me a concerned look. "I think it was an ent. Althan, the one that healed me."

"Why was it calling you?"

She slowly shakes her head. "I don't know."

Charlie points up. "They're leaving."

The growls finally die down, and the monsters turn away. With their tails low, they disappear from sight.

"Vic… ky…"

"Althan?"

"Have present… for you…" the voice answers.

A branch reaches down, holding a small bottle filled with some kind of brown-greenish liquid.

"Take… this…"

Vicky holds out her arm, but they're way too far apart, so I gesture for her to climb onto my shoulders while Maël holds on to her waist to make sure she doesn't tumble out of the portal.

The ent leans closer and stretches out his branch as far as he can. "This will… help you…"

The rest of his sentence is lost when his old, gray

149

eyes grow wide and he slips over the edge of the portal.

"No!" Vicky and I yell at the same time.

We both try to grab one of the ent's branches, but it's too late. With a splash, it lands in the lava stream and catches fire. The low moan it produces sends shivers down my back.

"Althan!" Vicky yells. "No!"

With his last strength, the ent holds his arm with the present in it high above the boiling sea.

"Quick, try to grab the bottle," I say, pointing at the tree fingers wrapped tightly around the glass.

Vicky leans closer. "I can't reach it."

With the sound of trickling sand, the Beach of Mu swoops down and grabs the bottle, dropping it safely into Vicky's hands. Then it dives into the portal, which starts to close. The round opening above us gets smaller, as does the monster with the toad skin that looks down on the burning ent with a menacing grin, up from its safe, dry place behind the other portal.

Charlie sees him too and conjures a ball of gel in his hand, but the portal closes too quickly.

A second later, there's nothing but red sky around us, illuminated by two yellow moons.

"How much longer before we can go home?" I ask the Beach, waiting for us to follow it again.

It gives me a wide smile, which I take to mean 'not much longer'.

When I turn and take in my new surroundings for

the first time, my mouth falls open.

After all the dark and depressing worlds we've gone through, this one feels so light and refreshing. Everything around us is colorful and warm. Sweet smells rise up from large orange flowers that sway from left to right, tinkling softly. When I look up at the sky, pink clouds drift away to reveal a giant green sun.

"It's so beautiful here," Taylar gasps, leaning on Jeep heavily.

"Hey, you're awake." I smile at him. "How are you holding up?"

"I'm not sure," he says evasively.

I give him the most confident look I can manage. "Don't worry, we'll find this Banks guy soon."

Gisella throws back her long, bright red locks. "I might have an idea."

"Shoot," I say.

"Well." She paces up and down in front of us. "There's an object that can store memories. You can replay them, sort of like a YouTube video. We can use it to record Taylar's memory of his brother's death and take it to the police. They'll arrest Shelton Banks and put him away for years."

With a sigh I shake my head. "That won't work. It's not enough evidence. Besides, it's the fairy that killed him, not Banks himself."

"True." She taps her lips with her index finger. "But… while he's being questioned, we can search his house for more evidence. A man like that has killed more than one person, don't you think?"

The corners of my mouth move up. "You're right." I scratch my head as another thought hits me. "But how do we find this object? And how will we get it to the police or whatever if we can't even return home ourselves?"

Taylar waves his hand in the air to catch my attention. "We can worry about that later. Just working on my unfinished business, making progress with it, gives me energy."

"And finding the object is not a problem," Gisella smiles. "One of my ancestors made it, so we can use my blood in a summoning spell to get it."

"Sounds good to me, if you know where to find such a spell."

She points at my pants. "It's in your father's notebook behind your waistband."

"My father's notebook?" My hand moves to my waistband on its own and pulls the two books out. As soon as I do, the weight and size of them seems to change. *Weird.*

The books look almost identical. They have the same red leather binding, but one of them has a couple of scratches on it, as if a bear or wolf ripped it. Or something else... When I open them, yellow symbols pulse at me, the same ones I saw on the Cards of Death. On the next page, our names are written, also in yellow ink. The scratched book says *John Banner.* The other one has my name in it.

Vicky takes the books from me before I can flip

more pages. "Let me look for it."

"But—"

"I'm sorry, babe. You can inspect them further once we're back home. Right now, we're in a hurry." She gestures at Taylar's almost faded face and my cheeks burn with shame.

"You're right."

She gives me a warm smile and starts walking, with her head buried in Dad's notebook. Briefly, she looks up at the swirling sand shape above us. "I can search and walk at the same time. Lead the way, please."

When I catch up with her, she hands me back my notebook, which has the title 'Book of Spells' written under my name on the first page in my handwriting. Pushing back my curiosity, I quickly slide it back behind my waistband, where it immediately feels lighter and smaller.

I have to admit, a lot of this magical stuff is really cool. If only there wasn't so much scary stuff too, I would be able to actually enjoy myself.

Vicky reaches inside her back pocket with her free hand while scanning the ingredients for the spell. She hands me all kinds of bottles with herbs in them, some candles, salt and an incense stick.

"Where did this all come from? I saw you put the bottle Althan gave you in that pocket. This can't possibly fit in there too, can it?"

She chuckles. "Sure it can, babe, it's a magical pocket." She hands me a chocolate bar. "Give this to Charlie."

I frown at it. "Why?"

"He needs it. It's fuel for this grease balls."

Charlie snatches it out of my hands and rips the wrapper off.

I raise my eyebrows at him. "Really?"

He swallows the first big bite and grins. "Really."

After a confirming nod from Gisella I shrug. "Well, I suppose it explains a lot. You're always eating after all, and you never gain weight."

He munches on contently, and I turn back to Vicky. "There's something I don't understand."

She glances up from the book. "About what?"

"Why did Althan save us, and why did he give his life to hand you that bottle?"

Vicky's shoulders sag immediately, and I stutter an apology. "I… I'm sorry, Vick. I didn't mean… I was just… Forget about it."

"No, it's fine." She blinks away her tears. "Althan said we were important, that there was a prophecy about us."

I hold my breath. *Another prophecy about me?* "What did it say?"

"That one day, a young couple would stumble into their woods, lost and injured. This couple was to be saved, or all worlds would fall."

I rearrange all the objects under my arm before gently stroking her hair with my free hand. "He died to save us, to save… the universe, I guess. It is an honorable way to go."

She pushes me away and I drop a candle, which

Charlie picks up. "He didn't have to die," Vicky says, raising her voice. "He only did because we messed up. He saved us, but we failed to save him in return."

With a heavy feeling, I shake my head. "We did the best we could, Vicky. And sometimes things are just meant to be. I wish we could've saved him, but we simply couldn't."

With an impatient gesture, she wipes her face. "I know. I don't blame you. I'm just mad at all the evil in the world." She stops so suddenly Jeep bumps into her.

"Sorry," he mumbles, but she doesn't seem to hear it.

She points at a small clearing, mostly hidden by trees with bright pink leaves. "That looks like a good spot to cast the spell. Hopefully, no one will bother us there."

I watch her walk away, baffled. "Right, I guess the conversation is over."

Charlie puts a hand on my shoulder. "Give her a break, she's been through a lot the last couple of days."

"I know. I just wish she'd talk to me about it."

He tilts his head. "She will. But she puts Taylar's well-being before her own struggles, you know."

I utter his unspoken words. "Which is exactly what I should do." I take the candle back from him. "Thanks. Let's get this done."

"That's the spirit."

CHAPTER 19

"Is this even possible in this world?" I ask when Vicky puts everything in place for the spell. "I thought Maël said our magic doesn't always work when we're in another world."

"True," Vicky answers without looking up from the circle she's making out of salt. "But we have to try."

One look at Taylar, slumped against a tree with his eyes closed, tells me she's right.

I rub my hands together. "Tell me what to do."

She hands me Dad's notebook back. "Here are the instructions. Make sure you don't change the words."

I scratch the back of my neck with my free hand. "I thought you said I had the ability to write my own spells."

She pauses her preparations. "You think it's wise to do that when you know so little about spells?"

"Probably not," I agree, bending over the book.

The instructions are pretty clear, so as soon as Vicky is done setting everything up for me, I begin.

I light the incense stick and follow the line of salt, inside the circle, reading from the book in my other hand.

"Powers that be, hear my call.
Help us out, before we fall.
Aid us in our time of need.
Give us strength before we bleed."

After I finish my walk around the circle, I push the stick into the ground in the middle and light the four candles one by one, meanwhile repeating the spell twice.

Then Vicky nods at Gisella to step forward.

She puts her hand in mine, and I pull her inside the circle. The thought of cutting her makes me nervous, but she seems fine with it. She just waits patiently, with her hand outstretched in confidence.

After reading the instructions one more time, I take my athame from behind my waistband, place the tip of the blade in the middle of her palm and pull it toward me. Blood wells up, and I drop the dagger in the grass. Together, we move from candle to candle and hold our hands above the flames.

"Powers that be, hear my plea.
Take this blood and set it free.
Turn it into smoke to find

157

the object that was left behind."

Every time I say the words, I squeeze Gisella's hand until a drop of blood lands in the flame.

When the last candle is done, we move to the middle of the circle, and I push her palm against the burning incense stick.

Her face contorts with pain, but only for a second. One by one, the candles are extinguished by an invisible force. The smoke that rises from them takes on the shape of a spiral above our heads. It twists faster and faster while the smoke gets thicker.

"It's working," Vicky says breathlessly from outside the circle.

The smoke spiral turns into two claws that dive into the ground. Clumps of earth fly everywhere, and I shake my head to get it out of my hair.

For a while, nothing happens, and I'm starting to worry. *What if it didn't work at all? Or… if we conjured some kind of evil by accident?*

Just when I lean forward to peer into the hole that the claws made, they shoot out of it. The smoky fingers are clutching something, which they take straight to me.

When I hold out my hand, they drop a small object in it and dissolve with a soft puff.

I look at the gizmo in my hand.

"Is this it?" I ask Gisella, while the others join us for a closer look.

The werecat girl slash witch gives me a wide smile.

"It is. It worked!" She holds up her hand, and I give her a high five.

"Well done," she says.

I grin. "You too."

After a glance over my shoulder at Taylar, my grin falters. "Tell me how to use it."

We hurry over to the young, white-haired ghost, who opens his eyes with a start. "It worked, didn't it? I can feel it."

My heart pounds loudly in my chest. "You can?"

"Yes, I felt a little jolt of energy in my power core. Do you have the object?"

I hold it out to him, and he picks it up gently.

"Are you sure this is it? It looks like a pocket watch."

There's not much I can say to that. He's right. It looks quite normal, like an antique, silver pocket watch.

Gisella sits down next to him and points at the engravings on the case. "What do you see?"

Taylar scrunches up his nose and squints. "It looks like a woman with two rats at her feet."

"My great-aunt," Gisella explains.

"The one who made this?"

"Exactly." She smiles again when Taylar's expression changes from fascinated to scared. "Don't worry. It won't harm you, and it won't turn you evil either. It has been cleansed a couple of years ago, and it hasn't been used since."

Taylar stares at her hard. "How do you know?"

She wiggles her fingers in front of him. "I used my witchy senses." She points at the pocket watch again. "What else do you see?"

"Well, this looks like... eh... like a..." He sighs. "I don't know what this is."

He points at a snake-like thing along the edge. The same things are carved along the other side.

"It's an elephant's trunk. It symbolizes a strong memory. The watch will keep any memory you want until you take it out again." Gisella places a hand on Taylar's arm. "Are you ready to use it?"

He blinks out of sight and grits his teeth when he appears again. "I don't have a choice."

Gisella squeezes his arm. "You'll be fine. Can you summon the memory of your brother dying?"

The young ghost swallows. "Of course."

"Make sure it's complete," Maël interrupts. "We need a clear view of the fairy and what she did."

Taylar nods solemnly and closes his eyes again.

With a sudden flash, several images come back to me. I remember what Taylar showed me not too long ago. The abandoned house, the fishbowl, his brother Lleyton climbing in through the window. And then the fairy, who turned everything upside down, literally. It must be horrible for him to relive this again. To see his brother getting killed and not being able to do anything about it.

"When you see it clearly," Gisella whispers, "open the watch."

Everyone is silent when Taylar opens his eyes and

breathes in slowly. Tears make their way down his cheeks as he pushes the small button on the front of the pocket watch. It springs open with a soft click and reveals an intricate set of tiny wheels and screws. From them, two light beams rise, the endings turning toward Taylar's face.

"Keep your eyes open and your mind focused on the memory," Gisella instructs, still in a whisper.

Taylar obeys. Perfectly still, he waits for the light beams to hit his eyes. When they do, he goes rigid. His blue irises turn yellow, and steam rises from them.

I wring my hands together. "Is this supposed to happen?"

Gisella nods.

The steam works its way out of Taylar's head and through the beams into the watch.

With every sliver, Taylar's face seems to relax a bit more, and he becomes more visible. His pants grow darker, and the green of his shirt becomes more vivid.

Finally, the light beams pull back. Taylar's irises turn back to their normal light blue, and the pocket watch slams shut.

We all jump a little at the sudden sound, and I kneel down next to Taylar. "Are you okay?"

He blinks several times before answering. "Yes, I think so. It's weird." He hands me the watch and rubs his face. "It feels like there's a hole inside my head."

Abruptly, he stops rubbing and lowers his hands. He turns his head to Gisella. "Is it gone? Did it take

161

my memory of Lley?"

The werecat presses her lips together.

"No!" Taylar yells. "You didn't tell me I'd lose this memory! I thought it would just make a copy!" He flings his hand forward. "Give it back to me! I want it back!"

She holds the watch behind her back and tries to catch Taylar's eyes. "Listen to me."

He shakes his head wildly. "No! You tricked me!"

I want to object, but I have to agree with him. She made it sound so simple. She never said he'd lose the memory.

"Listen to me, Taylar," she repeats sternly. "That memory was killing you. You're better off without it. Now we can use it to set things straight."

Tears flow down his cheeks. "No. Please…"

"You still remember everything," Gisella continues. "You just can't see it anymore."

Finally, he calms down. He stares at her, but his face is no longer a mask of despair and anger. "You're right, I can remember it all." He wipes the tears from his cheeks. "But you should've told me before that thing sucked my memory out of me."

"Would you have done it if I had?"

"Probably not."

She throws her red hair over her shoulder. "Which is why I didn't tell you. It was either this or dying."

"So it was a good choice," I interrupt. "No matter how hard, she's right, Taylar. We need to take care of your unfinished business, or more than just one

162

memory will be lost." I push myself to my feet and hold out my hand to him. "So, what do you say? Are you ready to get out of here? The sooner we do, the sooner we'll be able to send your memory to the authorities."

He grabs my hand and hugs me when I've helped him up. "Thank you, Dante." Then he turns to Gisella and hugs her too. "Thank you. I'm sorry I yelled at you."

She pats his back. "That's okay. I understand."

Charlie steps forward and pulls them apart. "Alright, alright, enough of that." He points at the red sky, where the Beach of Mu is moving in restless circles. "I think it's time to move on."

CHAPTER 20

"I wish we could stay here," I say after a couple of minutes. "Just move everyone we love here and build a new life."

Charlie chuckles. "And let everyone else on Earth die? That sounds like a great plan, mate."

I shove him lightly. "You know what I mean. Look at this world. It's so pretty and peaceful."

"Looks can be deceiving, Dante," Maël says behind me, and when I look over my shoulder, she points at an orange tree on our left.

Taylar, who is thankfully walking again, lets out a grumble of disgust. "That is so gross!"

At first, I have no idea what they're talking about, but then I see a trickle of red running down the bark of the tree, and when I move my gaze up, I can make out a large mouth with three rows of teeth.

"Is that an ent?" I ask, picking up my pace.

"I'm not sure," Vicky answers.

Then we all gasp as something jumps down from the tree.

"Definitely not an ent," I say, my voice slightly trembling.

"Where is its body?" Charlie asks in a hushed whisper.

No one has an answer to that question. I don't think any of us have ever seen anything like this before. The creature has no body. No feet, no arms, not even a head. It's just a giant orange mouth, gobbling up something that looks like a rodent, only purple.

Charlie is already three steps ahead of me. "Do you still want to live here?"

I grab Vicky's hand and hurry to catch up with him. "Not really."

The Beach of Mu is speeding up too. Above us clouds gather, and thick brown drops fall down. They splatter onto the road, leaving burning holes.

"We have to find shelter!" I shout above the racket of the impact.

Drops fall straight through the ghosts as they turn more transparent. Charlie, Gisella and me don't have that kind of protection though, which means we have to duck left and right to avoid the rain. A big drop hits Gisella on the shoulder, and she yells in pain and stumbles to her knees. Charlie and I pull her up immediately and take her with us under a tree with thick branches full of crawling white moss.

I look up at it gingerly before letting go of Gisella.

"Let me see," Charlie says, pulling at the tough fabric of her catsuit.

She holds up her hands. "I'm fine. I can heal myself." Her fingers gently press every side of her shoulder. "Besides, it's not that bad."

"And we have other things to worry about," Jeep adds, nodding at something behind us.

As soon as I whirl around, my breath catches in my throat.

Gliding through the maze of falling raindrops like a pro dodgeball player, the mouth advances.

Jeep takes off his hat and prepares to throw it, while I conjure a bolt of lightning.

"On three," I say. "One... two..."

I wait for the hat to soar through the sky before releasing my bolt. I aim a bit lower than the spot where Jeep's hat is heading, and a second later, a ball of gel the size of an ostrich's egg flies past my head, aimed a little higher.

With bated breath, we all watch the objects get closer to the mouth.

"Come on, come on," I whisper. *At least one of these should hit that monster. It needs a miracle to escape all three.*

Jeep's hat goes straight for it, and I wait for the monster to dodge it. If it does, it'll be hit by either my bolt or Charlie's ball of gel. Meanwhile, the killer drops are still falling down, ready to crush the abomination if our attacks miss it.

Only an inch before something hits it. But then

166

the monster does the unthinkable. The mouth opens. It shows one row of teeth, then two, then three, and still it opens wider. It moves sideways to avoid the hat and opens wide, swallowing the ball of gel in one giant gulp.

"No way!" Taylar shouts, and he moves closer to the bark of the tree.

My bolt extinguishes several feet behind the mouth, and Jeep's hat curves back like a boomerang.

"This thing is way too fast for us. We have to get out of here," I say, looking at the rain denting the road and wondering if we will ever be able to slip through unharmed.

No such luck. Even if we could, the drops are getting bigger by the second. If they keep growing, soon there won't be any room left between them. The road looks like a crater, dark and cracked, with brown liquid pouring out of it.

Maël slams her staff into the ground. "I'll try to freeze it."

We all gather behind her, our weapons ready, except for D'Maeo. He stays where he is, next to the ghost queen, with his eyes fixed on the incoming monster.

I expect him to raise his arms to block any power the mouth might have, but he just keeps still. When I reach out to touch his shoulder, he doesn't respond.

"Get ready," Charlie says, growing two balls of grease in his hands. "It's not slowing down."

Slipping between two huge rain drops, the mouth

reaches Maël. She stops mumbling and raises her staff when the monster goes for her throat. It tries to munch through the wood, but it's too strong and after several attempts to bite off Maël's head and a lot of shaking from the queen, it lets go and goes for the other target within reach: D'Maeo.

I conjure a lightning ball in my hands and turn to Charlie. "Get ready."

He nods and raises his hands.

The mouth lets out a high-pitched shriek as it jumps in front of the old ghost.

My muscles tense as I prepare to hit it with my ball of lightning.

Then something strange happens. The monster looks up at D'Maeo and freezes. Instead of attacking, it bows. Behind it, a large raindrop hits the road. Water splashes over the monster, and I see a glimpse of a body attached to the mouth. It's gone before I can take a better look though.

"What's it doing?" I mumble, and I feel Vicky tense up beside me.

A shadow seems to pass over D'Maeo's face as the rain suddenly stops falling, and the clouds dissolve.

Silence descends on us.

Slowly, the mouth opens. With a choking sound, it spits out balls of purple fur, covered in blood. I can make out little legs and a tail and avert my eyes before I throw up myself. From the corner of my eye, I see the monster smiling up at D'Maeo, who still doesn't move. The mouth closes and turns. Then it runs away

168

faster than it came, leaving us stumped.

It takes me several seconds and even more glances at the spot where I last saw the mouth to regain my posture. I'm the first to speak, and the only question that comes to mind is, "What the heck was that about?"

All eyes turn to the old ghost, standing frozen in place, as if he too has a hard time wrapping his head around it.

"D'Maeo?" Once more, I place a hand on his shoulder.

He shivers and shakes his head like a wet dog. "What is it?"

Since I have no idea how to explain what just happened, I just point at the mess in front of his feet.

"What's that?" D'Maeo asks. He blinks several times before looking up and scanning our surroundings. "Where did that monster go?"

"It left after bringing you this lovely gift," Charlie says sarcastically.

The old ghost stares at the remains of the squirrel some more and rubs his sideburns. "I don't understand."

With a sigh, I leave the shelter of the tree. "Neither do I. Let's go, the Beach is eager to move on. And to be honest, so am I. I don't want to run into any more of these weird creatures."

I beckon Charlie to walk with me and when the others are a couple of steps behind, I bend closer to him. "Did you see that shadow?"

He nods thoughtfully. "I thought I'd imagined it, but if you saw the same thing…"

I bite my lip. "This is all so weird. All this magic and other realms. The strange things happening to the members of my Shield. I don't know what to think of it. I don't know D'Maeo that well, or I can't remember, but I know something is wrong with him."

"I agree."

I look my best friend in the eye. "Would you mind keeping an eye on him? I'm not sure we can trust him anymore, and well… you're the only one here I remember. The only one I really trust."

He slaps me on the back. "Of course."

"I'm glad you're here, Charlie."

"I'd rather be lying on a beach with a cocktail somewhere," he winks, "but yeah, me too."

CHAPTER 21

After a while, the road smoothens again. The earth moves up by itself to fill up the holes created by the rain, and the brown liquid evaporates. I keep my eyes on the sand shape in the sky, wondering how something like that can be real and go over everything my friends have told me once again. *Maybe if I think about it long enough, my memories will return.*

I stop dead when the Beach of Mu drops from the sky and out of sight.

"What is it?" Vicky asks, giving me a worried look.

"Didn't you see that? The Beach! It just disappeared."

"I'm sorry, I was looking around. Where did you see it last?"

"Just further up the road."

We take out our weapons, and I gesture to the others to stay put while we check it out.

The athame feels strangely familiar in my hand. Although it's hard to imagine, I must have used it many times.

With careful steps, we walk to the spot where the beach vanished.

"Watch out!" Vicky yells so suddenly I almost trip.

She catches me, and I cling onto her arm when I see what's in front of us: a steep drop decorated with pointy branches sticking out. At the end of it, there's a bright blue lake above which the beach is hovering, shaped like a giant eagle. From the water rises an arc made of concrete blocks. *Another portal.* Inside it, a bright greenish light welcomes us.

"Oh great, another portal," Vicky mumbles before beckoning the others.

"How many have we already gone through?" I ask.

"Well, if I remember correctly, for you and Maël it's the fifth one."

The Beach of Mu swoops down and changes into a stairway again so we can descend.

"Thank you," I say, letting the others go first.

Taylar gives the portal a longing look. "I hope this one takes us home."

I step down after him. "I'm with you on that."

Everyone waits for me to catch up, but when I do, they still don't move. They all just stare at me from the bottom of the sand stairs.

"What are we waiting for?" I ask.

Charlie bursts out in laughter.

"What's so funny?"

Gisella smacks her boyfriend on the head. Not very hard, but he stops laughing.

"Sorry," he says, not looking sorry at all. "The thought that we were all waiting for you to lead us was just hilarious."

Gisella hits him again. "Be nice."

He kisses her on the cheek. "I'm always nice."

"You're waiting for me to take the lead?" I gulp. "I have to admit, Charlie has a point. I currently have no idea what I'm doing. It's probably better if someone else makes the decisions for a while."

The majority of my Shield looks at D'Maeo, but I quickly step forward and hold out my hand to the African queen. "Would you mind taking up this responsibility, Maël?"

From the corner of my eye, I see D'Maeo frown. Vicky told me he is—after me—the leader of the Shield. But I can't trust him right now, something is off about him.

Maël takes my hand and bows her head. "Of course, master. It would be my honor."

I bow back, feeling a bit silly, but it makes Maël smile. Both our heads turn to the portal with the pulsing green light several steps away from us.

The blue water from the lake splashes over our feet. Sweat prickles the skin on my back at the thought of entering another unknown world.

"Are we going in there?" I ask Maël, glad to leave the choice to her.

The Beach of Mu turns back into its eagle form

and pulls at my shirt with its beak. When I don't move, it lets go and flies to the portal. It lands on top of the concrete arc and makes a whistling sound that doesn't fit a bird. It's more like a coach whistling to get the players' attention.

Maël nods and holds out her staff. "I think we are indeed going in there."

She moves her staff through the water before stepping in fully—to check for anything deadly I suppose?

Nothing weird happens, so I follow her. Behind me, I hear the others splashing through the water. It's nice and warm. If I had the time—and if there was no chance of mouths or other body parts attacking me—I'd love to dive in and float around for half an hour at least. Just relax and talk to my friends.

But we've got a world to save. No, a universe.

I snort. I still find it hard to believe that I am the so-called chosen one. I feel like I've been sucked into a movie full of crazy creatures. Thankfully, the screenwriter put in some friends too.

A sideways glance at Vicky tells me she's studying me.

"Are you okay?" she asks. "You seem distracted." She moves a bit faster, and I follow.

When we're several steps ahead of the others, she leans over to me. "Why did you choose Maël to lead?"

I take in her expression, wondering if she's hurt because I didn't choose her. Maybe I should have.

But she looks worried rather than offended. *Should I tell her?*

"Maël used to lead a whole tribe, so I figured she'd be great at leading us," I say.

She drops her voice to a whisper. "You do know that D'Maeo is our leader, right?"

"I do… but…"

"But what?" she presses. "Is it because of what that mouth did?"

"Yes, but there's more." The portal is only a couple of steps away from us, so I'll need to speak quickly. "When that mouth monster attacked, did you see a shadow or something pass over D'Maeo?"

Vicky shakes her head. "I didn't, but he was acting really weird."

I look over my shoulder to check on the others. They're still several steps behind and discussing something. Charlie is watching D'Maeo like a hawk.

"Well, there was a shadow, and I've seen it before," I whisper. "When D'Maeo came to pick us up from the church. For a moment, he didn't look like himself. I'm not sure what is was, but it wasn't good."

"That sounds scary. We should keep an eye on him."

I nod. "I've asked Charlie to do so."

She stops dead and gives me an incredulous look.

"What?" I ask carefully.

"You asked Charlie? Why didn't you just ask me?"

"Well, I…" I stutter, raking my fingers through my

hair.

The others catch up, and Vicky waves them past impatiently.

"I get it," she says when we're alone again.

My mouth opens to tell her she doesn't look like she gets it, but I swallow my words.

"You don't trust me."

"What? Of course I trust you! You're my girlfriend."

"Yes, but you don't remember that, do you? You know I am because I told you."

I shake my head. "No, it's not just that. I feel it."

She crosses her arms, and I have to admit, she kind of scares me. The look in her eye is murderous.

But my love for her is stronger than my fear or my doubts, so I reach out and grab her hands.

She tries to pull away, but I won't let her. "Listen to me."

"Why?"

"Because I'm about to pour out my heart to you, that's why." It comes out blunt, a bit angry and way too loud, but maybe that's what dissolves her bitterness.

I bring my head closer to her, and the energy between us crackles. "Do you feel that? That is our love, our connection. It doesn't just come from you. It comes from both sides. When I woke up in that church, I didn't know you were my girlfriend, but I did know how I felt about you."

She closes her eyes and takes a couple of breaths.

"Then why didn't you confide in me about this?"

"Because…" I struggle to find the reason. "Because I'm just very very confused right now. It's all a bit too much, and I'm trying to stay strong. Nothing is as it should be…" I pause and wait for her to look at me. "…except for us."

The right corner of her mouth moves up a bit. "That sounds almost plausible."

I kiss her on the lips and whisper, "I want us to be perfect."

She grabs the back of my head and pulls me closer. When our lips meet again, electricity courses through my body, and everything around us is forgotten. That is, until something pushes me so hard I almost tumble over. When I regain my balance and look up, the sand eagle is hovering in front of me, looking rather angry.

"I'm sorry," I say, holding up my hands in defense. "We're coming."

After a curt, irritated nod, it returns to the top of the arc.

I clear my throat and try to act natural while I walk up to the portal where my friends are waiting. "So, let's go see what's on the other side, shall we?"

I'm grateful when no one comments, not even Charlie.

Maël holds out her staff to prevent us from stepping through the portal. "Give me a second to check for anything dangerous first."

"Great plan," I mumble, still flushed from shame.

I expect her to step through, but instead she

pierces the greenish light with her staff and closes her eyes.

Nothing seems to happen until suddenly she stumbles back and clutches her wand to her chest. She stares at the moving green light inside the arc. "That does not feel good." She looks up at the Beach of Mu. "Do we really need to go through this portal?"

The eagle's head moves up and down without hesitation.

When Maël sighs, the bird drops down from the arc and lands on her shoulder. Then it turns its head to us and whistles again, as if to say, 'Gather around! We should stick together!'

We obey and when the ghost queen walks through, we follow in one straight line.

I push Vicky through to make sure she's safe and close ranks.

CHAPTER 22

Everything is dark and chilly in here, and it takes a moment for my eyes to adjust.

"What a gloomy place," I say, looking around and breathing in the musky, steely smell.

Then my heart almost stops. Above us, three rivers decorate the dark sky, like giant moving ribbons. In the distance, there are two more. The sky seems to be never-ending.

"Tartarus," I mumble.

"What?"

The others turn around and stare at me.

"We're in Tartarus. I've been here before." I point at the sky. "Those are the five rivers of the Underworld."

Vicky's face lights up. "You've got your memory back!"

"No," I correct her with a shake of my head, "it's

just this I remember. This world."

I scratch my head and turn to Maël. "Didn't you say Purgatory is a part of Tartarus?"

She leans on her staff and nods. "I did."

"So, the beach is going home."

Gisella is turning round and round to take everything in. "I think it is, but why is it taking us with it?"

The sand eagle pushes itself off from Maël's shoulder, soars high into the sky and whistles.

The ghost queen beckons us with a determined expression on her face. "I think we will find out soon."

We walk until our feet are numb from exhaustion and cold. After several hours the three rivers and the portal are far behind us, and the other two rivers rage on above our heads. I've stopped looking up, because the movement in the water gives me the creeps. If you look closely, you can see arms, claws and torn faces, wide open mouths screaming for help without sound and eyes shimmering in the pale light of an invisible moon.

Charlie drops back a bit to talk to me. "D'Maeo seems normal again." He smirks. "Not that walking around in Tartarus and being a part of the chosen one's Shield is anything resembling normal, but you know what I mean."

"Good," I say. "Let's hope he stays that way."

Charlie rubs his arms. "Is it getting colder, or is

that just me?"

Vicky leans over from my other side. "No, I feel it too. Also darker and…" she shivers, "ominous."

As soon as the last word leaves her lips, the shivers running through her get stronger. At the same time, Jeep utters a moan and drops to his knees.

"What is it?" I ask and hurry over.

When I reach out to help him up, his muscles all tense up. The tattoos on his arms and neck wriggle under his skin.

He lifts his head and shows me his teeth. "Get away… from me."

I back up so fast I trip and fall. My head connects hard with the cold, rocky road. Halfway to the back of my head, my hand freezes as my gaze locks onto Vicky's. There's a murderous glint in it that makes me afraid to move. *This must be the start of one of those fits she was talking about.*

She opens her mouth and spits out a string of vicious syllables I don't understand. Her head tilts into an impossible angle, and she licks her lips.

Two hands grab the fabric around my shoulders and pull me back a millisecond before Vicky leaps.

She misses my feet by an inch when I pull them in, and growls like a rabid bear. She's about to charge again when Jeep knocks her over.

At first, I think he's protecting us, but soon, I realize he has turned into a raging beast himself.

"This can't be real," I pant when Charlie helps me up. "What are the odds of them having a fit at the exact same time?"

D'Maeo steps up next to me and rubs his beard. "Actually, it's not very surprising. Jeep has been having more and more trouble keeping the souls trapped inside his tattoos, and Vicky's fits are getting worse. On top of that, walking around in Tartarus, every step bringing us closer to Purgatory, breathing in the evil molecules floating around… These things will only make their conditions worse." He steps back as Vicky and Jeep roll our way, scratching, kicking and clawing at each other wildly. "And don't forget that everything is out of balance. That isn't helping either."

I suddenly remember Maël telling me about particles inside people being pulled in the wrong direction. I've felt okay since the white ents healed me, but D'Maeo is right, it was only a matter of time before we'd find ourselves in this situation.

We move back further, but the two ghosts only have eyes for each other. The sounds they make are awful. Jeep keeps moaning as if he's in terrible pain—which he probably is—and Vicky snarls and growls, emitting angry, incoherent words in between. Both are trying to bite the other's limbs off, but thankfully, they seem to have equal speed and agility.

"Is there anything we can do to stop them?" I ask Maël.

She shakes her head. "If we knew how to do that, we would not have to be afraid of these fits."

The two ghosts bump against each other at full

force. Both tumble to the ground in a daze, and I crouch down next to them.

"Enough of this!" I yell, imitating the tone of every drill sergeant I've ever seen in movies. "Get a grip, both of you! You are stronger than any curse or imbalance."

Both heads turn to me. Although their teeth haven't changed, they somehow look sharper now. Their eyes are dark, and rage contorts both of their features.

"Snap out of it, I mean it," I say threateningly. "Stop this, or I'll banish you from my Shield."

I hear Taylar gasping behind me and Gisella hushing him.

With balled up fists, I stare Jeep and Vicky down.

They don't move, but I'm not sure whether they're listening, fighting on the inside, or just thinking of the best way to rip me apart.

"Come back to us," I say, gently now, sending them both a pleading look.

They tilt their heads in unison, as if to size me up. I force my feet to stay where they are and keep telling myself, *they won't hurt me, they won't hurt me.*

Jeep's wrinkled forehead slowly relaxes, and I sigh with relief. But I let down my guard too soon. Vicky's eyes glisten with malice as her lips curl up further to form a manic grin.

"Vicky…" I say, but the weight in my voice is gone. I sound as scared as I feel. "Listen to—"

The rest of my sentence is lost when she hurls

herself at me with her mouth open and her fingers stretched out like claws.

I want to dive out of the way, but my feet don't move. Nothing moves anymore, except for the fear inside me.

Come on! Do something!

Vicky is about to knock me down and swallow me whole when I remember the power within me. I can take her down with a hurricane or a wave. If only I had more than a millisecond to conjure something.

My brain freezes. I'm out of options.

"Remember who you are," I say, looking her in the eye.

Then I brace myself for impact.

It doesn't come.

At the last moment, a tattooed arm pushes me aside, and Jeep's body takes the full blow. The two of them tumble to the ground again, grunting and struggling.

Vicky lurches for his throat, but Jeep moves his hand to the side of her head, and with a well-aimed blow to the temple, she goes down.

I snap out of my frozen state and kneel down next to Vicky. She's out cold.

I look up at Jeep. "Thanks." I narrow my eyes. "Are you back?"

He holds up his thumb.

"Good. Just checking."

When I push myself back up, Charlie steps up to me. "That was tense. And that last part!" He places his hands on my shoulder and stares into my eyes.

"Remember who you aaare," he breathes, and then collapses into a fit of laughter.

Gisella elbows him in the side with a scowl. "Don't mind my boyfriend. He can act like a jerk sometimes, as you might know."

"Come on, that was funny," Charlie says, rubbing his side. "Such a beautiful imitation of Mufasa."

"Who's Mufasa?" D'Maeo and Maël ask at the same time.

Charlie's mouth falls open. "Really? You're kidding, right? Mufasa was Simba's father."

He holds up his hand when they open their mouths for the obvious question. "No, don't ask." He sighs and shakes his head. "You should really teach your Shield more about contemporary art, Dante." With a smile, he turns back to the two oldest ghosts. "You've never heard of the Lion King? It's a classic."

Gisella's elbow shoots out again.

"Ouch! Stop that!"

"I'm sorry to interrupt," Gisella says, her voice dripping with sarcasm, "but we've got more important things to do. Like find out why Dante froze like that and move on to see what the Beach of Mu wants."

All eyes turn to me.

"What happened, Dante?" Jeep wants to know. "Why didn't you step away or try to stop her?"

I shrug. "I don't know. Is it that uncommon, to freeze? I didn't want to hurt my girlfriend and…" I

185

shrug again, realizing I have no idea why I couldn't just step aside or block her attack.

"I saw something," Gisella confesses. "A dark shape climbing onto your back. I wanted to help, to get it off you, but somehow, it dazed me too."

A dark shape? I exchange a quick look with Charlie. "You mean like a shadow?"

She nods. "Something like that."

"Was it…" I force myself not to stare at D'Maeo. Inside, I nudge my power core. "Was it attached to someone?"

Gisella bites her lip. "Eh… I'm not sure. I didn't pay attention to it. I was just trying to move. But then Jeep knocked Vicky out of the way, and it was all gone: the shape, the daze."

Taylar clears his throat. "I saw it too."

"And?" I ask, dreading the answer.

"It *was* attached to someone." He turns slowly to where D'Maeo is watching quietly. "It was attached to you."

CHAPTER 23

In a matter of seconds, we've all pulled out our weapons and created distance between us and the old ghost. I pull Vicky, who's still unconscious, with me as I join my friends.

"Wait a minute," D'Maeo says, holding up both hands. "I don't know what you think you saw, but I am not the enemy. I could never hurt you. Any of you."

Maël narrows her eyes at him. "I am not certain anymore."

"Something is wrong with you, D'Maeo," I say. "I saw it in the church and later with that mouth monster. Something isn't right."

A soft groan makes me look down.

"Keep an eye on him," I tell the others while I bend over Vicky. "How are you feeling?"

She rubs the side of her head with a frown. "Tired,

and my temple hurts a bit."

"Sorry about that," Jeep says without turning his head.

"I heard you," Vicky tells me. "I tried to come back. I fought. I really did." Tears flow from her eyes.

"Hey." I wrap my arms around her and hold her tight. "Don't worry about it. It's not your fault."

"I don't want to hurt anyone, but it's so strong."

"I know. You didn't hurt anyone, don't worry."

I wipe the tears from her cheeks and eyes and help her up.

The others keep their eyes on D'Maeo, who is waiting with his hands in the air for us to continue the interrogation.

Vicky drops the hand still rubbing her head. "What's going on?"

After a quick summary, she gives D'Maeo a once-over before crossing the distance between them.

I reach out to stop her, but Maël pushes her staff against my chest. "She will be fine. She will use her power to read his feelings. If he wants to hurt her, she will know in time."

"Okay," I say, but I'm not convinced.

Vicky comes to a halt in front of the gray-haired ghost. "Look at me," she orders.

He does, and for several tense seconds, she falls silent.

"How do you feel?" she asks him then. "Different than usual?"

"No."

"How do you feel about being a part of Dante's Shield?"

D'Maeo shifts his feet but doesn't break eye contact. He knows Vicky will sense it if he doesn't tell her the truth. "I am proud and nervous about it."

Without pausing, Vicky interrogates him further. "Do you have the intention to hurt any of us?"

"Of course not." He sounds a bit impatient.

"Are you carrying something that could be dangerous to any of us, including yourself? On or inside you?"

He shakes his head. "Not that I'm aware of."

Vicky turns to us, but it's not with the smile I was hoping for. "He's telling the truth, but there was a tiny disruption in his eyes when he answered the last two questions."

"What does that mean? What kind of disruption?" I ask, rubbing my arms against the sudden cold that takes over my bones.

"I've never seen anything like it before. It was like a ripple in his eyes. It went by so fast I almost didn't catch it. But there was also a small blind spot in his emotions." She shakes her head. "I'm not explaining this right. But I've never experienced this before, and it's hard to put into words."

"I think you did great," I tell her, forcing a smile onto my lips. "Your questions were spot on, and now we know that D'Maeo doesn't mean us any harm, but that there's probably something inside him that doesn't have good intentions."

The old ghost stares down at his body when we all look at him. "I don't feel any different. All I know is that I sometimes lose time. Not much, just a couple of minutes."

I turn back to Vicky. "You know a lot about spells, right?"

"Sure."

"Is there a spell that can draw out whatever is inside of D'Maeo? Or keep it locked inside until we can figure out a way to get it out?"

Vicky scratches her head. "I think there is, but I don't know it by heart. You could check your father's notebook."

Maël points at the sky. "Maybe we should do that later. The beach is getting restless."

She's right. The sand eagle soars over our heads, whistling loudly.

"Mighty Beach of Mu!" I call out, and it stops in front of me, hovering in the air with ease.

"Is there time for us to cast a spell? We want to make sure the entity inside D'Maeo doesn't attack us."

The eagle moves its head from left to right and lets out a high-pitched whistle.

"I guess that's a no." I close my eyes. *We've trusted the beach so far. It has led us into dangerous worlds, but it also saved us several times. It reunited me and Maël with our friends, and it crossed all of these worlds to get me and lead me here. D'Maeo hasn't hurt any of us... yet. The thing inside him got rid of that mouth monster.*

I press my lips together. *It also froze me when Vicky attacked. It's a good thing Jeep snapped out of his episode in time to push me away.*

Sighing deeply, I open my eyes. *We'll just have to trust that we can keep each other safe.*

"D'Maeo, now that you know something is inside you, trying to hurt us, will you be able to keep it from taking over?" I ask.

Finally, he shakes off the shroud of defeat hanging over him and pulls back his shoulders. "I cannot guarantee anything, but as always, I will fight to keep you safe."

"All of us," I press.

He smiles. "Of course. And if anything feels wrong, I will let you know."

"Great. Then I guess we're good to go."

The eagle must have been listening in, because it whistles again and takes off at top speed.

"I think we're almost there, guys," I say as we set off after it.

Let's just hope we're not walking straight into a trap.

Soon, we leave the last two rivers in the sky behind us and walk into even darker territory.

I rub my arms again, but this cold can't be driven out. It's not just physical cold, but a combination of fear, longing and despondency lingering in the air.

The vast space around us narrows as the thick darkness crawls closer. Several steps further, the dark turns into two solid walls with a small path leading to more blackness. I hesitate, but when I see the Beach of Mu continuing without even pausing, I follow.

I let everyone pass and keep an eye on the road behind us. In the distance, the flowing rivers are no more than specks. There's a small light even further away, but it doesn't move.

Charlie is the last in the row of worried faces.

"Did you see anything strange?" I ask, nodding at D'Maeo's back.

He shakes his head while we walk on. "Nothing."

"Good."

We walk and walk. Around us, everything has grown silent. No more voices coming from the river or the blackness behind the walls. The path gets narrower, and eventually we're forced to walk in single file.

After what feels like several hours, the sand eagle finally slows down.

"Be ready to fight," I tell the others, and we all take out our weapons. Shoulders are straightened, and the expressions of weariness change to relief.

I tilt my head in an effort to filter out any noises besides our footsteps and the wingbeat of the beach.

Everything is still silent, but something else has changed.

"Do you feel that?" I ask no one in particular.

They all nod without speaking.

I hold my free hand closer to the wall on my left. A warm draft makes my cold fingers tingle. A wave of frozen air follows, and then another warm one lingers for a second.

"Weird," I say softly.

"Not really," Maël answers. "We're getting close to Purgatory, where souls fight to get to one side or the other. Good and evil clash there, creating hot and cold waves.

"Plus darkness and light," I add, pointing at a spark making its way along the wall on our right.

"Good to know it's not all evil in there," Jeep mumbles.

"So, we're really going into Purgatory?" I ask, reluctant to move closer to it even after what I've recently heard about it. After all, most stories about Purgatory aren't exactly laughter and sunshine.

"The Beach of Mu wants us to go in there," Charlie points out. "And we still trust it, don't we?"

I press the space between my eyes to stop the pounding coming to life there. "Yes, but why does it want us in Purgatory? What are we going to find there? What are we supposed to do?"

"Fix the balance we disturbed, I suppose," Vicky answers.

I drop my hand to look at her. "And we're throwing ourselves in there blindly?"

We hold each other's gaze for several seconds. I wonder if she's reading my emotions. If she can feel my fear. Not that I would care. I have a right to be scared. We don't know what we're getting ourselves into, and we've seen a lot of bad and dangerous things lately. Enough to stop and think about this, I'd say.

Suddenly, Vicky's mouth splits into a wide smile. "That's it!"

I shake my head, confused. "What's what?"

"You're right, we shouldn't go in blind if we don't have to. And we don't." She claps her hands excitedly. "If I'm not mistaken, we have a way to see what's going on in Purgatory. Or at least in a part of it."

I frown. "We do?"

She nods feverishly, her eyes gleaming with elation. The others crowd around her as far as that's possible on the narrow path.

"You see," Vicky explains, "we were told we upset the balance of the universe when we sent Trevor and his demons somewhere unknown with our defensive spell. We didn't know where they ended up. But…" She gives me a crooked grin, "we did reverse the spell he put on your mom and Mona, meaning we can look through his eyes now, instead of him looking through theirs. And I'm guessing Trevor is in Purgatory." She crosses her arms with a satisfied expression. "That's why the beach is taking us there."

I can't hold back the triumphant whoop that rises in my throat. I pick Vicky up and her feet go through the walls as I spin her around. "You are brilliant!"

"I know," she chuckles when I set her down again.

CHAPTER 24

"Okay," I rub my hands together to warm them up, "how do we look through Trevor's eyes?"

Vicky shrugs. "We haven't seen him since we reversed his spell, so I think we need to say the words of the original spell."

I stop rubbing my hands. "And you know this spell?"

She rolls her eyes. "Of course I do. Would I be this happy if I didn't?"

I pull her head closer and plant a kiss on her temple. "Great. Just write it down, and I'll try it."

She pulls a piece of paper and a pen from her endless pocket and starts scribbling the words down while I enjoy the frequent warm waves passing by.

Too soon, she nudges me and hands me the note.

I scan it quickly. "That's all?"

She puts away the pen and smiles. "Yep, it's only a

195

small part of the spell. Just the words to activate everything we prepared earlier."

In the glow of the passing sparks, I read the lines to myself first.

When I open my mouth to say them out loud, Vicky pushes a candle and matchbox into my hands. "You do need to light this candle first and burn the words while you read them." She takes the piece of paper back and waits for me to ignite the wick.

I blow out the match and exchange it for the paper. "Here we go."

When it catches fire, I read the words out loud.

"Activate our spell of sight.
Make our vision clear and light.
Show us now what his eyes see
and make us hear it all clearly."

There's not much left of the piece of paper when I finish the last sentence. The flame makes it way to my fingers in a hurry, and I prepare to drop it, but then it vanishes with a soft whoosh, leaving nothing but a trail of white smoke dotted with black spots. It swirls in front of me like a mini tornado, and now I see that the dots are more than random shapes. They are letters, the letters from the spell. They mix with the white smoke that used to be the paper and climb up and up until I can no longer see them.

Above us, a thick mist breaks up the dark. Inch by inch, it drops and widens.

I step back and move to blow out the candle, but Vicky's hand shoots out to stop me. "Don't. Blowing it out will end the spell." She points at the mist coming to a halt and forming a square, like a screen. "Watch."

The blackness inside the "screen" turns brighter and brighter until it's impossible to look at. With my eyes closed, I wait for the light to become bearable.

"It's working!" Taylar exclaims, as if he didn't expect it to.

I want to give him a witty response, but when my gaze falls onto the screen, all I can do is gape.

"Do you think this is Purgatory?" Charlie asks Maël, who is clutching her staff tightly.

"I am not sure," she answers.

I'm still not able to say anything. While I stare at the scene above us, my mind whirls. *Is this real? Do things like this and places like this really exist?*

It's like watching a horror movie, in which the good are battling the evil. Bodies in all shapes, sizes and colors jump and fly left and right. They bump into each other and roll around on a road made of floating logs, like a long wooden raft. Under it, there are two gaping holes. One is a pit of fire, with sharp rocks sticking out of the walls, the other is a pool filled with clouds surrounded by purple flowers. Between the two holes, in the middle of the wooden pathway, lies a glass mold with black and white pebbles in it. I can barely make out what it used to portray with all the scattered pebbles around it, but when no one dives over it for a second, I see it. A yin and yang symbol.

My insides knot together when I realize we are the reason the balance here was disturbed. We were the ones who sent creatures here that belong in Hell. Now, big two-headed wolves with flames for fur pin down the souls who were supposed to be judged here. Out of all the places Trevor and his demons could have ended up, this is one of the worst. Here, they have found hundreds of souls tiptoeing the line between good and evil, easily pushed in any direction. They can create allies in a matter of seconds. And they do. I see humans trying to outrun the demons and failing. Some surrender quickly. Others fight for what they're worth. It's not hard to see where each belongs. But instead of ending up in one of the two holes, like they should, all of the souls are herded onto a wooden platform that floats from the pathway to a vertical, yellow flickering line in the sky. One by one, the souls step through and disappear. As soon as they're all gone, the platform turns back, like an automated ferry, to pick up more passengers. I concentrate on the woman hesitating in front of the portal. If I can remember her features, I can scry for her later, if I need to. There's not much time, but she has an interesting face. I should be able to... She steps through, and I close my eyes briefly to hold onto the image. When I open them again, my gaze shifts to the person steering the platform in the right direction. I squint, thinking I'm hallucinating.

With my right hand, I feel around for Charlie's arm.

"What?" he says, looking up from the holes below.

"Is that... Paul?"

As soon as I say his name, the person on the platform looks up, as if he can hear me. Even though he's too far away to make out his exact features, I no longer doubt what I'm seeing. I'd recognize that triangle-shaped face surrounded by thick black hair anywhere.

"Is he helping Trevor? Helping the Devil?" I ask in an incredulous whisper.

Charlie doesn't answer. When I look at him, his forehead is wrinkled up, and his teeth make a grinding noise.

"Yes, he is," he finally says. "I told you he and Simon had gone crazy, didn't I?"

"You did but seeing this makes it more real than anything you could've said." I rake my hand through my short hair. "I guess I was still hoping you got it wrong somehow."

Unable to look at our former friend any longer, I move my eyes over the rest of the scene.

The souls that put up a fight are brought closer to our vantage point, closer to Trevor.

A voice rises above the noise of the battle. "Come here."

One of the wolf demons pushes the resisting people forward.

"That's Trevor's voice," Vicky says beside me.

A hand is raised in front of us. It beckons the souls that should be send to Heaven. An itch makes its way through my stomach and up to my throat. I cough, and Vicky hushes me.

"Don't be afraid," Trevor tells the souls in a drawling tone. "I have a good offer for you all."

He holds out his arm, indicating the vertical portal that swings into view as he turns his head. "Instead of suffering here for eternity, you can choose to join us."

I can almost see the grin on his face as he continues. "Help us free Lucifer, and you will earn a place in his kingdom."

Most of the people shake their heads. Some avoid Trevor's eyes, trembling from head to toe. Hope flares up in my chest when not one of them agrees to help him.

"I don't ask for much," Trevor says with a soothing undertone. "And it shouldn't be hard, considering our numbers." He starts pacing up and down the narrow floating path. Two steps to the right, turn, two steps to the left. "All we need is some help getting a couple of souls. Starting with a small nature fairy. The prepping has already been done. It wasn't that hard to make her angry." He chuckles. "We poisoned her home."

Disgust and disbelief glides over the faces of the souls.

Trevor keeps pacing. "She was forgiving at first, said she could restore most of it. Then her little animal friends started to die. She couldn't save them.

Nor could she save any of the trees that withered away. Or her fairy friends." He laughs out loud now, startling his audience. "Oh, that face! I've never seen anything more beautiful. A heavenly creature with fury etched into her tiny forehead. It was a pleasure to order my army to electrocute her." An irritated expression takes over his face. "Then she escaped, but that's okay. We'll find her soon and take her to Hell."

He stops to face his listeners, who back up as one. "A fate much worse than that awaits you all if you don't help me. I can send you to Heaven now, but your happiness won't last long. We will get what we want with or without your help. I prefer with, since patience isn't my master's biggest virtue." Our view is cut in half as he winks. "So that's your choice: help us and live happily in our new world, or don't help and suffer for eternity."

The people shuffle their feet nervously. Some are mumbling things like, 'I'll do it' and 'I guess we have no choice'. Others are still looking for a way out, but the wolf demons with the flaming bodies block their way.

"Alright, enough of this!" Trevor suddenly thunders, making all of the souls jump. "Decide now before I think of a better place to put you all."

My insides cringe as they all agree. They're led to Paul on his floating ferry as sheep to the slaughterhouse.

"Don't do it! We're coming!" I yell.

The screen flickers, and the mist swallows it up, leaving nothing but dark sky, broken now and then by a hesitant sparkle.

"What happened?" I ask, looking at my friends.

Vicky points at the candle in my hand. "You blew it out with your futile shout."

My mouth forms a shameful O when she takes the candle and drops it back into her pocket.

"Sorry," I say.

"No need to feel sorry," Maël says, slamming her staff down. "We have seen enough. We know what awaits us in Purgatory. Trevor is sending souls back to Earth to take this fairy's soul. We need to stop him, close that portal and make sure everyone is brought back to where they belong."

I nod. "This must be the fairy the Cards of Death point to." I think back to the lightning bolt on the first card and bite my lip. *They electrocuted the poor thing. How cruel can you be?*

"I know she's already dead, but I think they haven't taken her soul yet. That's why they're sending this private army to Earth, right? We can still save the fairy."

Maël throws me a bitter smile. "Maybe, but we should prepare ourselves for another loss."

For once, I don't agree with her. Shaking my head, I squeeze myself past the others until I'm close enough to put a hand on Maël's shoulder. "No, we should always keep the faith and trust in our own strengths. We will defeat this Trevor and save the fifth soul."

The bitterness disappears from her face, and her smile becomes genuine. "It is good to see you are slowly coming back to us, master."

CHAPTER 25

The Beach of Mu lands on my shoulder as I take the lead. My heart beats deafeningly in my ears.

I can't believe I'm walking into Purgatory voluntarily.

I know we have faced demons and other magical creatures before, but since I don't remember any of that, it's hard to keep the faith I so convincingly portrayed a minute ago.

My legs seem to know what they're doing though. Without hesitation, they keep carrying me forward. *I hope my powers work by themselves just as well.*

Suddenly, the narrow road is blocked by a dark ripple hovering in front of me.

I stop and raise my athame.

"This is it, guys." My voice knows it before I do. We have arrived at our destination.

The sand eagle on my shoulder whistles happily and bounces up and down with delight.

"Well, at least someone's happy to be here," Jeep observes dryly.

I turn to face my friends. "We probably need some kind of plan."

"Right." Jeep grins. "How about we storm in there, kill every last one of those demons, your former friend and Trevor and make sure no souls fall off the path."

Charlie gives him a high five. "Great plan."

I roll my eyes. "Yes, but how?"

Jeep pushes past me and winks. "It'll come to you."

He steps forward and is swallowed by the ripple.

The Beach of Mu lets out a shrill whistle as if to say, 'what are you waiting for? Follow him!', so that's exactly what I do.

Trust your instinct, trust your instinct, I tell myself while I walk through the slimy stuff.

But all my thoughts come to a halt when I step onto the wooden pathway.

Everything around me looks just as it did when I was looking at it on the screen, but at the same time, it's totally different. Thanks to the spell, we could only see what Trevor saw. Now I can see everything, and there's so much more than just the path, the portal and the two holes below. There's screaming and howling in the distance, but also soft voices saying prayers. The sparks we saw on the road leading here crawl through the sky like snakes. They shoot up from the heavenly hole below, paint artful patterns left and right and touch the souls that drift to us from all around. The smell lingering in the air is a mixture of flowers, fresh apple pie, burnt skin and musk.

It's all so overwhelming that it takes me a minute to notice Paul is no longer here, and neither is Trevor. Also, three two-headed wolves are pounding my way.

Without realizing what I'm doing, I take the short stick with the small ball from my pocket and thrust it forward with force. The stick extends, and the ball grows considerably in size on its way to the target. In the blink of an eye, it hits the front demon square between the two heads. With a loud yelp, the monster goes down. *Well, I guess the spell to make them vanish doesn't work anymore. Not that it would help. They would just end up here again.*

I shake the thoughts from my mind when the two other wolf demons stomp over their comrade's body without a single pause, their fiery eyes locked on me.

"I'm here," Vicky's voice suddenly says on my right. "We've got this."

I haul in my Morningstar—that's what it's called!—catching another demon in the rear, and clutch my athame with my other hand.

I wait for my Morningstar to fully fold back, whispering words of courage to myself. Apparently, Vicky doesn't possess that kind of fear or patience. With a battle cry that frightens even me, she charges the incoming demons.

My muscles tense as I prepare to follow her, but before I can, Gisella tears past me. With a couple of somersaults, she kicks one of the wolves in the heads before piercing its flaming body with her blades. I lower my weapon as I watch the two girls take down three more demons without much trouble.

Charlie nudges my shoulder. "Your mouth is open."

I close it and swallow a couple of times. "Are you sure I'm not dreaming?"

He smacks me in the back of the head.

"Ouch!"

With a grin, he conjures a ball of grease in his hand and throws it at another charging demon, blinding it so Gisella is able to take it down with one sweep of her arm. "You're not dreaming."

I nod at the small army of wolves on fire, creeping along the path, growling like rabid dogs. "In that case, we should give the girls a hand."

Charlie flicks back his hair. "Love to."

As one, we move forward, the rest of the Shield close behind. Balls of gel and light fly everywhere, swords reflect the flames on the demons' bodies and soon instinct takes over my every move.

I'm surprised at the ease with which I fling my Morningstar and lash out with my athame at the same time. I duck before I even know I need to. I throw a lightning ball into the gaping mouth of an incoming monster when my Morningstar gets stuck. When I almost tumble into the flaming pit below, Taylar grabs my hand and pulls me back onto the floating path. I return the favor when he's knocked onto his back and almost slides off the logs. I jump onto the back of a charging wolf and use its strength to pull my Morningstar free. Immediately, I swing it, and it latches onto the log right next to Taylar, who grabs it and pulls himself back up.

As the wolf turns its heads to bite me, I blind it with a lightning bolt. D'Maeo finishes it off with his sword, and I grin. "We make a great team!"

He gives me a grave nod before turning to face another incoming attack when suddenly the sound of Trevor's voice rolls toward us. "Drop your weapons now, or she's dead."

It's as if the whole scene before me freezes, and for a split second, I think Maël has used her power to stop time. But the demons are backing up, and everyone on my team is panting hard, even though most of them don't need to breathe. It must be a habit that's hard to lose.

I have to blink several times to convince myself that what I'm seeing is real.

How did Mom get here? And why isn't she trying to escape?

Trevor walks up the path to where we're standing, Mom at his side. He's wearing a burgundy suit with shiny black shoes under it. His hair is neatly combed to the side. Mom's face is pale. Her blonde hair is pulled up, and one lock is draped around her face. She's wearing an evening dress I've never seen before. They both look like they're on their way to the opera or something. Watching them together makes me nauseous.

The demons shrink back to the sides of the path to let them pass. Without a word, me and my friends move closer to form a solid line of defense.

I want to ask Mom if she's okay, tell her to run, tell her everything will be okay, but my lips are frozen. No sound comes through.

It seems to take forever for them to reach us. It's as if they're taking a stroll in the park.

Finally, they come to a halt. With a smirk that's almost wider than his face, Trevor opens his arms.

"Well well, look who's here, Susan." He pats the hand clutching his left arm. "It's your son. I think he has come to kill me. Tell him how you feel about that, my love."

My love? Nausea rises in my throat as I watch them approach.

"Mom? What's going on?"

"I would hate for that to happen," she says with a smile that looks fake, plastered on. Her face is like a doll's, stiff and unmoving, her eyes blank. "Hello, Dante. Trevor and I are together. Please don't kill him."

Fuming from head to toe, I ball my hands around my weapons. My power core pulses wildly inside my chest. I step forward. "What did you do to her?"

Trevor calmly raises his free hand and inspects his nails. "Nothing. We love each other. Is that so hard to believe?"

"It's not hard to believe. It's impossible," I hiss

through clenched teeth while memories of him flood back into my mind. I see him talking to a demon in an alley, threatening the priest we saved and showing his slick smile to Mom at the bird park.

"The potion," Vicky breathes from behind me. "The love potion we made for that man at the black market, as payment for your pendant."

Trevor grins and raises an eyebrow. "You got me. I saw you lurking around and decided to have a little chat with that salesman. Offered him a pretty sweet deal to trick you into making a love potion." He pulls Mom closer, and she throws him a smile, apparently deaf to his foul words. "You didn't know love potions made by family members of the target are stronger, did you?"

I cross my arms and tilt my head. "You know what? It doesn't matter. We'll get her back, no matter what. That potion won't last forever. And you're not going to kill her." I imitate his evil grin. "You love her. So while we fight to save the world from your master, at least I'll know she's safe. I should thank you actually, for giving me one less thing to worry about."

I expect his smile to falter at this, but he still seems very content with himself. He shakes his head like a schoolteacher that's tired of hearing the wrong answer over and over. "You're right... and you're wrong."

I tap my foot and sigh theatrically. "Is that so?"

He chuckles. "Sure, you got me on the whole

'you're not going to hurt her' part. Of course I would never hurt her. But there was something else you said… what was it?" He taps his lips with his finger, pretending to think hard. "Something about getting her back no matter what?"

"We will," I say, balling my fists to keep myself from going for his throat.

"Of course you will," he calls out jovially. "If you keep out of my business. Otherwise…" He squeezes Mom's shoulder. "I kind of like the idea of keeping her with me for eternity." He looks down on her with a nauseating smile. "Wouldn't that be lovely?"

She smiles back like a frozen doll. "That would be wonderful."

Trevor presses a kiss on her temple. His eyes flit back to me, inviting me to attack.

Vicky places a hand on my shoulder to keep me from diving forward.

"Oh love," Trevor says, "isn't it a beautiful thing?" He turns his back to us and starts walking away, Mom still clinging to his arm.

After two steps, he stops and looks over his shoulder. "Oh, I almost forgot to give you an important piece of information… Susan is only safe because she's with me. If you kill me…" He traces the line of his neck with his finger.

As I watch them walk away from us, anger shoots through me in waves of heat. My fingers hurt from the force with which I clench my fists.

"We'll get her back," Vicky says softly.

A tear escapes my eye when I blink. "I can't let him walk away with her like that. I just… can't."

As Jeep grabs my left arm, Vicky holds the right. "You have to. He won't harm her."

I'm panting with the effort to stay where I am. "What if he forces her to… you know."

Silence answers me. When I finally manage to tear my gaze from the two figures walking away from us, I find Vicky gritting her teeth so hard they squeak in protest.

"You're right," she says as she lets go of my arm. "We can't let them leave."

I breathe a sigh of relief. "So, you're with me?"

"I'm always with you." She points at our friends behind us, who step forward with determined looks and raised weapons. "We all are."

CHAPTER 26

As if on cue, the Beach of Mu swoops down from somewhere above our heads. In the blink of an eye, it has reached Trevor and Mom and picked her up as if she's as light as a feather. They both give a surprised cry and reach for each other, but the sand eagle is already too high up.

Mom struggles to break free while the beach carries her back above the path.

"Don't fight, Mom!" I yell at her. "He's with us. He's trying to save you!"

To my relief, she stops kicking and wriggling. That is, until Trevor interferes.

"Susan! Don't let it take you from me!"

She reaches up and pulls at the bird's claws.

"Mom, don't!" I call out, but the effects of the love potion are too strong. She pulls one toe loose, then another.

They both drop down several inches, and Mom

dangles from one claw.

The beach tries to grab her again, but she keeps wriggling.

"Mom, listen to me!" I yell as loud as I can. "You have to stay still, or you'll get hurt."

She doesn't respond and reaches up again to wrench loose the other claw.

"Beach of Mu, fly lower!" I shout.

It obeys, swaying as Mom kicks her feet.

Behind them, Trevor shouts a command at a particularly large wolf demon. It leaps as Mom's feet get closer to the floating pathway.

"Watch out!" I yell.

The beach makes a sudden turn, and Mom sways left just as the demon pounces. But one of its jaws catches the tail of the sand eagle. Instinctively, it changes form, and Mom slips from its grip.

It all seems to happen in slow motion. Mom's eyes go wide as she reaches for a handhold that isn't there. A collective 'No!' from Trevor, me and Vicky mixes in the air. I throw myself forward, even though I know I'll be too late to catch her.

Fear takes a hold of Mom's face as the momentum of the turn carries her over the edge of the floating pathway. A cold hand folds around my heart when she plunges toward the hole that leads to Hell. I drop onto my belly and reach for her, but she's already too far away. Tears of panic run down her cheek, and her mouth forms a cry for help that is lost in the noise of the raging fires below.

The Beach of Mu dives after her, back in its eagle form. I haul myself back onto my feet and take a deep breath.

When I close my eyes, ready to leap, a hand wraps around my wrist.

"What are you doing?" Vicky asks.

I tear myself loose and shoot her an angry look. "Going after her! What else?"

A sad smile slides across her face. "Well of course, silly. But you aren't planning on going alone, are you? We're in this together. Wherever you go, I go."

A voice dripping with sarcasm makes me turn my head. "Oh, that's so sweet!"

Trevor has caught up with us. His eyes are full of hate but hidden beneath that is real hurt and worry. If I had any doubts about his feelings for Mom, they would vanish now.

"No really, it's sweet," he says. "But it won't do you much good to go after her. You won't last long in there. There's a welcoming committee in the form of an army of demons waiting at the bottom of that pit."

I raise my eyebrows. "Is that so?"

"It is. That's why *I* am going in there. The demons won't harm me. I can get her out."

I feel my mouth dropping open, but I can't stop it. *Is he seriously trying to save us now?*

Trevor grins and smacks me on the back hard. "Don't confuse common sense with caring, boy. I put some protection on Susan, in case I lost sight of her." He winks. "We're in a dangerous place, after all. And in case you showed up, I put in an extra… fail safe, so to speak." He laughs out loud, but it doesn't sound very cheerful. I'm not sure whether he's trying to fool *me* into thinking everything is fine, or himself. "If you or any of your lovely friends touch her, the protection will shatter. Therefore, it's in Susan's best interest if I go down there to get her back, and you stay here." He smirks. "Or wherever you like, as long as it's far away from us."

"He's bluffing," Jeep says.

Maël steps forward. "I do not think he is. When the Beach of Mu lifted your mother, I sensed something. I could not put my finger on it, but this must have been what I felt. I think he is telling the truth, Dante."

"He is," Vicky confirms, looking into Trevor's eyes.

Trevor lifts his hands and claps in mock admiration. "Well observed. I guess that's settled then."

He turns to the pit below and waves. "It was lovely to see you all again. I hope it is the last time."

"So do I," I say through gritted teeth.

Trevor nods at the wolf demons, ready to pounce us again. "You probably won't last long. Meanwhile, stay out of my business. If you meddle with our plans again, you will never see your mother again." He takes a deep breath and steps off the path. Without a sound, he drops into the smoldering hole below and disappears from sight.

Vicky gives my hand a comforting squeeze. "She'll be fine. The Beach of Mu will keep an eye on her too."

"Great," I sigh and turn away from the gaping hole below. It's probably best to focus on something else. "Let's close this portal and get the souls that he sent to Earth back, okay?"

"We can't," Charlie says. "He told us not to meddle anymore, remember? Which means we can't do anything until we get your mom back."

"Sure we can," Vicky responds with glinting eyes. "Because he didn't say anything about someone else interfering."

When we all stare at her blankly, she pulls Dad's notebook from behind my waistband and waves it around. "We've used the cloaking spell several times. What if we use it again but cloak ourselves with different appearances this time?"

"That's brilliant!" I call out. There's more I want to say, but behind Vicky, the demons are moving. I pull Dad's notebook out of her hands and stuff it back behind my waistband while Vicky turns to see what's happening.

"I guess we have some fighting to do before we can cast the spell," I say.

A look over my shoulder tells me the others are ready for another round of slaying. They all have determined expressions on their faces and weapons in their hands.

Just in time too, because with a loud growl, the

remaining group of demons pounces. Within seconds, it's as if the fight has never stopped. Trevor pushed pause, and now that he's gone, the scene comes to life again.

Since my Morningstar is still stuck in the spot where Taylar almost went over the edge, I swing my athame with my right hand and throw bolts of lightning from my left hand.

When a wolf knocks me over from behind, I turn onto my back quickly and hit its two heads with lightning. The monster howls in pain and backs up, but not before setting my pants on fire with its flaming fur. I roll over in an attempt to extinguish it and bump into Charlie, who loses his balance.

My hand shoots forward and catches his ankle just before he tumbles from the pathway.

"Help!" I yell, dropping my athame so I can use both hands to hold his weight. I could probably haul him up by myself if it wasn't for another demon towering over me. Its left head shoots down and misses my head by half an inch as I pull it back.

"Somebody?" I shout, using one hand to fire several balls of lightning at the demon.

This monster is more agile than the others. Not a single ball hits it as it moves left and right, and from behind it, another wolf steps forward, licking its lips.

"Pull me up!" Charlie yells.

I shoot some lightning at the second demon, and it backs up a little. "I can't! I need one hand to keep these demons away!"

With a whoosh, Maël's staff splits the air between me and the wolf. It looks up a fraction too late. The tip of the staff hits it in the chin hard, and it tips over sideways. Maël slams the wand down onto one of the second demon's heads before taking care of the first.

Meanwhile, I pull Charlie back onto the path. He holds up a hand filled with grease balls and aims it over my shoulder, hitting another demon in the eyes. Then he pushes himself up and holds out his hand to me. "Come on, we've got more monsters to kill."

We turn to where the others are fighting. There are only a couple of demons left, so I take a few seconds to steady my breathing.

Then I nod. "Okay, let's finish this."

Charlie pulls some sweets from his pocket and shoves them into his mouth. Then he conjures two large grease balls and raises them above his head with an exhilarated cry. He dives forward, and I follow with a less enthusiastic yell.

I brace myself, but inches from impact, the battling monsters all freeze and back up with their tails between their legs and their heads down. Even the largest one seems afraid.

We all lower our weapons and frown.

A chill creeps from my toes to my neck at the thought of what could have made them run so suddenly.

Then I see the boat, decorated with skulls and bones, and with a jolt, memories flood back into my head. I have to lean on Charlie to prevent myself from falling over. The light from the lantern attached to the bow of the boat seems to hypnotize me. I can't tear my eyes away from it to look at the figure standing behind it. Not that I need to; I already know who he is and what he looks like. I've met him before. Charon, the ferryman of the Underworld. *Has he come to punish us for screwing up the whole universe?* It sure feels like it.

I sink to my knees and grab my head, that feels as if it's splitting in half. The tunnels of the silver mine appear before my eyes in hot flashes. The black void in the wall, the spider demon grabbing Mom, the premonitions of the Devil coming back to me.

I press my hands against my eyes and scream.

"Stop it!" I hear Vicky call out. "What are you doing to him?"

"Just giving back what was taken in another world," Charon's raspy voice answers.

Vicky's response gets lost in the noise in my head, but the images sooth the pain somewhat.

I see Vicky lying on the bed at Darkwood Manor and giving me the provocative look I have grown to love. I vaguely register rolling onto my side while flashes of kisses and more slide by. Touches with electricity, smiles and conversations heat me up further. Then the nice memories are pushed aside by battles, blood, swirling black smoke, an evil tree, Trevor holding a priest, the soul of a young man dragged away from me and the body of an old woman draped over a stack of suitcases.

"NO!" I scream, curling up into a ball.

A hand is placed on my back, and a soothing voice speaks to me, but I can't understand the words. My memories drown out all sounds in the present. Mona's face hovers in front of me, smiling as usual.

"I'm your fairy godmother," she says, and she turns and turns until she's nothing but sparkles that warm my body with their soft touch.

The pounding in my head finally stops, and reality trickles back in. I relax my limbs, push myself into a sitting position and blink several times. "Let's not do that again."

Vicky, sitting next to me, still stroking my back, lets out a shrill laugh. "I agree."

Then I remember who gave me my memories back. Charon must have used his Lake of Remembrance somehow to bring them back. I scramble to my feet and bow deep, trying not to topple over as dizziness hits me. "Thank you for your help."

The skinny figure dressed in dark rags towers over me. Although I can't see his eyes, I can feel them bore into me disapprovingly.

"I would say it was my pleasure," he booms, "but your respect is not enough to erase my rage." He points a bony finger at me. "You upset the balance of the universe."

If I could shrink into oblivion, I would. Instead, I keep my head down and put all my regret in my words. "I know, and I am really sorry, Charon. It was a grave mistake, and we will do everything within our power to set things right."

There's a short silence before he pulls back his arm. "You may rise."

I straighten up and pull at my clothes to give my shaking hands something to do.

The silence between us pricks my skin. I open my mouth to apologize again when Gisella takes a step forward.

"Can you tell us what happened, ferryman?"

She seems to be the only one here not impressed by Charon's presence, and I'm not sure whether to admire or disapprove of that.

To my surprise, Charon answers without scolding her. "Your spell landed Trevor and the demons here and made sure they couldn't get back to Earth. That is why he sent the souls from Purgatory to Earth instead, which in turn disturbed the balance of the universe even more."

"So we have to undo the spell?" I ask.

He shakes his head, making the bones crunch. "No, it is too late for that."

Gisella throws down her arms, changing her hands into blades. "Don't worry. We'll get all the souls back here and take care of Trevor."

Charon tilts his head, and the dark holes where his eyes should be gleam in the passing sparks. "Your courage and determination are admirable, but you must remember that you are not alone. You are all part of a team in which some members are more important than others."

Gisella frowns at him. "Yes, I know I'm not as important as Dante. How could I ever forget? Everyone keeps reminding us he's the chosen one."

"He is," Charon replies calmly. "But he cannot finish his quest without all of you. You are all a part of this. In a way, you were all chosen to play a part, small or big."

Taylar clears his throat. "Are you saying he can't succeed without us?"

I hear the unspoken 'without me?' in his voice.

The ferryman nods slowly. "That is what I am saying."

When no one else speaks, I bow again. "Allow me to apologize once more for our mistake. We'll be more careful from now on." He stares at me without uttering a word, so I continue. "And thank you again for returning my memories to me."

Charon floats back onto his boat through the side. His staff changes into an oar, and water rises up from the path under it. "Do not disappoint me again, young Dante. We all depend on you."

No answer seems good enough for that, so I settle for a 'Yes, sir.'

The corners of his mouth go up far enough to reveal his sharp teeth. "I took care of the remaining wolf demons for you. They won't bother you again."

I recoil. "You did?"

He bends forward, closer to me than physically possible. "Don't tell anyone," he says in a hoarse whisper, "but I've been keeping an eye on you since even before we met, and I've grown quite fond of you, boy."

He gives a small bow back, and when I blink, he's vanished into a thick mist beside the floating path.

The lantern attached to the high bow of the boat is the last thing we see, swinging gently from left to right, before the vessel disappears completely.

Charlie breathes out audibly. "That was something you don't see every day." He wipes his forehead. "A bit scary too."

Gisella shrugs. "He wasn't *that* impressive."

Vicky nudges me. "How do you feel, now that you know the ferryman of the Underworld is fond of you?"

I'm still staring at the spot where Charon was standing just a couple of seconds ago. "You know... I'm not sure that's such a good thing."

"Why not?" Jeep asks, rubbing the tattoos on his arms. "You told us he's neither good nor bad. And he helped you before, didn't he? When you were trapped in the Shadow World with Vicky and she zapped home without you?"

"Sure," I nod. "For his own good. If I fail, he'll die, or perish, or whatever you call it in his case."

Jeep pulls down his sleeves. "Well, I think he meant it. He really likes you. And that could come in handy again."

My muscles scream at me to lie down while my mind buzzes with all the memories that have come back. I swallow a sigh. "Maybe."

"Well," Vicky says cheerily, hooking her arm in mine, "I'm glad he stopped by. He saved us a lot of time getting rid of those wolf demons, and more important: we've got you back."

Maël takes me in, leaning on her staff. "Speaking of this... how do you feel?"

I look at her and try to find the words to describe what's going on inside me.

"Confused," Vicky says. "And scared, determined and..." I meet her eye. "Grateful."

I shake my head with a smile. "Thank you for that assessment, Doctor Vick." I turn back to Maël. "I'll be fine. But the world will not be if we don't do something now. So, who's ready to dive through that portal and fight?"

They all raise their hands and howl like a pack of hyenas. I laugh and beckon them. "Let's do this!"

CHAPTER 27

The wooden platform is empty when we reach it.

"Where did Paul go?" Charlie asks as I hold out my hand to Vicky. "Do you think Charon got rid of him too?"

I shake my head, anger waking up in my stomach again. "No, he was gone when we came here. He probably fled as soon as he saw us. The coward."

Rage flares up in my best friend's eyes. "Yeah, I think you're right. But I'm sure we'll see him again."

Once we're all on the platform, it takes us to the portal without trouble. I stare into it and scratch my head. "If we close it, how do we get back home?"

Charlie pulls his hair together. "We could go through and block it using a spell, you know."

"That's a good idea," I nod. "And I can write another spell to get the souls back where they belong."

Vicky kisses my cheek. "It's good to have you back."

Her touch gives me energy, and I kiss her back. "It feels good to me too."

Okay, no time to linger. We have to get everyone back in Purgatory before they catch the fairy's soul.

Reluctantly, I pull back and take a last look at the pit leading to Hell. *I'm coming for you as soon as I can, Mom.*

"Right." Straightening my shoulders, I turn to my friends. "I'll go first, with Vicky, to see where we end up. Wait for one of us to give the all-clear before following, please. I don't want anyone else to get hurt or lost."

And with that, I take Vicky's hand and step through the portal.

It's different than the last couple of portals we went through. We don't arrive on the other side immediately. Instead, we land on some sort of slide. I feel us slipping downhill, faster and faster, going from left to right. There's no sound or light around us, and suddenly, I wonder if this is actually a trap.

But then we slow down, and Vicky's cold hand wraps tighter around mine. *Of course she senses my unease.* I want to ask her if she's worried too, but I'm afraid to disturb the silence. Darkness often hides the most horrible things, and I don't want to wake anything.

The slide ends, and we get up. Behind us, the air seems to change. It becomes more solid with every passing second, until finally it pushes us forward through a blackness I mistook for a wall. It's all sticky, and it smells like a combination of rotten eggs and decaying flesh. It clings to every part of me and makes my skin itch. I try to move faster, but it's like struggling through glue. I shake my head as it crawls up to my mouth and eyes.

I knew it. It's a trap. Thank heavens we didn't all go in at once.

The air behind us is still pushing, and hope ignites in my chest when I see a sliver of light in the distance.

When I try to pull Vicky closer, my whole body grows cold. She's no longer there. I'm clinging to the slick substance instead of to her.

Reflexively, I nudge my power core. A blue ball comes to life in my hand and chases away the black mud. I concentrate on a bigger ball, and once the light spreads further, I'm able to move my head and arms. I look around and scream when two eyes and a mouth appear in front of me.

"Shh, it's me," Vicky hisses. "Come. The exit is right here."

She takes my unlit hand and pulls me along. The oily substance tries to grab onto her barely visible form but fails.

The light gets bigger, and suddenly, we tumble forward. Vicky catches me before my nose hits the rocky ground. She's almost as solid as a living girl now, and I pull her into a hug.

"We're fine," she soothes me. "But how are we going to let the others know they can come? We're far from the entrance."

I rub the last bits of mud from my pants and freeze. "Wait a minute. I know this place!"

In the dim light of the pulsing red symbols on the walls, I turn in all directions. "I can't believe it! We're in the silver mine!"

"What?" Vicky furrows her eyebrows. "You mean our silver mine? In Blackford?"

"Exactly." I conjure a new lightning ball and illuminate the walls. "This is amazing. There's not a single sign of the porthole to Darkwood Manor."

I wave at the spot where it should be. "Mona! Are you in there by any chance? Open up!"

All remains quiet, except for the bubbling surface behind us.

Oh right, we need a way to reach the others or get a message to them.

"I can call the rest of the Shield to me," I suggest.

"Sure, but what about Charlie and Gisella? When they see the others disappear, they won't know what to do."

"Good point. So, what then? Is there a way to send them a message?"

She shakes her head. "I don't think so." She stares at the wriggling portal. "We could go back?"

She sounds about as thrilled at the idea as I am.

"There must be a better—" My last word changes to a shriek when a voice interrupts me.

"You're back!"

We both whirl around and whip out our weapons.

I slam my free hand against my chest when I spot Mona's head sticking out of the open porthole just outside the tunnel.

She smiles brightly. "I'm glad to see you're still in one piece. I lost sight of you for a while, and a minute ago, you suddenly popped up." She sticks her head through further to check the rest of the tunnel. "Where are the others?"

"Still in Purgatory," I say, lowering my athame.

Mona wrinkles her forehead. "Did you by any chance bump into your mother? She fell off the grid too."

I exchange a quick look with Vicky.

"What is it?" Mona asks.

I can't look at her, so I pretend to concentrate on putting away my athame. "Trevor got her. But she should be safe with him. He actually loves her."

Mona gasps. "How did that happen?"

A distant scream makes us all turn our heads to the portal.

"I'll tell you all about it later," I say, conjuring a bolt of lightning in each hand. "Close the porthole. We don't want anyone to find this secret passage."

"I'll keep an eye on you from here," Mona says before stepping back. "Be careful!"

Inch by inch, we move back to the portal, which seems to be swirling more violently again.

"Do you hear that?" I ask in a hushed voice.

Vicky tilts her head. "What?"

"Voices."

Her face lights up. "It must be the others!" Without warning, she calls out, "Jeep! Maël! Is that you?"

There's a muffled response that could mean anything.

Vicky sticks her hand in.

"No!" I yell. "What are you doing?"

But she's already up to her elbow in the muddy substance.

I yank at her arm, but it's stuck. "Are you crazy? What were you thinking?"

"That our friends are probably just as stuck as we were," she responds calmly.

"And we got out on our own, didn't we? They'll be fine without us."

"Do you want to gamble their lives on that assumption?"

I groan and stick my hands in too. "Guys? Take our hands."

Something touches my fingers, and I almost pull back. Not that I would be able too, because as soon as I try to pull the person inside toward me, something sticky wraps around my arms and hands and pulls me further inside.

"I knew this was a bad idea!" I call out as I watch Vicky getting pulled in up to her shoulders.

The darkness claws its way from my arms into my neck, and I shake my head in an attempt to get rid of it. Meanwhile, I'm pulling like crazy, but it's like fighting cement.

There's a draft behind us, and a warm sparkle lands on my nose.

"Keep still for a moment," Mona's voice says.

I obey without hesitation, and when Vicky stops wriggling, a cloud of sparks drifts between us and splits in two. Half of the lights jump onto my arms, and the other half makes its way to Vicky's shoulders. As soon as they touch the mud, there's a high shriek, and the sticky stuff crawls back. The sparks follow it, but it's not done fighting. In the blink of an eye, the strings of black form into claws that slam down onto the dots of light.

"Enough of this," Mona says. There's a whoosh, and a warm whirlwind passes between me and Vicky. Sparks escape from it and rain down on us. A bunch of them cling onto the blackness of the portal, and part of the mud evaporates. The claws let go and retreat hastily.

Simultaneously, Vicky and I pull as hard as we can. The resistance breaks, and we tumble backwards. Taylar lands on top of me while Vicky and Maël are a mess of intertwined see-through limbs and clothes.

"Thanks," Taylar mumbles, and we jump back onto our feet and help the ladies up.

When we turn back to the portal, the Mona whirlwind is grabbing one arm after the other and hurling the people attached in our direction. Soon, we have D'Maeo, Gisella and Charlie at our side and a hole in the portal surrounded by sparks.

"Look at that," I say. "It's turning."

The vortex behind the dark mud rotates right, then backs up a bit and proceeds to turn.

"Now I understand why we were sliding down," I mumble.

Gradually, the hole in the portal starts to close as the whirlwind spins slower.

I hold out my hand. "Wait! Where's Jeep?"

"He was right behind me," Charlie says.

"Mona, can you see Jeep?" I call out to the whirlwind.

She doesn't answer, but more sparks rise from her and dive deeper into the vortex as it spins and spins. At the end of it, I can make out the vague form of the wooden pathway and the dark sky of Purgatory, until a black bowler hat blocks my view.

"There he is!"

The sparks shoot forward, but when they reach the spot, the hat is gone.

"Jeep!" I yell. "Can you hear us?"

When there's no answer, I turn to face the others. "I have to go in to get him."

I take a deep breath, but before I can make a move, Charlie grabs my shirt. "Wait! Look!"

I follow his gaze and gasp. The scenery at the end of the vortex is changing. Purgatory moves out of sight bit by bit as something else slides into its place.

"Guys?" A low voice echoes through the tunnel.

"We're here!" three of us yell at the same time.

For a second, I see something resembling a stretched-out hand. Then a shrill howl makes us slam

233

our hands against our ears. A cold wind extinguishes every single spark with one violent blast. The whirlwind is shot out of the portal with such force that it knocks us all off our feet.

Mona lands in a heap against the back wall of the tunnel and doesn't move.

The rest of us are scratched up, but otherwise fine.

Gisella hurries over to Mona while I try to stay on my swaying feet. I must have hit my head harder than I thought. There are now two vortexes instead of one. That is, until I blink several times, and they merge into one again.

I breathe in sharply. "It's closing!"

Vicky throws herself forward. "No! Jeep!"

We squint into the darkening hole in front of us, but there's no sign of him or his hat.

Our hands find each other, and we exchange a quick look. Then we face the portal again and jump… only to bump into a solid black wall.

Vicky drops down to her knees, tears falling from her eyes. "It took him! It took Jeep!"

I squat down next to her and pull her head against my shoulder, searching for words of hope.

There must be something we can do to get him back. A way to go after him.

But we don't even know where he went. We don't even know if his soul is still intact. Even if we can open this portal again, the world behind it will have changed.

I close my eyes as visions of Jeep being ripped apart swim before my eyes. Another memory returns to me. The memory of my body and mind being taken over by cold. And I realize an important rule was broken. *There was a chapter 13. A chapter that I should've skipped in my story. But I didn't realize I was in it at the time. The Shield warned me never to write a thirteenth chapter. And now, because I did, bad luck has found us. It found us, and it took Jeep. We've lost him. We've lost a member of the Shield.*

CHAPTER 28

My hands form into fists as I squeeze Vicky harder. *No,* I think to myself. *No more negative thoughts. We have accomplished impossible things before, so we can do it again. Jeep is not lost yet.*

Wiping the tears from my eyes, I kiss Vicky on her forehead, get up and pull out Dad's notebook. I flip through it at record speed.

Vicky looks up at me in confusion. "What are you doing?"

"Looking for a lost and found spell of course. We have magic. We can get Jeep back."

"You know there's nothing I want more than that right now," she says, pushing herself to her feet, "but he'll have to wait."

Without looking up from the notebook, I shake my head. "No. We have no idea where he went. He might be fighting a whole army of demons right now.

We can't leave him."

"There's no other choice right now." Vicky sounds desperate, and I lower the book to meet her eye.

"Sure there is. We try everything we can think of until we have him back in one piece."

Another tear forms in the corner of her eye. "What about the soul, Dante? The fifth soul? Shouldn't we save that first? We're already way behind on Trevor. He's got dozens of minions looking for it."

"She is right, Jeep will have to wait." Maël pulls Mona to her feet. They both look tired.

When I drop my gaze back to the book in my hands, Maël continues. "You know there is a reason why Lucifer keeps hunting these souls. Evidently, he is able to use them even if he fails to obtain them all. Another soul will bring him closer to his goal. We cannot let that happen, Dante."

D'Maeo clears his throat, and I know nothing good will come out of his mouth.

I'm right.

"I hate to say this, but I agree. Jeep will have to take care of himself until we have saved the fifth soul."

"And he wouldn't want it any other way," Taylar adds. "He would want us to finish what we started together. To keep fighting."

Vicky pushes my arm with the book down. "Yes, he would."

I sigh. "Fine. We'll find the soul first. But as soon

as it's safe, we're going after Jeep and Mom. We're not giving up on anyone. That's an order." I give them all a stern look, and they nod, even Charlie and Gisella, who aren't obliged to obey me.

"Good." I tap the book in my hand. "So, what now? We can't simply go after that soul. If we do, the chances of getting my mother back are slim. A cloaking spell probably won't hold for very long."

There's a moment of silence in which everyone straightens their clothes and hair and frowns or mumbles to themselves.

Then Mona suddenly raises a finger. "I've got it!"

A handful of sparks hops from her hands onto her head and jumps down, showering her in light. When the sparks touch the ground, Mona doesn't look like Mona anymore. She's a ten-year-old girl with pigtails and a dress covered in ribbons.

Gisella grins and claps. "That's amazing, Mona!"

I frown. "It is, but can you do that to all of us at the same time? And can you keep our fake appearances up for hours on end?"

Mona clicks the heels of her shoes together and changes back into her perfect self. "I cannot. But…" she gives me a wide smile, "I've got friends." She shoos us back through the porthole. "Have something to eat and drink while I find some help. Go on!"

After one last look at the closed portal, I step into the hidden room at Darkwood Manor. Immediately, a weight seems to fall from my shoulders. I close the porthole behind Mona and pull her into a hug.

She utters a muffled cry of surprise.

"Thanks for saving us," I whisper.

"Oh, honey, there's no need to thank me for that. It's my job. I wish I could do more."

I kiss her on the cheek. "You do plenty. We're blessed to have you around."

She glistens from head to toe, both literally and figuratively. "Well, you're very welcome. Now hurry downstairs, and I'll go see some of my friends."

"Yes, ma'am."

She giggles and goes up in sparks.

When I walk into the kitchen, the others are pulling all kinds of snacks from the closets while Vicky heats up water for tea. Soon we're all sitting in our usual spots around the table. Except for me, because I'm staring at the two empty chairs where Mom and Jeep should be sitting.

I squeeze my eyes shut to drive out the vivid images of them both suffering.

They're fine. Mom is under Trevor's protection, and Jeep can handle himself. They'll be okay for now.

A flash of the closing portal passes before my eyes. I gasp.

"What's wrong?" Vicky asks.

Slowly, I close my mouth and open my eyes. Everyone's attention is focused on me.

"It suddenly hit me," I say. "The reason why those wolf demons were trying to open the portal in the silver mine."

Vicky frowns. "Why?"

I drop down onto my chair and stare at the table. "The vortex behind that portal rotates past different worlds." I pause and look around the table, but no one seems to grasp what I'm trying to say, so I explain further. "Eventually, it will pass Hell too. That's what the demons were preparing for. They probably know when the vortex passes Hell, and they want to make sure it's open then."

D'Maeo scratches his sideburn. "That doesn't make sense. If someone from Hell wanted to get through, they could do so just as easily as we did now from Purgatory."

Maël nods. "Opening gateways from Hell to Earth is not easy. I think the demons were not only opening the portal, they were also trying to steer it in the right direction."

I press my temples with both hands. *The Devil is planning to enter Earth through a portal in my town. And we're the only ones who can stop him.*

I slam my hands on the table, startling everyone. "Well, it's a good thing we found out about this, because now we can do something about it. We were already keeping the portal closed using the Bell of Izme, but now we can figure out a way to keep the vortex from reaching Hell. This is actually good news."

"Sure, if we ever get to it," Charlie sulks.

"We will. We've gotten this far and conquered some situations that seemed impossible before." I raise my mug high. "So I want to make a toast…" I wait for the others to raise their mugs too. "To our golden team. We will succeed, no matter what!"

My words are greeted by cheering, and when everyone takes a sip, I see Vicky giving me a curious look.

"What?" I ask.

"You've changed."

I lean closer to her. "Is that a good thing?"

She grins. "I have to admit, I like this new positive attitude. And it's a good trait for a leader."

I put away my mug with the intention of kissing her when there's a loud whoosh.

We all look up and shield our eyes as seven women arrive in whirls of different colors.

They're all different, but all as perfect as Mona is: smooth skin, unwrinkled clothes, not a single hair out of place and glowing from within as they touch down in a row next to the kitchen table.

I hastily get to my feet and bow. "Welcome. We are grateful for your presence."

They bow back in unison, and Mona steps up next to me. "I have found some friends who are willing to help us. May I introduce…" She gestures at the beautiful women. "Hanna, Bella, Emma, Flora, Donna and Kara."

We all mumble our hellos. Mona smiles brightly. "I've given them a quick summary of what happened. Each of them will put a spell on one of you. This way, the magic won't run out too soon. You will have plenty of time to search for the soul, save it, send all the souls from Purgatory back and find your mother. Once you've got her back, you won't need our spell anymore." She lifts her right foot, takes of her shoe and holds it up. "I think you all know the story of Cinderella. Of course, it was twisted a little. In the story, the spell on her shoes isn't broken when the magic runs out. In reality, your shoes will be the first to return to normal, so please keep an eye on them." She puts her shoe back on and searches for something in her pockets. "Hold on, it's here somewhere. Ah! Here it is." Showing us a yellow ring, she continues her instructions. "You will all be given a ring for the duration of the spell. This ring belongs to the fairy godmother who enchants you, and with it, you can summon her in case something goes wrong." She walks over to D'Maeo and slides the ring onto his finger.

"I had imagined a different setting for this," D'Maeo jokes. "And shouldn't there be a proposal first?"

Mona's cheeks turn bright red, and she fiddles with her hair.

D'Maeo kisses her on the lips and sparks rise from her chest.

"We'll get to that later," he whispers in her ear, loud enough for me to hear it across the table.

All the other fairy godmothers are watching the scene with upturned mouths, like dolls. It's a good thing I know Mona so well, otherwise I would've thought they were robots. Still, seeing them together gives me an uneasy feeling. They're just too perfect to be real.

"Anyway," Mona continues when she manages to pull free from D'Maeo. "Each ring has the color of the godmother's sparks. Mine is yellow."

"Wait, your sparks all have different colors?"

Mona nods at the godmothers, who throw a handful of sparks in the air one by one.

It's like watching fireworks. Red, blue, purple, pink, orange and green clouds fill the kitchen, and we all gasp.

"Each ring is made of two parts. Turn the upper part three times to the left and two times to the right to contact your temporary fairy godmother. Go ahead, try it." She vanishes, and D'Maeo studies the ring.

He turns the upper part to the left until it clicks three times, then he turns it back two clicks.

In a cloud of yellow, Mona lands in front of him. "Yes, like that! Easy, right?"

"But please only do this in case of an emergency," the second godmother says. "We all have our own charges to take care of too."

"Of course," I say hastily. "We won't bother you unless it's absolutely necessary. I can't thank you all enough for stepping in on such short notice and helping us out like this."

"You're very welcome," they all say in unison, showing rows of perfect white teeth.

Mona slams her hands together. "Okay, if everyone is ready, we can start. No time to lose, right?"

CHAPTER 29

The fairy godmothers each pick a person to change. I end up with a stout, dark-haired woman.

I'm relieved when she introduces herself again. "Hi, I'm Flora."

"I'm Dante, it's nice to meet you."

"Oh!" She presses both hands against her cheeks and stares at me wide-eyed. "I've got the chosen one? Oh jolly!" She bends over until her nose nearly touches mine and whispers, "I'll give you the best transformation I've ever done. Don't you worry."

"I'm not worried," I say truthfully.

"Good." She straightens up and taps my nose gently. "Now stand up, close your eyes and relax."

I do as she says. Through my eyelids, I can see pink flashes of light moving around me. My whole body tingles, and I have to concentrate to keep myself from moving or opening my eyes.

"A bit more hair," Flora mumbles. "How about a beard?"

Something soft moves over my chin.

"Apparently not."

The feeling disappears, and I feel fabric wrapping around my arms.

"Very nice," Flora says to herself. "Let me see…"

Her hand touches the hair on my head. "I think, maybe…" There's a breath of air, and suddenly my head feels colder.

"Yes, that's it."

Mona's voice interrupts her musings. "You could add some hair to the back. It will make him blend in better."

"Great idea!" Flora answers cheerfully, and the back of my head gets a bit warmer again.

"And a bit of stretching to finish it up," she mumbles. Something pulls at my limbs, and I grunt, although it's more a strange than a painful feeling.

"Alright, Dante," Flora says, grabbing my hands. "I think you're all done."

As soon as I open my eyes, pink sparks dance along Flora's hand, revealing a mirror, which she holds up to me.

I recoil. "Wow!"

Blue eyes stare back at me from a frowning fortyish face. Most of my hair is gone, except for thin layers on the sides and back of my head and some stubbles on my chin and under my nose. I'm wearing jeans, a plain dark blue T-shirt and a black leather jacket. My sneakers have changed into brown leather shoes.

"This is amazing, Flora. Thank you," I say. I tilt my head. "Hey, I still sound like me."

"Only to us, love," she says with a wink. "To everyone else, you sound like a forty-three-year-old tough guy." She lowers the mirror.

"Dude, you look like an action hero!"

I narrow my eyes at the guy using Charlie's voice. He's no longer a young, blond surfer. "You're Asian!"

Next to him, a pretty young woman with short black hair leans forward. "So am I."

"Gisella?" I shake my head. "This is crazy!"

"Where are you from?" I ask.

"We were both born here in the United States, which is why we don't speak Japanese," Charlie says with a wink. "Our families are from Japan though, and we'd like to visit our relatives there one day."

I chuckle. "Very convincing."

My gaze shifts to the other unfamiliar faces at the table. It's a good thing all of us always sit in the same spot at the kitchen table, or I'd have no idea who was who.

On my left, next to Charlie, there's a pale, chubby man with glasses, dressed in a cheap black suit. I'm not sure what stands out more, the coffee stain on his shirt or the way his brown hair is glued to his head. He's got a sulky expression on his face, and he keeps pushing his glasses higher up his nose.

I stare at him until he finally sighs and says, "Yes, it's me, Taylar. I look like an idiot."

Charlie looks him up and down with a grin. "You

look like a man who has seen nothing but the inside of an office for years."

"Oh good!" the fairy godmother with the wavy red hair calls out. "That's what I was going for."

The grumpy office guy crosses his arms and stares at the empty mug in front of him.

I look up to the head of the table, across from my seat, where D'Maeo was sitting several minutes ago. He's the only one who has been made younger. Instead of sixtyish, he's now around fifty years old. He stands up and turns as if he's in a fashion show.

We all applaud, except for Taylar, who's still sulking.

Mona took away some of D'Maeo's arm muscle and added some length, making him taller and more slender than my fake appearance. I love how he still looks like the leader of the Shield. His unwrinkled face and pristine suit somehow scream 'manager', and I have a feeling that was exactly what Mona was going for.

"You're still wearing a suit," Charlie comments.

"Yes," the old ghost answers in his own voice, sitting down again, "but I've never worn anything other than black, so this feels a bit strange." He strokes the fabric of his dark blue jacket.

"You look great," Mona tells him, raking her fingers through his brown hair. "You're like a cross between Jude Law and Bradley Cooper."

D'Maeo rubs his bare chin and cheeks. "Really? I feel so… bald."

"It looks great," Asian Gisella assures him.

"Sure," D'Maeo huffs. "On this face."

While they chat, I take a look at the person sitting in Maël's chair. "No way!"

Everyone falls silent and Charlie chuckles. "Donna did a great job with Maël, didn't she?"

My head is spinning from trying to take in all these changes. By now, I'm afraid to look at Vicky. She's the only one I don't want to change. I don't care what the others look like, and as long as I don't look too bad myself, I'm fine with it, but Vicky is a different story. I love the way she looks, feels and smells. I love everything about her. She's my dream girl. I don't want to kiss or hold anyone else.

Which is why I'm glad there's one more transformation for me to admire before turning to the girl sitting to my right. I try to block out any glimpse I pick up from the corner of my eye while I take in Maël.

She's turned into a blonde, white thirty-something woman wearing a navy colored two-piece suit with a tight skirt around her small hips. Her hair is wound into a neat bun at the back of her head.

I want to burst into laughter, but I can't do that, so instead I ask her, "How do you feel?"

I can't help but laugh when she answers in her own deep, dark voice. The combination makes me think of an alien.

"I'm sorry," I say, swallowing hard. "It takes some getting used to your new look. But what do you

249

think?"

"Honestly," she says, "it is a wonderful disguise, but I think fighting in this skirt will be difficult." She shoots Donna an apologetic look.

"You're right," the fairy godmother says with a nod. She waves her hand and orange sparks wrap around Maël's waist. In the blink of an eye, a pair of navy pants replace the skirt.

"Thank you," the blonde woman says, "that is much better."

"What do you think of my new look?" Vicky whispers in my ear.

"I'm not sure I'm ready to see it."

"Sure you are," she says, grabbing my face with two hands and turning my head.

My mouth falls open when a woman in her mid-forties smiles at me. She's got a head full of short, blonde curls and dark brown eyes that are almost as mesmerizing as Vicky's own blue ones.

"Well?" she asks.

When I don't answer, Charlie laughs. "I think you still make a pretty couple."

Flora and Hanna glow. "We thought you'd like it."

"Right, so you've made everyone handsome, except for me," Taylar pouts.

Mona gives him a sympathetic look. "I'm sorry, but we have to keep it realistic. Not everyone is good-looking. We're not in the movies after all."

"We can switch," Vicky offers. "I don't mind looking like that."

The godmother with the black bob cut shakes her head. "We can't do that. It's too risky to change genders. We want you to blend in."

Taylar shrugs. "It's okay really, I was just being sarcastic. I like being solid." He grins. "It just didn't have to be this solid."

"Oh right!" I call out. "You're all no longer transparent. That's amazing!"

The fairy godmothers give a small bow.

"Well, darlings," Mona claps to get everyone's attention, "I think we're done!"

"There's something I wanted to ask before you all leave," Asian Charlie says.

All the godmothers turn their perfect faces toward him. "Yes?"

"Dante and his Mom have a fairy godmother, but apparently Gisella and I do not. Why is that? Why doesn't everyone have a fairy godmother?"

The godmother with the long black curls, Kara I think, gives him a wide smile. "That's a good question."

Mona waves her friends away. "You girls go back to your charges. I'll explain it to them. Thanks for your help, darlings!"

"You're welcome!" they say in cheery voices and whirl by whirl they vanish into colorful sparks.

I shift my attention to Mona, curious about her answer.

"Fairy godmothers are assigned to people who need help making the world a better place."

Charlie's forehead wrinkles up, reminding me of what Jackie Chan looked like every time he was about to start a fight. "Gisella and I can also make the world a better place!"

"I never said you couldn't," Mona answers calmly.

Taylar leans back in his chair. "I think it's a compliment that you don't have one, Charlie. It means you don't need help saving the world."

I press my lips together when I realize what that means for me.

"No, Dante," Mona says, shaking her head. "It doesn't mean you're weak. It just means you're getting more trouble in life than anyone could handle on their own. And so does your mother."

"Never mind," I say, shaking my head to lose the voice telling me I'm a failure. "It's fine."

Vicky grabs my hand. "You're just as brave as the rest of us."

I snort. "No, I'm not."

"You keep going, don't you?" Her brown eyes staring into mine makes me itchy. They don't match her voice. And the solid hand holding mine feels weird too. Still I resist pulling back. Instead, I force a smile on my face. "Let's get to work, shall we?"

Vicky's curls jump up and down as she nods. "That's the spirit. Where do you want to start?"

I yawn. "By going to bed?" I hold up my hand when she frowns. "I'm kidding. Sleep will have to wait until we've found the soul. We can't risk these spells wearing off." I glance through the back door.

"I'm hoping to find all of the souls from Purgatory before dark. I don't know what time it…"

The last words get caught in my throat as something approaches in the dim light of the rainy afternoon—or morning, I'm not sure. "What's that?"

CHAPTER 30

All heads turn, and everyone goes silent.

"It looks like a man," office-guy Taylar says quietly. "I think he's wounded."

Our brand-new blue-suited manager turns in his chair. "That man is not wounded. He's dead."

We all jump from our seats at the same time and pull out our weapons.

"It doesn't look hostile," blonde Maël comments as the corpse stumbles closer.

As bad as the guy looks—covered in blood, his bones bent at awkward angles, his clothes torn and his hair a mess of dirt and leaves—I have to admit, he looks more like he's trying to find help than someone to kill. But I'm pretty confident he's beyond help, and I'm also pretty sure he didn't stumble into my garden by accident.

He reaches the door and knocks. I'm serious, he

doesn't bang on it, he knocks.

"We're not letting him in, are we?" Charlie asks, moving his head to shake the blond locks he no longer has over his shoulder.

"Of course not." I walk to the door and hesitate. "Should I open it and see what he wants?"

The zombie takes a step back and waits patiently. *Very strange behavior for a dead guy.*

"Maybe Jeep sent it?" Gisella's words sound hesitant, but they give me a sudden boast of hope.

With one quick move, I press down the door handle and swing the door open.

"What do you want?" I ask, raising my athame in case the zombie tries something.

From up close, I can see large scratches across his cheeks and forehead. He looks as if he's been tortured to death. Blood is dripping from his right hand, and he leans on his ankles instead of on his feet. He doesn't speak, but that's not a surprise. Most zombies don't.

My patience is running out as the man stares at me in silence. I'm about to shoo him away when he walks to the wall next to the back door and starts writing words with his bloodied finger.

Carefully, I move around him and try to make out what he's writing.

The others step outside too, weapons at the ready.

Charlie is the one who breaks the silence. "It's a message from the Devil."

I grit my teeth while I take in the words.

My offer expires in two minutes. We will make a good team. Think hard and choose wisely.

L.

Slowly, I shake my head. "I thought the Devil was supposed to be smart? Did he really think I was going to work with him?"

What is your answer? the zombie writes.

"The answer is no, of course! We will beat you no matter what."

More words in blood appear on the wall as the zombie moves his finger slowly and deliberately.

Don't be so hasty. Your decision has consequences for your loved ones. I've already captured two of you, and the rest will follow if you don't agree to work with me. They will all suffer.

"You have no one!" I yell. "No one!"

The zombie doesn't even flinch. He just takes two steps to his right and keeps writing.

I have your mother. She's such a lovely lady. So much fighting spirit. And for my other prisoner... how do you think I found my messenger?

Rage and despair build up inside me until my head explodes. My jaws ache with the effort to keep myself from screaming. My eyes burn from the tears I hold back. If I grab my weapon any tighter, the bones in my hand will snap.

The zombie waits patiently while I steady my breathing and search for the right words.

"If you think grabbing the people I care about will

force me to join you, you're way off. It will only force me to fight harder. And I can promise you this…" I point my finger at the zombie as if he's the Devil himself. "I will fight you until my death if I have to, and if you're not defeated then, I will find you from beyond the grave. I will build my own army in Heaven and hunt you until you beg for mercy. And I will never give you any."

"And we'll fight with you!" Charlie calls out. The others let out a battle cry that can probably be heard on the other side of Blackford.

Without warning, the zombie turns and leaps at me faster than I presumed possible. Thankfully my reflexes are as fast as they were before I lost my memory. Besides, I was expecting the guy to attack, so with one quick move, I raise my arm, and he walks straight into the blade of my dagger. I pull it out before he gets the change to wrap his bloody hands around my neck. With one swipe, I take off his head. Then I kick the body until all the bones are split into little pieces. I pick up the head and fling it with all my might at the message on the wall.

"Dante…" Vicky's voice says softly.

Panting loudly, I kick the body some more. Blood stains my new leather shoes.

"Dante? Babe?" Her hand is on my arm. "Look at me."

My head is pounding so hard I squeeze my eyes shut. "He's got them, Vick!"

"No, he doesn't." She pulls me into a hug, and I

rest my head on her solid shoulder. "He's bluffing, babe. He's just bluffing."

Tears force themselves out of the corners of my eyes, and I no longer hold them back.

My new determination to stop sulking and be positive kicks in soon. I check my weapons and straighten my back before raising my hand to ask for silence. "There's something I want to say before we go hunting." My eyes glide over the unfamiliar faces. "We've been through a lot already, but I have a feeling that things will get a lot harder before the end. But we cannot lose faith." I ball my hand into a fist and raise it. "There's no reason to lose faith, no matter how bad things look. We cannot let Lucifer win, and we won't. We're strong, and we've got each other, even when we're not together. We'll keep fighting no matter what and for the right reasons. And that is why we will win this."

They all take out their weapons and raise them with a loud cheer. I almost laugh out loud at the sight of them. They look like a bunch of office clerks cheering on a company merger. *If only that was all we had to worry about.*

The woman with the short curls steps up to me and gives me a cheeky grin that doesn't really fit her looks. "Where to, boss?" she asks with Vicky's voice.

"Do you have a map of the United States?"

"Of course."

She digs into the back pocket of her pants and

hands me a folded map. "Here you go, Jason."

I snort. "My name is not Jason."

"Well, it isn't Dante either now. We'd better think of something to call each other while we look like this. We can't go around calling each other by our real names."

I give her a quick kiss on the lips. "You're so smart." I turn to the others. "I'm going to scry for a soul I saw in Purgatory. It was one of the souls that was sent here by Trevor to collect the fairy soul. It should lead us to the fairy or at least somewhere near it." I hate how insecure I sound, so I try to make up for it with a broad smile. "While I scry, you guys can think of some names to match our new bodies. Try to pick something that's easy to remember."

"No problem!" Vicky says cheerily, and they gather around D'Maeo while I unfold the map at my end of the kitchen table and take the pendant in the form of my athame from the cupboard.

It's not hard to bring up the woman's face in my head. I focused on her hard when I saw her, knowing I might need to find her later, and I chose her because she stood out between the other souls. I knew she'd be easy to remember even with the short time I had to study every detail of her face. Her eyes were small and upturned, her cheekbones high. Her skin was a beautiful light brown, her nose small and her lips thin. The fear coursing through her couldn't hide her elegance as she stepped through the portal back to Earth.

With her face in mind, I release my pendant, my hand high above the map to make sure the pendant can reach any corner of the country. It scans the map with wide circles and spins until my hand gets heavy.

With clenched teeth, I wonder if I need a map of the world instead. Curly Vicky pops up next to me and shakes her head. "Looks like your soul isn't in this country."

"Yes, that had just occurred to me too. Do you have a map of—"

I cut off my question when she slams another map onto the table.

"Thanks." I pull up the pendant, fold the US map and unfold the new one.

Vicky rejoins the others, and I start again.

This time, the pendant slows down fast and drops down on… "New Zealand?"

Vicky looks up with a wide smile. "We're going to New Zealand? I've always wanted to go there."

I lift the pendant and bend over the map. "Looks like our destination is Goblin Forest, in the west."

"Great!" Vicky says, making a little jump for joy.

"Awesome," I reply dryly. "Except we don't have a clue how to get there."

"Sure we do," she says. "We can cast a spell. Or ask Quinn to take us."

There's a brush of air on my neck, followed by a familiar voice. "Did somebody call?"

Vicky's smile widens even more. "Quinn! Just the angel we were looking for."

"Hi V… What do I call you now?"

"Valery," she answers proudly.

Quinn's heavy footsteps pass me. He takes in the new faces and finally rests his gaze on me. "Dante."

I can't say I'm surprised he recognizes us. *Our souls probably shine through our disguises.*

"Mona's friends disguised us so we can save the next soul without the risk of losing my mother," I explain.

He scratches his short curls. "Looks like I missed something."

"You missed a lot, but that's okay," I say, and I mean it. "We can use your help now though." I point at the tiny hole the pendant made in the map. "We have to go to New Zealand. We can probably get there on our own, but it'll be much faster if you take us."

"No problem," he says without hesitation. He narrows his eyes and takes us in one by one once more. "Where's Jeep?"

I pull back my shoulders. "We don't know. He's the next *to do* on our list, along with my mother."

"I knew I should've kept her in Heaven," Quinn mumbles.

"What?"

He shakes his head sadly. "She's Lucifer's best leverage. She's one of the most important people in your life, and she can't defend herself. I should've kept her in Heaven where she would've been safe."

"You can do that?"

"If I have a good reason, yes. And I do."

The tall manager in the blue suit steps forward and places a hand on Quinn's arm while staring at me hard. "It's too late for that now, and to be honest, I think Susan has a role to play in all this, just like we do. She's not just your weak spot, Dante, but also Trevor's."

I give D'Maeo an appreciative nod. "You're right. And my mom might not have any magical powers, but she does have a strong will. She lived with those fits for years, remember?"

Vicky drops into a chair. "And that's not easy."

Quinn's lips curl up. "Sounds like I underestimated her." He spreads his arms. "Are you all ready for a trip to New Zealand?"

"Almost," Vicky says, pushing herself to her feet again. "First, we need to remember our new names. We cannot use our real ones for a while. For Susan's sake."

"Agreed," I say. "So what did you come up with?"

They fall back in line, and Vicky points at everyone. "From now on we will no longer be knows as Vicky, Taylar, Charlie, Gisella, D'Maeo, Maël and Dante, but as Valery, Ted, Chung, Grace, David, Mabel and Dean."

I give them a one-man applause. "Nice. Give me a second to remember them all."

I repeat the names in my head. Two of them are easy. They fit their appearances so well. The nerdy office guy is Ted/Taylar, and the good-looking manager is David/D'Maeo. Chung isn't that hard either, and I'm sure the other names will stick too once I've said them a couple of times.

I nod. "Okay, I'm ready." I step up to Quinn. "Take us to Goblin Forest New Zealand, please."

"Yes, sir," he says with a small bow, and a second later, bright light envelops him.

After blinking several times, I can see his angel form. The change still amazes me: the glow from within him, his white curls, his broad, hulking form and of course his giant wings.

When I look sideways, I see that Grace/Gisella is gaping at Quinn. It's the first time she's seen him in his true form, and even she is impressed.

"You look great, Quinn," she says before joining us under his wings.

Her words result in a pinch from Chung/Charlie, and she chuckles. "Well, he does, Char... I mean Chung, you can't deny that." She snuggles up closer to him. "But don't worry, I don't fall for big and winged. I'm not trading you in."

"Okay, everyone," Quinn interrupts, "get ready. Remember to inhale deeply as soon as my feathers touch you, and keep your eyes closed until we land."

"Yes, please do," I say, remembering my temporary blindness the last time we travelled like this.

Something soft touches my shoulder, and I take a deep breath. I can feel the feathers wrapping around my body, and the next moment, I'm lifted from the ground. Wind pulls at my clothes, and my skin starts to prickle. I don't know if I'm upside down or inside out, until suddenly my feet touch solid ground again.

"We're here. Open your eyes."

Just to be sure, I wait for several seconds before I obey.

Quinn is still in his angel form, almost too bright to look at. We're standing on a small dirt path surrounded by moss-covered trees that seem to dance. They are bent in all directions, with trunks and branches of trees growing out of other trees, as if they're lost in an intimate dance. More branches close off most of the sunlight seeping in from above, but still the forest looks friendly. Like ents having the time of their lives.

"Hippie trees," Vicky voices my thoughts.

"Exactly!"

"I have to go now," Quinn says with a guilty expression on his face. "Call me when you're ready to go back home, and I'll pick you up." He points to a dark spot to my right. "I think the place you're looking for is over there. Be careful."

I hold out my hand to shake his, and an incredible warmth goes through me when we do. "Thank you, Quinn."

"No problem. See you soon."

With a blinding flash, he soars up into the sky and disappears.

Valery/Vicky dances around me with her arms in the air. Her blonde curls bob up and down around her brown eyes. "It's so beautiful here!"

I can't argue with that. I've never seen anything like this. It's like stepping into a fairy world.

Then I realize, we probably did step into a fairy world.

I tap my Asian best friend on the arm. "Do you think this is the home of the fairy that the Devil is after?"

He nods, looking more serious than I've ever seen him, with his small eyes and short dark hair. "I think so."

I shake my head at the sound of his low voice. "This is so weird."

"It sure is," he says, taking in my new face with a grin.

"We should go," our 'manager' says, beckoning us.

Blonde Maël joins him and peers into the darkness up ahead. "I agree with D'Ma— I mean David. There is a lot of sorrow and anger out there. We might be able to track it to the fairy."

"Good." I touch the hilt of my athame and walk up to them. "Lead the way, please."

We walk silently toward the dark, scanning the trees and sky on all sides. Beetles crawl around and birds sing. Butterflies flutter above the moss on the ground, and a squirrel jumps from tree to tree. It looks so peaceful that I can't imagine a fairy's soul was snatched here.

That is, until we suddenly step out of the slivers of light and into total darkness.

A chill clings to my bones immediately, and I rub my arms hard, not just to drive out the cold, but also the fear that rises in my chest. My legs get heavier with every step I take, and no matter how hard I blink, I can't see anything anymore.

When I carefully stick out my arms, I feel David and Mabel in front of me, also standing still, and Valery behind me. She grabs my hand. "What happened?"

"This must be the part of the forest that Trevor poisoned," I say in a hushed tone. "The home of the nature fairy they need."

I gently nudge my power core to create a small ball of lightning in my hand. When I lift it to illuminate the others, I see Mabel nodding gravely. "I think you are right. I can smell the poison all around us, but there is also a lot of grief and anger here."

"Anger, the sin of the fifth circle of Hell," I whisper.

"Exactly." Mabel turns slowly, holding out her hands as if to feel the air. After several seconds of silence, she shakes her head. "I sense death."

My heart stops beating. "Yes, Trevor said they killed her. But is her soul still here?"

"Pain still lingers in the air. She suffered." Her eyes find mine. They are so sad.

"Look." She steps aside, and I search the ground and trees. It's hard to make out anything, so I light another ball in my other hand.

I gasp. "Oh no!"

CHAPTER 31

Without thinking, I throw myself forward and kneel next to the small broken body lying on the mossy ground. I make one of the lightning balls float above the fairy while my hand hovers over her still form.

She looks so fragile and so... crushed. Cracked. Burnt. I don't think there's a word for all that's been done to her. Just looking at her burned skin and twisted arms and legs makes me nauseous. Her blonde hair is covered in mud, her beautiful features contorted in frozen pain. When I see the gaping hole in her small chest, I turn away. "It looks so... empty. I think she's not here anymore. Maybe we're too late."

Valery reaches into her pocket and pulls out the Cards of Death. She stares at them briefly before looking up with a wide smile. "No, we're not."

It takes me a moment to understand what she means. Then I sigh with relief. "You're right, the cards didn't crumble to ash. That must mean they don't have the fairy's soul yet." I peer into the darkness around us. "But where do we start looking for her?"

Valery puts the cards away and shrugs. "I think a spell would be the best way to find her."

"On it," I say, yanking Dad's notebook from behind my waistband and flipping through it at Superman speed.

"How can you read anything when you turn the pages this fast?" the woman with the short black hair, Grace, asks.

"I can't," I say, stopping for a second. "I'm hoping the book will take me to the right page."

She nods appreciatively. "I'll let you concentrate then."

Please, show me a spell to find the fairy's soul. Please, please!

I start flipping the pages again while I repeat my request, and suddenly, I can't move my hand anymore. "Found it!"

I bend over the page and scan the words quickly.

"Tell me what you need," Valery says, her hand already in her endless pocket again.

"Do you have any caraway in there?" I scratch my head. "Not sure what that is."

"It's a plant, and yes I do," she says, pulling out some crescent-shaped, brown seeds with light edges.

"Great, and two sachets and two green ribbons, that's it." I slam the book shut and put it back behind my waistband while Valery searches for the items.

"I love how prepared you always are," I whisper to her as she hands me what I requested.

"I learned the hard way," she responds, putting some white and red ribbons back in her pocket.

"How did you get that pocket anyway?" I ask while I throw a handful of caraway seeds into one sachet and tie one of the ribbons around it.

"It was a gift from someone I helped a long time ago."

I meet her eyes. There's sadness in there, and I reach out to squeeze her hand.

"It's fine," she says. "We all lose people."

I kiss her on her solid cheek. "We do, but it's never fine. It's okay to miss your friend."

She turns her head and wipes a tear from her eye. Her voice is hoarse when she responds. "You're right. I'm just glad I always carry something of hers with me."

When I don't move, she waves her hand at the sachet. "Go on, finish the spell, I'm fine."

"Hey, guys, look at all this water here," Chung, a.k.a Charlie, calls out. He has wandered off to the edge of the illuminated spot created by my floating ball of lightning. "It's like a puddle but very deep." He pulls out a stick longer than his arm and holds it up. "See, only the part I'm holding is still dry. Isn't that strange?"

I shrug. "We're in a magical forest, Chung. Nothing is strange here."

"But it doesn't even feel like water, you know," he persists.

I meet his worried eyes and sigh. "Step back a little, please. I don't want you to fall in. Mabel, can you check out that puddle? Carefully, please."

"Of course, Dean," the blonde woman says.

I give the others a stern look. "I have to focus now, or we won't find our fairy's soul in time."

They all nod, and 'manager' David follows Mabel to the puddle for back-up. I turn away from them and try to imagine the fairy alive and well, fluttering in front of me, healthy and glowing. My thoughts reach out to her while I hold up the sachet.

I whisper the extra words I made up to strengthen the spell.

"Bring this lost soul to this place.
Keep her safe through time and space."

I untie the ribbon, take half of the seeds out and put them in the other sachet, which I tie with the second ribbon. Then I close the first sachet again and place it next to the fairy's body. The other sachet goes in my jeans pocket.

"All is ready for this soul.
Return her to us safe and whole."

The sachet in my pocket vibrates, and the one on the ground moves in small circles.

"Get ready," I tell the others. "She might not be alone."

The light from my lightning ball reflects onto the blades and swords that are drawn.

A noise like a swarm of whispering bees comes closer. I search the gaps between the trees, but nothing moves.

Until…

"Something's coming," chubby Ted says, moving his shield a little higher to protect his face.

It's more the sound that tells me he's right than me actually seeing something. The soft buzzing is close now, and I can pinpoint it to a spot just behind the fairy's broken body. Then the light hits it, and my mouth falls open. The fairy's soul is so much more beautiful than I could have imagined.

Her wings and hair are made of golden pollen, and her skin looks as soft as a cloud. Bright green leaves make up her long dress. Even after all the torture she's been through, kindness emanates from her eyes and smile as she looks up at me.

I give a small bow. "Sweet fairy, I am sad to be too late to save you from such a horrible death, but I will do what I can to take your soul to a safe place." I gesture at my friends. "We all will."

"Thank you," the fairy says with a voice like a summer breeze.

Since I'm not sure what else to do, I open my arms invitingly. Without hesitation, the fairy flutters into them, filling my whole body with warmth.

Valery throws me a small cloth to wrap her in, and while I do, I address the others. "Is everyone ready to leave?"

Mabel, Chung and David are still investigating the puddle, Chung munching on something of course.

"There is something evil in here," Mabel says. At the same time, the water explodes.

We all watch in horror as a dozen snakes made of water jump from the puddle. Their mouths open wide as they loom over us, spitting drops of steaming liquid. Small bubbles appear and pop open all over their bodies constantly.

"Watch out, they're boiling!" I yell, stepping back to protect the fairy.

I want to tell Maël to freeze them. Just in time, I remember I can't call her that. "These must be the demons from the fifth circle of Hell, since they are covered in water, like the Cards of Death hinted. They were guarding the dead body. Mabel, can you use your power?"

She doesn't respond until Chung nudges her. "He's talking to you."

She shakes her blonde head in confusion. "Yes, of course. I forgot."

"Can you do it?" Without her staff, I'm not sure how much she'll be able to do.

To my surprise, she pulls out a whiteboard pointing stick and unfolds it with one quick wrist movement. *Extra credit to the fairy godmother who thought of that disguise.*

Unfortunately, the water snakes don't wait for her to finish her spell. After a sharp hiss from the one on the left, they all swoop down at once.

Ted jumps in front of Mabel with his shield raised. I'm glad to see that despite the bigger body, he's just as fast as before.

I use my free hand to throw as many bolts of lightning as I can manage, but they don't have much effect. The snakes just shudder and continue their attack.

While I concentrate on freezing them instead, the others form a line of defense between me and the demons. Chung and Grace drop back a little to keep from getting burned. Chung flings balls of gel around, hitting several snakes in the eye. Grace joins me at the back and holds out her hands. "Give the fairy to me. I'm of no use in this fight. I can't do anything from a distance. But you can."

I hesitate. My doubts about her wash over me once more. I've trusted her so far, but was I right to do so?

"Don't worry, I'll keep her safe," Grace assures me. In her eyes there's only kindness and honesty.

I nod and hand the wrapped-up fairy over to her.

"I can try an old incantation that might hide us," she says.

It feels as if lightning shoots through my head. *An incantation? Is she planning on using her witch powers?*

My hands fold around the edge of the cloth. With all my heart, I hope I didn't make a horrible mistake.

"Don't, the risk of them taking you over is too great."

She stares at me for a moment with her small, dark eyes. Somewhere deep within them, I can see a glimpse of Gisella.

She tilts her head. "Alright, I'll only use them if I have no other choice."

It feels like the truth, so I let go of the cloth.

"It won't come to that," I promise her. Then I step forward, next to Chung, and focus only on freezing the snakes.

With snake heads hitting Ted's shield and spitting boiling drops around it, I can tell it's hard for Mabel to concentrate on stopping time. The demons' movements stutter somewhat, but that's all she's able to achieve. We're slowly driven back as we try to evade the drops flying around. Valery lands on her back, slashing at the snake above her like a maniac.

I focus on its head and think of ice as hard as I can.

Just as it opens its mouth wide, its whole head freezes. Without blinking, Valery cuts the head right off and kicks it into the undergrowth. The body collapses on the ground, no longer boiling.

The other demons rise higher up out of the puddle, their tales lashing out angrily at everything they can reach.

Quinn, can you take us and the fairy out of here? I call out in my head.

The snakes' stuttering movements are getting more frequent, but someone is bound to get hurt before

Mabel manages to fully freeze them in time. And I have trouble concentrating too.

"I cannot do it!" Mabel calls out. "There is too much misery and pain here. It is draining my energy core."

So that's what it is. The destruction here has hurt so many living things that it left a remanence.

Quinn, can you heal this place?

There's no answer.

"Is there a spell we can use?" I call out to no one in particular.

"Dean…"

It takes me a couple of seconds to realize David is talking to me. His face is scrunched up in concentration and pain.

"What's wrong?" I ask, even though I have a feeling I know the answer.

He grits his teeth so hard I can hear them crunch. "That shadow we talked about earlier, the one inside me?"

I nod apprehensively.

"It's trying to take over."

The snake demons push Ted further back, and I throw some ice cubes in their direction.

"Can you hold it back?" I call out to David.

Silence answers me, and I throw some more cubes at the snakes. It slows them down a bit, but other than that, it doesn't seem to hurt them much. They're getting more and more impatient and are throwing in every bit of force they've got to take one of us out.

Come on, focus! With all my might I picture the snakes getting frozen over.

With a soft crackling, ice starts to crawl from their tails up to their heads. They shake their bodies vigorously, but I hold on to the image of ice wrapping around them.

"What are you doing?" Grace's voice says behind me. "Stay back."

Mabel leaves her safe spot behind Ted's shield and passes me.

"Step away from Grace, David," she says, her voice firm and unafraid.

My focus is wavering. Normally I would trust Gisella and Maël to take care of D'Maeo's shadow, but the rottenness lingering here is affecting us all. I can feel it seeping through my skin, weakening my powers, while it only feeds the darkness inside D'Maeo.

"Valery, Ted…" I say with trembling voice, "cut those demons' heads off, please. I can't hold them much longer."

Gel balls shower down onto the water snakes, keeping the bodies from moving.

Chung appears at my side, a determined expression on his face. "We've got this."

Valery and Ted jump forward and slice the heads off one by one.

I breathe out, my head pounding and my hands trembling from the effort of fighting off the remanence and conjuring ice at the same time.

Valery pulls at my arm. "Dean." She nods at the scene behind me.

My heartbeat rises to a deafening volume in my head when I turn around.

Grace and David are standing face to face, their noses inches from touching.

Grace clutches the fairy to her chest, her eyes pinned onto David's face, which is darker than before.

"Give me the fairy," he says in a low voice that doesn't suit him.

"We are here to protect it, David," she says. "Step away from us."

My chest contracts at the thought that I put my faith in the wrong person. I doubted Gisella so much because of her ancestry, while I kept trusting D'Maeo even though I knew a shadow had nestled inside him. *How could I be so stupid?*

"David," I say. "Be strong. Fight the shadow."

He doesn't respond. I wish I could use his real name, but you never know who's listening.

I take a step toward them just when David reaches out for the bundle in Grace's arms.

Time seems to speed up. Suddenly, a dozen things happen at once. My mouth opens to utter a 'NO!'. Valery leaps forward with her hands outstretched. Ted hurls his shield at David's head. Balls of gel zoom past my ear. Grace lifts one hand and utters several words I can't make out above the screaming in my head. With a jerk, David is lifted off his feet and pushed back, his arms and feet held out in front of him as if he was punched in the stomach hard.

Time slows down again. Two parts of David seem to hover in the air. One is his body, the other a dark copy of it. For a split second, I can see their true forms. A gray-haired ghost in a black suit and... I gasp. I recognize the shape that pulls itself back into David's body: black smoke with two red eyes.

"It's the black void that killed him, the thing we fought behind that portal when we were looking for Trevor. The thing that took parts of D'Ma... David's soul."

Valery comes to a halt next to me. "I thought we freed him from that?"

"Some part of it must have still clung to him when we escaped."

David finally lands, him and the dark void reunited. He tries to stand up but starts sinking into the ground. Within seconds, only his hair is visible.

I hold up my hand to Grace. "There's no need to use your powers anymore. With the water demons out of the way, we can handle him."

She shakes her head. "I'm not doing anything. I just pushed him away from us with an incantation."

"Help!" David calls out. "Dean! Mabel!" His voice sounds normal again, and I dive forward to pull him out.

When I reach him, his face is turned up, his forehead already covered in mud. By the time I kneel down, all I can see are his eyes, filled with fear.

"I'll get you out," I promise him. "Don't worry."

I start digging away the scorched earth around him. Valery, Chung and Ted join me, but David is sinking fast. *No amount of digging will get him out of there in time.*

Just before he closes them, I can see regret in his eyes, but also peace. *He's given up.*

"You keep fighting!" I yell at him. "Do you hear me?"

A second later, he is gone, and the earth closes above him.

I dig some more, but even when I get some of the earth out, there's no sign of D'Maeo. Finally, I lean against the nearest tree and shake my head. "He's gone."

CHAPTER 32

For about a minute, I just sit there, looking at David's face with D'Maeo's eyes floating in my vision. Then Jeep and Mom's faces follow, and I grit my teeth.

I look at the mud and broken twigs beneath me and try to imagine the huge form of Satan miles and miles below us, on a throne maybe, who knows. "If you think I'm giving up, you're mistaken! You can beat me down as much as you want, but I'll keep going. I'll keep fighting until everyone I love is safe."

When I look up, my friends are eyeing me with sad expressions on their new faces.

Valery walks up to me, and our gazes lock. Warmth flows through my body, slowing down my heartbeat.

"I'm not giving up," I repeat, "and I'm getting everyone back. Mom, Jeep, D'Maeo and anyone else we're going to lose."

Valery nods. "I like that plan."

Her gaze shifts to Grace, who steps out in front of me and gently places the fairy back against my chest. The creature looks up at me with loving eyes. I smile at her, thankful for the warmth that's spreading through me again.

"Don't worry," I whisper, even though she doesn't seem worried at all, "we'll protect you."

I push myself up and wipe the dust and sand from my pants. "Quaddisin, are you there?"

Patiently I wait for the familiar whoosh that announces his arrival.

It doesn't come.

"Quinn?" I turn my head in all directions. "Can you take the fairy to a safe place, please?"

Still nothing.

I meet Valery's eyes. The frown on her forehead tells me she's as concerned as I am.

Why isn't Quinn answering? He knew we'd be calling for a ride back home. He knew we were looking for the fairy here. Something must be wrong.

Now what? Where can we take this fairy? We can't get to Heaven on our own, and we have no way of sending her there.

Suddenly, Chung raises a finger and tilts his head. "I heard something."

We all stay very still and hold our breaths.

Chung is right, there's a rustling in the trees up ahead. Instinctively, my hand moves up to shield the fairy from whatever is coming. *Please let it be Quinn.*

Of course it isn't. Quinn would have landed in

front of us, not try to creep closer unnoticed. Besides, I scried for the woman I saw in Purgatory, so I knew she'd be nearby. But I wasn't expecting the things approaching now.

There's a disgusted look on Chung's face, and I can't blame him. A similar grimace is probably visible around my mouth as I try to figure out what the things actually are. They're not zombies, judging by the lively glint in their eyes, and not ghosts either. Still they show some resemblance to both. They look human in some ways, but I'm not sure they are. Something is… I don't know… *off* about them. As if they were in an experiment that went wrong.

They have human arms, legs and a torso, all sort of see-through, but not quite. It's more as if a layer of brownish mist has been placed upon them. Their sole focus on us causes collisions with trees. Hard collisions that should hurt them but don't. Their bodies seem to be unbreakable, and it appears they don't feel pain. Also, their heads have contorted into weird bumpy shapes, as if they're made of wax.

Grace backs up two steps and changes her hands into blades with one swift move. "What the heck are they?"

Mabel holds out her hand in front of her, sensing the air. "These are lost souls, tainted by the journey back to Earth. Their minds are broken, their temporary bodies falling apart. They will do anything to get back to Purgatory."

My mouth falls open. "These are the souls Trevor

sent back from Purgatory?"

Mabel straightens up. "Yes, get ready to fight."

While I conjure a lightning bolt in my free hand, I call out to Quinn again in my mind. *We're under attack. Please come as soon as you can. We've got the fairy.*

"Hold on tight," I tell the fairy in a whisper.

I think about hiding her under my shirt, but it's too late for that. The souls already know I've got her, judging by the way their eyes focus only on me.

I step forward until I'm next to Mabel.

"Should we use our powers?" I whisper. "The enemy is probably watching these souls. He'll know it's us."

She nods slowly. "You are right. We should fight the old-fashioned way. We have risked too much already." She turns to the nearest tree and breaks off a thick branch.

I frown at her strength, then extinguish the bolt in my hand quickly.

I turn to the others. "Don't use your powers unless you have no other choice. They will give us away."

Chung clenches his jaws before turning and throwing his balls of gels into the forest behind us. At the same time, Grace changes her blades back into hands. She meets my eyes. "I can still do an incantation, if you want. I don't think Tre... our enemy knows I can do that."

"Only as a last resort," I tell her, and I pull out my athame.

Just in time too, because the first soul has reached Mabel. She hits it square between the eyes, leaving a dent the size of a baseball in the woman's head. Still, she keeps coming, her fists outstretched. Mabel swats her out of the way with ease, and she slams into a tree, where she crumbles to the ground and tries to get up on broken legs. The rest of the crowd doesn't even look in her direction, and they completely ignore Mabel too, swaying sideways to get to me.

Mabel reaches out and pushes me behind her. "You should stay back."

She's right, of course. It's not a good idea to risk the fairy getting snatched. But my heart aches at the thought of hiding behind the others and doing nothing.

Valery pulls me back and takes my place. Sensing my aversion, she calls to me over her shoulder. "Just use your Morningstar to help us out."

I groan in frustration. "I can't, it'll give me away."

But sulking won't do me any good, so instead I try to figure out how to get this fairy to Heaven. *A spell to send her up might be too dangerous, she could be intercepted halfway there. So maybe a spell that takes all of us to the gates of Heaven? That should do it, right? Unless everything there is turned upside down too, just like in Purgatory.*

I breathe in sharply. That might be why Quinn is no longer responding.

Suddenly, I remember something important. I look up. "Guys!"

No one responds. Of course not, they're all busy

fighting back the souls that try to overrun them, their eyes glinting whenever they catch sight of me. But I know they're listening, so I tell them my thoughts anyway. "Just fighting them off isn't enough. To restore the balance, we need to send them all back to Purgatory."

"Can you build a cage to put them in until we're ready to send them back?" Valery shoots me a quick look over her shoulder while stabbing one of the souls in the neck. It hisses angrily and pulls at her leg with its last strength.

"Sure," I say, more confident than I feel, because how am I supposed to build a cage that fits all of these souls, without any help?

The fairy flutters against my chest, and heat comforts me.

When I look down, she blinks at me with gentle, trusting eyes.

"Can you help me?" I ask softly.

She gives me a small smile, which I take as a yes.

After making sure the others can handle the attack, I sit down on a log a couple of steps back and put my brain to work. To my surprise, an idea pops into my head instantly, and the words for the spell I need float in front of my eyes.

There's a soft giggle from below, and I gasp. The fairy is holding up one tiny hand, and from it, a bright green vine twists all the way up to my head. I can feel the end of it tickling my forehead.

I blow her a small kiss. "Thank you."

She pulls the vine back in with a simple wrist movement and snuggles closer again.

The others are still doing a great job, slamming down souls and denting heads to make sure no one can reach the fairy. A feeling of pride rises in my chest at the sight of them fighting without using their powers. I know we trained for this, but still, they're awesome.

I duck when a screaming soul soars straight at me. It slams into a tree, rolls over a couple of times and gets up, swaying. Part of its face is missing, one eye dangling from the socket as it stares down at its flattened arm. Then it raises its head and squeals with delight as it catches sight of me. Without hesitation, it charges.

I fumble for my athame and jump to the side to distract the soul while aiming my weapon at the busted side of its face.

It lets out a holler that sounds like 'Mine!' before speeding up, drool dripping from its lips when it spots the fairy clinging to my chest. Because of this, my weapon misses its target. It still hits the soul in the side though, and it tumbles to the ground.

I don't wait for it to get up but pull back my athame and slam it into its back. It creates a gaping hole and the skin around it pulls back in waves when I retrieve my weapon. I shake my head in disgust. *It looks like a three-year-old tried to make a monster out of clay and threw a tantrum before it was finished.*

It's hard to imagine this was once a human being. I

have to remember that this isn't the soul's fault. It was sent back to where it doesn't belong anymore.

I squat down next to the deformed body. "I'm sorry. I'll get you all back to where you belong. I promise."

A low growl rises from the mess, and I back up quickly. "Be like that then."

I look around, pick up a sharp stick and return to the body.

"You'll make a fine binder," I say, driving the stick through the flat part of the back, pinning it to the ground.

Behind me, the souls are getting angrier and more impatient by the second. Judging by the grunts and slower movements, my friends are getting tired, and I know more and more souls will find their way past them if I don't hurry up. So I grab my Book of Spells and start writing.

It takes me about three minutes to jot down all the ingredients plus the words for the spell. I don't think I've ever written this fast before. I'm sure it's because of the heat coming from the fairy. It flows through me, feeding me all the energy I need.

When I'm done, the fairy reaches within her chest and pulls out the herbs I need. I watch in awe as she hands everything to me. The last thing she gives me is a long, glowing vine.

"Thank you," I say softly, and she gives me that radiant smile again.

When I glance back to where my friends are

fighting, I freeze. Not only are more deformed souls approaching, but following them with big strides is a familiar figure I hoped I wouldn't meet again.

"You can't be serious," I whisper to myself, bending down to set everything up for the spell. "How did he get back here?"

My hands move so fast they're almost a blur. Within seconds, I'm done, and I lay my Book of Spells in front of me to read the words. *I can still finish this before he reaches me. And the others will keep him busy. Or so I hope.*

> *"Powers of earth, help me now.*
> *Make these creatures stop and bow.*
> *Lock them up so they can't fight*
> *for what they think is wrong or right.*
>
> *Once they're all inside the cage,*
> *prepare them for the final stage.*
> *Take them back where they belong.*
> *Restore the balance that has gone wrong."*

The glowing vine comes to life on the ground. It slithers around for a second before rising in the air, like a snake ready to attack. One of the souls slips past Chung and launches itself at me. My hand flies to my athame, but there's no need. The vine shoots up and snatches the soul out of the air midflight. It kicks and flails and screams, but the vine is too strong. With ease, it pins the body down next to the one I took out and shoots forward to grab a second soul. One by one, the vine pulls the souls into the invisible cage, where they wriggle and moan like tortured maggots.

"What is going on here? Who are you people?" My former friend's voice sends shivers down my spine. He sounds aggravated, not at all like the person I used to know. Or thought I knew.

"Is there another prophecy we don't know about?" Paul says when no one answers. He narrows his green eyes. "Because I thought getting rid of Dante and his gang would do the trick."

"Of course you did," I mumble, balling my hands into fists.

Deep breaths keep me calm enough to stay where I am. It's not wise to give myself away.

Paul stops in front of Valery and Mabel and takes them in from head to toe.

"Who are you?" he demands. "And why are you interfering in our business?"

Valery's muscles tense. I can tell she wants to beat him up as much as I do. But she stays calm and raises her chin. "We are the Keepers of Life, here to restore the balance in the world. Please stay out of our way."

I almost laugh out loud at Paul's stunned face. Inside, I applaud Vicky for her quick thinking. The Keepers of Life are the ones tasked with keeping the Book of a Thousand Deaths safe. As far as I know, they have no other tasks, but this sounds plausible. By the looks of it, Paul certainly believes her.

"Well, pretty lady," he says in a low voice, raising his finger, "in that case, we have the same objective. We don't need all of you interfering in our business. We don't need your help, so please step aside." Anger flickers across his small face, but Valery isn't impressed. She just smiles sweetly and gestures at the last soul lifted from the ground and taken to the cage.

"We'll be out of here before you know it. We've gotten this far already. We might as well finish the spell." She gives him a pat on his freckled cheek. "Save you the trouble of starting over."

Paul slowly wipes his cheek and pushes his thick, dark hair out of his eye. "Get out of my way."

Valery folds her arms. "In a minute."

The vine has dropped the last of the souls from Purgatory. It starts circling its prisoners, growing longer and longer, until they are surrounded by bars of green. Their wide eyes are no longer angry, but sad, and their skin becomes more transparent, more like a ghost's. Their bodies take on human forms again and then, with the sound of a large tree hitting the ground and a flash of green, they all disappear.

I look down at the fairy. "It worked!"

She nods, but her eyes flick nervously over to where Paul is standing, his path still blocked by Valery and Mabel, with Chung, Grace and Ted forming a barrier behind them.

"Don't worry," I tell her. "We'll keep you away from him."

I put away my Book of Spells and cover the fairy

with my shirt. When I straighten up, Mabel and Valery step aside, and Paul walks up to me.

He scrutinizes me before asking, "Why did those souls attack you?"

I shrug. "They probably didn't want to go home."

"Right." He taps his foot impatiently. "Are you sure it didn't have anything to do with a certain nature fairy?" He steps closer, his nose almost touching mine. "You see, I need that fairy."

I cross my arms loosely over my chest, hiding the tiny creature. "Really? What for?"

"She ended up in the wrong place, like those souls you just sent back," Paul answers with an intimidating stare.

I shrug again and turn away from him. "Well, good luck with your search then. We have to get back to our daily tasks now, but if you need help, let us know." Over my shoulder, I give him the best smile I can manage.

He raises one eyebrow. "Will do, mister…?"

"Dean," I say without hesitation. Then add, after a quick look around, "Dean Wood."

He smirks. "How fitting."

I beckon the others. "Time to go, our work here is done."

"Don't you want to know my name?" Paul says calmly.

"Not really," I answer without looking at him.

"Or do you already know it?" he continues.

I feel myself freezing mid-motion before I can

stop it. But I have to try to bluff my way out of it, or I might never see Mom again.

"How would I know, and why would I care?" I tell him, showing him my most bored expression. I gesture at the silent trees around us. "We came here to restore the balance, and we did. We don't really care about anything else."

He gives me another intense stare. "Not even about your mother?"

I feel the muscles in my jaw tensing. *He knows who I am, and he also knows exactly which buttons to push.*

Valery moves so close to me her arm touches mine. "Let me kill him."

I want to shake my head, tell her that's a bad idea, that it will give us away, but it's already too late. Paul knows who we are, and he will make sure Trevor hears about this.

It takes just a small nod for Valery to propel herself forward. But Paul is prepared. The smirk never leaves his face while he changes into his stone form.

Since he already knows who I am, I whip out my Morningstar. But I watch helplessly from the sideline, highly aware of the fact that I can't risk getting the fairy closer to Paul.

He swats Valery's fragile form away with ease, but before he can charge me, the others block his way. A low chuckle escapes his lips as he takes them all in. "You think you can beat me with sticks and knives? I'll pulverize all of you."

"I've got a better idea." Grace lifts her arms so quickly Paul is too late to pull away. Her hands fold around his stone cheeks, and she mumbles something in a dark voice.

Paul tries to pull away, but she's got him in a strong hold. He kicks at her legs, and her face crunches up in pain. Chung and Ted both bend down and grab Paul's legs while Mabel and Valery each take an arm.

"Let go of me," Paul says, but he no longer sounds threatening.

I almost feel sorry for him as cracks appear in his stone face. A shadow falls over him. Bit by bit, he turns darker, and parts of his arms and legs crumble to dust.

Grace stops mumbling and pulls back her hands. Paul sways on what remains of his feet, his eyes wide with fear. His lips are moving, but no sound comes out.

"Keep going," Valery says. "We can't let him go."

I take a step closer, ready to object, to plead for my former friend's life. But I know Vicky is right. If we let him go, he will run back to Trevor without hesitation and blow our cover. He will come back with reinforcements and keep going until we're all dead. No matter how much I hate it, it's either him or us.

Paul's efforts to break free are getting more frantic.

"Finish it, Grace," Valery urges Gisella.

Grace closes her dark eyes and takes a deep breath. "Okay."

She grabs Paul's face again and continues her incantation.

"Please don't," Paul begs. His eyes search for someone who will listen. "Charlie? Dante?" he says. "I know we've had our differences, but we don't want to kill each other, do we?"

Half of his hand is blown away by the wind, and a tear crawls down his cheek over Grace's hand. He sounds so much like the Paul I thought I knew that I almost want to step forward and pull Grace back. Almost. Because I also remember the many times he tried to kill us.

My heart beats loudly in my chest as I ignore his words and watch him slowly crumble to dust.

First his arms disappear, followed by the top of his head and large chunks of his legs.

The others let go of him, since he's no longer able to defend himself. A steady flow of tears paints lines across Grace's face. Chung puts a hand on her shoulder in comfort. She keeps repeating the incantation until what's left of Paul collapses and crumbles into a million pieces on the ground.

I avert my eyes and wrap my arms firmly around the fairy under my shirt. Still, a soft sob rises in my throat. I know we had no other option, but it still hurts to see a former friend die.

"Rest in peace," I whisper at the dust the wind spreads into the forest.

CHAPTER 33

We walk in silence for several minutes, without purpose, except to get as far away from that place as we can. Still clinging to my chest, but no longer hidden by my shirt, the fairy is humming a comforting song, which seems to have a calming effect on all of us.

After about five minutes, I slow down until I'm walking next to Grace.

"Thank you," I say softly. "That must have been hard."

She bites her lip and shakes her head. "Hard is not the right word for it, Dean. It was horrible. It just felt… wrong. Very wrong."

I've never seen her so small and fragile, and that has nothing to do with her new Asian look. Using her witch powers broke something inside her, and there's nothing I can do to fix it.

"I'm so sorry. If there was another way, I would never have let you do it." I rake my hand through my hair. "Just try to remember that what you did was important. You helped us save the fairy *and* my mother."

She nods but keeps her eyes on the ground. The fairy sends warmth through me as my heart contracts with pain. It gives me an idea.

"Hey, would you mind carrying the fairy again for a while?"

I come to a halt, and so does Grace. She looks up, surprise in her eyes. "Why?"

I shrug, not knowing how to answer that. Carefully, I lift the fairy and place it against her chest. "Just trust me, okay?"

At first, I think she's going to hand the creature back to me, but then her face changes. Peace falls over it and some color rises to her cheeks.

I stroke the fairy's golden hair and thank her silently. Without looking up, she wraps her tiny fingers around my thumb.

"She is amazing," Grace whispers.

I smile. "She sure is."

Chung wraps his arm around her shoulder, and we start walking again.

"Where to?" Valery asks when I catch up with her.

My gaze moves over everything around us. The trees look normal here and bugs, birds and other animals scurry through the undergrowth. "To a place where we can safely cast a spell to take the fairy to

Heaven."

"Is there such a place?"

With a grin, I pull her close to me. "Probably not. You want to do it here?"

"The sooner the better, right?"

"True."

I turn back to the others. "We're going to do the spell here. Keep an eye on the forest and let me know if you see anything strange. Grace, stay close to me."

Mabel steps forward. "I could freeze everything around us, as a precaution."

I shake my head. "What if someone is watching?"

She holds out her hands and turns until she has checked every direction. "There is no one here but us."

Valery senses I'm still not convinced and repeats what Mabel did. "I don't sense anyone either."

"They could've cloaked themselves." I shake my head again. "I'm sorry, I can't risk Mom's life on this. We already made the mistake of fighting the water demons with our powers."

Valery nods. "You're right, we have to be careful." She pulls a knife from her pocket and gestures for the others to do the same. "Just hurry up," she tells me.

I take out Dad's notebook for inspiration. While I flip through it, my mind goes in overdrive, trying to come up with a way to get this fairy to safety. *Can a simple spell get us to Heaven? Probably not, because if it could, everyone with magic would try it. Still, I have to try, I'm out of other ideas.*

Impatiently, I turn the pages the wind keeps blowing back. Then I understand that it's not the wind, but the book flipping back. I let go and wait until the pages stop moving. It shows me an empty page.

"Okay… so what now?"

The book remains still.

Carefully, I move my hand over the white paper. Nothing happens.

"Come on, book, show me the spell," I mumble, shaking the notebook feverishly.

Valery glances over her shoulder with a frown. "What's wrong?"

I hold up the book. "It flipped to an empty page."

"Maybe the words are hidden to protect the spell?" she suggests, before turning her gaze back on the trees in front of her.

I bite my lip. *So, I need to cast a reveal what's hidden spell on the book first?*

Deciding it's worth a try, I take out my own Book of Spells and look up what I need. After all, Dad's notebook has never failed me so far. If it's trying to tell me something, I should try to find out what it is. And it makes sense to cloak a spell to get to Heaven. I just wish I wasn't in such a hurry to get this done.

I walk over to Valery and stick my hand into her back pocket. "Sorry," I mumble. "I just need a couple of things."

"No problem," she says with a grin.

After some searching, I find everything I need,

including a small mirror. I can't remember her fetching a new one, but there's no time to ask her about it. I suppose she used her magic to get it.

I quickly mix the herbs in a bowl and put everything in place. Then I light a white candle and hold it up against the mirror, which I've placed against a tree.

"Powers of high, hear my cry.
Send your vision through the sky.
Send it through to make us see
what lies beyond reality.

Powers that be, hear my call.
Make sure that we see it all.
Send your eyes through this reflection,
but keep us safe in your protection.

Through this mirror send your power
to these herbs for just one hour.
In these herbs your sight will stay,
to reveal what's hidden away."

A gust of wind blows the candle flame onto the mirror, where it dances inside the reflection. Then, it grows and grows until I can see nothing but fire in the mirror. It returns to the real world, passing the candle and settling inside the bowl in my other hand. The herbs ignite with the sound of fireworks, and I stretch my arm to prevent my shirt from catching fire.

The mixture goes up in smoke, and the flame dies.

I put down the bowl and pick up Dad's notebook. *Please work, please work.*

My heartbeat quickens when nothing happens. *Maybe the book was just confused, and there's nothing on this page.*

Just when I'm about to close it, I see movement. Letters flicker before my eyes, slowly morphing into full words and then sentences. I breathe out in relief as the words at the top of the page get clear.

How to reach Heaven.

My relief is short-lived, however, when I take a look at the ingredients.

"Golden candles?" I scratch my head. "And what is agalloch supposed to be?"

"It's a type of wood, with a strong smell," Valery says without looking back.

"Great, where can we find some?"

She shrugs. "No idea."

My shoulders sag. "You're kidding."

"Do not panic yet," Mabel interrupts. "I have a small box made of agalloch wood. We can use that."

"Good, where is it?"

"It is at Darkwood Manor, in my closet."

This keeps getting better and better. It's only a matter of time before Trevor and more demons from the fifth circle find us, and I doubt we'll be able to keep the fairy safe once more.

Pacing up and down between the trees, I try to stay calm. *There has to be a quick way to get Maël's wooden box here.*

Shaking my head in frustration, I open my Book of Spells again. "Our best shot is probably for Mabel to go home and for me to summon her back." I almost drop the book in my haste to find the right page. "Now where is that spell?"

There's a soft crackle in the air in front of me, and I take a step back. I let out a cry of surprise when Mona appears in a cloud of sparks.

"Is this what you need, honey?" She holds out a small wooden box to me.

I just gape at her. "How did you…? Where…?" I stutter.

She takes my hand and presses the box into it. "I was fixing my car and decided to check on you. I sensed that you needed something I could help you with." She glances at Mabel. "I hope this is the right box."

Mabel turns her head and nods. "That is the one. Can you take the contents back with you, please?"

Mona places a hand on her heart. "I already put them in a safe place."

Mabel gives her a small bow. "Thank you."

When I give her a questioning look, she smiles. "I kept some memories in there. Agalloch is a strong protector, combined with certain herbs."

Mona pulls me into a quick hug. "Be careful."

Some of her sparks jump onto me, and a feeling of comfort eases my mind. "Of course. Thank you, Mona."

With a cheerful wave, she says goodbye and explodes into a thousand lights.

I shake my head at the strangeness of it all. Just like that I'm holding the agalloch box in my hands. *If only everything was this easy.*

"Hurry up, Dean, something is coming," Mabel says. It sounds as if she's telling me what's for dinner tonight, but her body is on full alert.

I glance at the list of ingredients and walk over to Valery again. To prevent confusion, I first put everything I don't need anymore back into her endless pocket. Then I pull out some thyme, needed to contact another world, acacia leaves to symbolize the afterlife, some barberry to make sure our enemies won't be able to follow us, and black snake root for protection. Then I concentrate on golden candles, and my hand wraps around them. Finally, I take out matches, a small bottle of holy water, a clean bowl and an incense stick.

"They are coming closer," Mabel warns me as I set up all of the ingredients.

"Can you sense what they are?" I ask, crushing the herbs in the bowl.

"Demons."

"What about Trevor?"

"I am not sure."

As fast as I can, I burn the herbs, add three drops of holy water and draw a circle with the substance.

"Step inside, everyone," I say. "I don't want anyone to get left behind."

I place the three golden candles inside the circle and light them. Then, from the middle of the circle, I light the incense stick, hold up the bowl with the remains of the herbs and start turning slowly, facing the candles one by one, while I say the words of the spell.

"Powers that be, hear my cry.
Open a gateway to Heaven up high.
Grant us safe passage but keep us alive.
Keep us together until we arrive.

Powers of High, hear my plea.
Keep us safe and keep us free.
Let us travel to the heavenly gate,
and please don't let this change our fate."

The circle lights up, and the flames of the candles burn bright as I finish my third turn. The fog from the incense gets thicker just as several water snakes crawl out from behind the trees. Grace steps back and hands me the fairy before returning to the line of defense.

"Make sure they don't enter the circle!" I call out to my friends.

I step to the right and prepare to throw my Morningstar. Just in time I remember it will give my identity away.

I look at Chung. His gaze is fixed on the water demon slithering toward him at dazzling speed.

Valery throws her knife. It hits the snake square in the face, and it falls apart into a thousand drops. But the moment they hit the ground, the drops flow back to form a snake's body again.

As the mist around us pulls at our limbs, I call out to Valery. "Do you have any oil?"

She digs her hand into her pocket and pulls out two bottles. Before I can tell her not to throw it all at once, she hurls the bottles away from her with force. Oil spatters everywhere when the glass breaks. The snakes are pulled apart, hissing in frustration.

Just when I think we've beaten them, a man made of stone steps out between two trees. "If you think that will save you, you're wrong."

It takes me half a second to recognize the earth elemental, and my heartbeat quickens. Just in time, I resist the urge to ask him where Mom is. He doesn't know who we are and losing Jeep and D'Maeo means we're two people short. Hopefully he won't suspect a thing, so it would be foolish to blow our cover.

To my relief, Charlie is thinking the same thing.

"Who are you, and what do you want?" he asks.

Trevor laughs loudly. "Who I am doesn't matter, and you know what I want. You've got something that belongs to me."

He holds out his hand, pointing a finger at me. "Give up the fairy, or you all die."

My friends raise their weapons in unison.

Valery is fuming. "Never."

My head starts to hurt from the loud pounding of

my heart. I try to relax. *We only need to keep Trevor out of the circle for about a minute. Then the spell should take us to Heaven, where the fairy will finally be safe.*

But as Trevor charges, it becomes clear that non-magical weapons won't do us much good as long as he's in his stone form. The blades don't penetrate his solid skin, and he's stronger than we are.

With a simple push, he knocks over Chung and Grace. When he reaches for Valery, I throw a candle at him. It doesn't hurt him, of course, but it knocks him off balance a bit, giving Valery a chance to drive the tip of her blade into his eye.

With a holler that turns my skin into ice, he slams his hand against his eye and stumbles back. Ted uses the momentum to push him over.

"Stay inside the circle!" I scream when he steps over the line to finish the job.

The fog is quickly changing into a bright light. It wraps around my arms and legs, cutting off the oxygen flowing into my lungs.

The last thing I think before I close my eyes against the brightness is, *please don't make me lose another friend.*

CHAPER 34

I'm lying on something soft, all drowsy and peaceful. It feels as if I've slept for a week, but still I don't want to get up. My bed has never felt so comfortable, and my troubles seem to have left me. *There's nothing to worry about, so why wouldn't I stay here a while longer?*

There's movement on my chest, and I open one eye to take a peek. A tiny face surrounded by golden hair looks up at me with utter adoration.

"Oh, hello," I whisper, trying to remember why there's a fairy dressed in green leaves clinging to me.

I open the other eye and slowly look around. My friends are lying beside me, in deep, peaceful sleep.

It's not until I sit up that I wonder where we are. We're not at Darkwood Manor or at Mom's house. We're also not lying on beds or matrasses.

I reach down and touch the fluff on the floor. It feels like a cross between whipped cream and cotton.

Slowly, I stretch my arms above my head and sit up. Another look at my sleeping friends tells me something is wrong.

"Where are Jeep and D'Maeo?" I whisper to myself.

It's as if a sharp knife pierces my brain, and I squeeze my eyes shut. Memories flood back to me. I have to lean back on my arms to prevent myself from tipping over. I see Mom's hypnotized face, Jeep getting stuck inside the portal in the mine and D'Maeo/David sinking into the earth. Then Taylar's new face hovers in front of me, and my vision zooms in on his stubby form stepping out of the circle.

My eyes snap open, and I look around again. Tears of relief cover my cheeks when Taylar is still there. He mumbles something in his sleep and rolls onto his left side. Another check tells me Trevor was left behind.

I push myself to my feet. "Guys? We made it." *At least, I think so. Other than a dream, what could this place be?*

I pinch my arm and flinch. *Nope, not a dream.*

"Guys?" I say again, louder this time. "Wake up."

Maël shoots upright, her hand reaching for her staff. The others just moan and blink. Charlie covers his head with his arm.

"Everything okay?" I ask Maël as she stands up and takes in our surroundings.

She blinks several times, as if she can't believe where we are. I can't blame her. It's pretty amazing. I lost count of the number of worlds I've seen in the last couple of days, and this one must be the weirdest to visit. Maybe even weirder than the Underworld. Somehow, this seems more real. It's a world I have always been able to imagine. And it looks just like I thought it would.

Vicky walks over to me and rests her head on my shoulder. "You did it. You got us into Heaven." Her hand searches for mine and squeezes it. "It's so peaceful here."

My heart misses a beat. "You don't want to stay here, do you? I mean, I wish you all the happiness in the world, but..."

"Shhh." She places a finger on my lips and smiles. "I'd never choose to stay here if it wasn't with you."

Before I can utter another 'but', she kisses me. My heart settles down, and I pull her close. "I'm so glad you're safe. I can't bear losing anyone else."

She strokes my neck. "We'll get them all back. But the fairy's safety is our first priority."

"Right." I pull back, remembering the tiny creature still clinging to my chest. Heat rises to my cheeks when I realize she was smack in the middle of our embrace. But when I look down, she's fast asleep.

I gesture at the clouds below us. "So which way do we go? All these clouds look the same to me."

Vicky's eyebrows pull together in confusion. "Clouds? What clouds?"

"The ones we're standing on?"

She shakes her head. "I'm not sure what you mean."

"You don't see clouds?" I look back at the others, all on their feet now, looking rested and relaxed.

"I don't see clouds either," Charlie says, straightening his long locks with one hand. "Except in the sky, where they belong."

"What are you seeing then?"

He breathes in deeply, with a content expression on his face. "An endless beach, with swaying palm trees." He grins. "And a bar."

Vicky lets out a sigh. "Mountains covered in soft grass." She spreads her arms and lifts her chin. "I feel like Julie Andrews in The Sound of Music."

Maël wipes a tear from her eye as she looks around. I decide not to ask her what she sees and change the subject instead. "So, what do you think happened to our disguises? We all look normal again."

The ghost queen straightens her back. "Probably something similar. To us, we look like this. We project the way we see ourselves and each other onto our bodies."

I make a full turn. "So, we're really in Heaven, huh?"

She nods. "I think so."

Charlie yawns and scratches his head. "What now? We just leave the fairy here and try to find the exit?"

"No…" I think back to the spell I cast. "I asked for the spell to transport us to the gates of Heaven, not into Heaven."

The second I say the word 'gates', something shimmers in the distance.

309

I squint against the bright light. "Did you see that?"

Charlie takes Gisella's hand. "Yup, that's where we're going."

Still looking around, each enjoying our own view, we start walking.

Three steps further, we come to a sudden halt.

"Wow," I say, lifting my head to take in the shiny, white iron gate rising high above us.

"Welcome," a low, friendly voice says from our right.

We all turn toward it at the same time and take in the old man dressed in white robes towering over us. Suddenly, the urge to bow falls over me, and I get down on one knee. The others follow my example.

The words I say next roll out of my mouth without my permission. "Saint Peter, we've come to deliver a soul that belongs in Heaven. She was hunted down, and we strive to leave her only when she is truly safe."

When I look up, Saint Peter holds out his hand. "Come here, son. Show me this soul you speak of."

I step closer and try not to gape at the saint. He is almost as tall as a giant, but although he looms over me, I don't feel threatened. The smile behind his long, white beard is inviting, his eyes friendly.

When I come to a halt and show him the sleeping fairy, he nods. "Oh yes, this one disappeared from my sight. I have been searching for her, but it has been difficult to focus lately. All worlds have been disturbed, and panic has risen in Heaven."

I swallow the lump rising in my throat and hope he doesn't see the guilt on my face.

I lower my head. "We have done everything in our power to restore the balance of the universe. We hope you can keep this soul safe."

Saint Peter brings down both of his hands and cups them. "I can, and I will. Just place her here, and I will open the gates for her."

Gently, I place my hands on the fairy's back. "Wake up, little one."

The creature opens her eyes and smiles.

"We're here. Are you ready?"

I expect her to nod and wait for me to hand her over to Saint Peter, but instead, she pushes herself up until she reaches my face and places her tiny hands on my cheeks.

Thank you, Dante Banner. I will never forget this, she says in my head.

"You're welcome. I'm sorry we were too late to keep you alive."

Do not worry yourself with such thoughts. Everything happens for a reason.

"I'm grateful to have met you. Go in peace."

With a smile, she closes her eyes and kisses me on the lips. A feeling of utter calmness falls down on me, and the corners of my mouth go up. Then the comfortable warmth leaves my body as she spreads her wings and flies over to Saint Peter.

He turns to the gate, which opens on its own. He

holds the fairy up into the sunbeam that shines down onto the gate, and bit by bit, she gets even brighter than she already was. Her skin is a radiant white-green, and her hair curls up. With a pirouette, she rises from Peter's hands and takes off at lightning speed, leaving a trail of green leaves in her wake.

Saint Peter turns back, and the gates close behind him.

"Thank you," he says. "You did well."

Before I can respond, he starts to fade.

"Wait!" I say. "Can I ask you one more thing?"

Peter becomes solid again. "Yes?"

I clear my throat. "Eh… how do we get back to Earth?"

A wide smile chases away Peter's thoughtful expression. "Oh yes, of course," he chuckles.

He lifts his arm and points at something behind us.

When I look back, bit by bit, a road made of golden tiles becomes visible.

"Just follow that road," Peter says. "It will take you home. I wish you all the best."

I turn back to thank him, but he's already gone.

Charlie wipes a couple of drops of sweat from his forehead. "Well, that was interesting. Does anyone else think it's a bit too hot here?"

I shrug. "You're the one imagining the tropical beach. Just turn down the heat a bit." I turn to the others. "Are you ready to go home and get our friends back?"

"Hell yeah!" Taylar calls out. Then he flinches. "I mean, definitely!" He glances back to where Peter was standing only seconds ago, but nothing happens. The gate has also disappeared. It's time to go.

We follow the golden path in silence, each of us enjoying our own version of a perfect landscape while we can. I'm just starting to wonder how long this road is, when a dark shape shoots up from between two tiles.

It takes us all two seconds to pull out our weapons. A lightning bolt burns in my left hand.

The black mist in front of us keeps stretching.

"It's the black void that killed D'Maeo," I say, just as Vicky whispers, "I've seen this before."

She wraps her hand firmer around her sword. "You're right. But it's different somehow."

We watch in fearful anticipation as the black void takes on the shape of a man. A very familiar man.

"Is that…?" Charlie doesn't finish his sentence. I can almost hear his mouth falling open as a face appears in the mist. Half of it is darker than the night, with red lines indicating the eye and half of the nose and mouth. The other half is without a doubt D'Maeo's. Black lines run along the cheek, and his eye is as red as the other.

"We meet again," the darkness says in a rumbling voice that shakes the ground. "But this will be the last time."

* * *

Dante Banner returns in *The Sixth Ghost* – Choosing between the mission and the lives of your friends is never easy. Not even when your mission is to save the whole world. Will Dante have to give up one of his friends?

Turn the page for a sneak peek! Or pre-order the book online NOW!

Preview

Cards of Death book 6
The Sixth Ghost

CHAPTER 1

Is this bravery? I ask myself, staring at the black smoke that has half morphed into D'Maeo. *Or is it just common sense that all I can think of is 'I can't let this thing get into Heaven'?*

"What do we do?" Vicky whispers. "We can't attack D'Maeo."

Of course we can, but I don't want to.

I remember the words of the ferryman of the Underworld, Charon. He said all my friends are a part of my battle against the Devil. We can't afford to lose anyone. But we fought this black void before and it almost beat us. That was still with the help of D'Maeo and Jeep. If running away from it was our best option then, where does that leave us now?

"Dante?" Vicky sounds a bit desperate as she pulls at my sleeve.

When I blink to clear my head and my view, I see

the smoke growing rapidly. D'Maeo's face is contorted as it stretches higher and higher. The smoke gets thicker and looms over us.

"Our best option is to capture it," I say. "Lock it somewhere until we figure out how to separate it from D'Maeo, and kill it."

"With a spell?" Charlie asks, without looking up from the gel wall he's building.

I conjure a ball of lightning in each hand when the smoke hisses. "Yes, but not just any spell. We need to enhance it." I glance sideways at Gisella. "With dark magic."

"What?" She ducks as the void swoops down, the mouth in the monstrous face opening wide.

The rest of us dives sideways. Balls of grease and lightning hit the dark form, but all the smoke does is part.

"I'm sorry," I tell Gisella, "but I can't think of another way to beat this thing. We tried it before, remember? We barely escaped. It's too powerful."

"What do you think it wants?" Vicky asks as the mist spirals up, forming something that resembles a tornado.

I aim some more lightning at it, but get no more than a slight shiver as a response. "I'm not sure. We'd have to find out what it is first."

Taylar points at my waist. "Maybe John's notebook can give us some answers."

With a loud hiss the smoke dives down again, half of D'Maeo's nose and mouth still visible, but in the wrong places. It hits my shoulder and I grab at it as heat stings my skin. It leaves a hole in my shirt.

Vicky shoots me a concerned look, which I dismiss with a wave of my hand. "I'll be okay." I tilt my head to observe the shape in the sky above us. "It's as if the black void is holding back. It was a lot stronger before, wasn't it?"

Maël pauses her time bending mumbling. "That could be D'Maeo's doing. He is fighting it from the inside."

"Can you freeze it?" I ask her.

Her hand wraps tighter around her staff. "No, I can only slow it down. It is still too strong."

"Okay, slow it down as much as you can." I whip out Dad's notebook and open it at a random page.

Show me how to trap this entity, I think as hard as I can. To my relief the pages start flipping instantly. Three-quarters of the book have already filled up. I can't wait to find out what will appear on the remaining blank pages. Secretly I'm hoping for a spell to lock the Devil in Hell, but I don't think we'll get that lucky.

The pages come to a rest. Before reading the text on the page I look up to make sure the smoke isn't about to attack again. It's moving left and right, as if it's waiting for something. *No wait, it's something else. It's struggling. Maël is right, it's fighting to stay in control.* While it wriggles and stretches, more of the mouth become visible. It opens wide and lets out a scream.

I shiver. "That was him. D'Maeo."

I bend over the notebook, gritting my teeth. *Come on, give me something useful.*

My eyes scan the lines, then the letters one by one. I blink. "I know what it is."

Taylar moves a bit closer. "What what is?"

"That black void." I look up at it and then back at the notebook.

Taylar nudges me. "Well, what is it?"

"It's a Chaos Residue. Listen to this. *A Chaos Residue comes to life in a place of complete disorder, pain and confusion. Once it escapes its place of origin, it goes in search of places where it can wreak havoc. Whenever it succeeds, it grows in size and strength. After its hundredth kill, it will change into a Chaos Demon, which means it can take on solid shape. Once it does, it will be twice as hard to kill.*"

"Oh great," Charlie sighs. "So if we don't kill it now, we never will?"

Vicky frowns. "I don't get it. If this thing is out to create chaos, why did it go after D'Maeo? I mean, it killed him, but obviously that wasn't enough."

I feel my own eyebrows moving up too. "Maybe D'Maeo is the only one who can beat it?"

Vicky shakes her head. "No, that doesn't make sense. If he was, how come the dark void took over? It shouldn't have been able to do that then, should it?"

Maël stops her mumbling again for a second. "Remember what I told you about molecules and balance, Dante?"

I tilt my head. "Eh… sure." *Molecules and balance?* It

hits me. "Of course! When we disturbed the balance of the universe, the molecules inside each one of us could be pulled in any direction." My shoulders sag. "D'Maeo was already struggling with this thing. The imbalance inside him must have given it the opportunity to take over."

A smile creeps upon my lips. "So what we need… is someone who can pull the molecules back to where they belong."

Vicky's face lights up. "Mrs. Delaney!"

"Exactly."

"But how will we get the void to her?"

"And without endangering her life in the process, you know," Charlie adds.

"Give me a sec." I bend over the notebook again. My eyes fly over the rest of the page. "Okay, here's what I think. D'Maeo was the one who brought this thing here, to us. If we return to Darkwood Manor now, while they're busy fighting each other, the black void a.k.a. Chaos Residue shouldn't be too hard to lure. All we have to do is create the perfect circumstances for chaos. D'Maeo will give it the last push in the right direction."

"And then what?" Gisella asks skeptically. "Why would we be able to defeat it now?"

"Because one of us is fighting it from the inside. Once we're back on Earth Mona can get Mrs. Delaney, who will try to separate D'Maeo's molecules from the Chaos Residue's. Meanwhile I'll cast a spell to trap it, in case we can't kill it."

"Sounds like a plan to me." Taylar raises his shield as the dark smoke attacks again. It slams down hard, forcing him onto his knees. I follow it with my eyes as it moves up and prepares to charge again. I picture it freezing over and getting stuck halfway down, completely surrounded by ice.

"Nice job!" Vicky calls out when the images in my head become reality.

"Thanks." I smile, but I'm not completely reassured. "D'Maeo!" I call out. "I hope you can hear me. We've got a plan. Keep the black void busy while we return to Darkwood Manor. Then follow us."

I'm hoping for another scream in reply, but the smoke is still frozen, unable to move.

Before I beckon the others, I shout out one more message. "We'll get you back, I promise."

Then I take Vicky's hand and start running down the path.

WANT TO READ ON?

Buy the next book now, on Amazon!

Make a difference

Reviews are very important to authors. Even a short or negative review can be of tremendous value to me as a writer. Therefore I would be very grateful if you could leave a review at your place of purchase. And don't forget to tell your friends about this book!

Thank you very much in advance.

Newsletter, social media and website

Want to receive exclusive first looks at covers and upcoming book releases, get a heads-up on pre-order and release dates and special offers, receive book recommendations and an exclusive 'look into my (writing) life'? Then please sign up now for my monthly newsletter through my website: www.tamarageraeds.com.

You can also follow me on Facebook, Instagram and Twitter for updates and more fun stuff!

Have a great day!   Tamara Geraeds

Found a mistake?

The Fifth Portal has gone through several rounds of beta reading and editing. If you found a typographical, grammatical, or other error which impacted your enjoyment of the book, we offer our apologies and ask that you let us know, so we can fix it for future readers.

You can email your feedback to: info@tamarageraeds.com.

ABOUT THE AUTHOR

Tamara Geraeds was born in 1981. When she was 6 years old, she wrote her first poem, which basically translates as:

A hug for you and a hug for me
and that's how life should be

She started writing books at the age of 15 and her first book was published in 2012. After 6 books in Dutch she decided to write a young adult fantasy series in English: *Cards of Death*.

Tamara's bibliography consists of books for children, young adults and adults, and can be placed under fantasy and thrillers.

Besides writing she runs her own business, in which she teaches English, Dutch and writing, (re)writes texts and edits books.

She's been playing badminton for over 20 years and met the love of her life Frans on the court. She loves going out for dinner, watching movies, and of course reading, writing and hugging her husband. She's crazy about sushi and Indian curries, and her favorite color is pink.

Printed in Great Britain
by Amazon